The C[illegible] Casket
and The Spectres of Light

Katie Paterson

To Natalie.
love
Katie
Paterson.

due for publication in 2010

'The Battle of The Underworld' the third book
in 'The Chronicles of Valonia'

Titles by Katie Paterson

The Jewels of Valonia
The Golden Casket and the Spectres of Light

The Chronicles of Valonia

The Golden Casket and the Spectres of Light

Katie Paterson

HandE Publishers Ltd

Published by HandE Publishers Ltd
Epping Film Studios, Brickfield Business Centre,
Thornwood High Road, Epping, CM16 6TH
www.handepublishers.co.uk

First published in the United Kingdom 2009
First Edition

ISBN 978-1-906873-11-0

A CIP catalogue record for this book is available from
The British Library

With the exception of the legendary but possible existence of figures such as King Arthur and the Knights of the Round Table, all the characters and events in this book are fictitious and any resemblance to actual persons, living or dead, is purely coincidental.

Illustration design concept by Katie Paterson
Illustrations by Charles Tomlinson
Cover design by Ruth Mahoney and Charles Tomlinson
Typeset by Ruth Mahoney
Edited by Natalie-Jane Revell, Kayleigh Hart and Caroline Petherbridge.

Printed and bound in England
by CPI Bookmarque, Croydon, Surrey

To Olive.
A much loved, inspirational lady.
Better known to me as
Mum

Tyntagyle

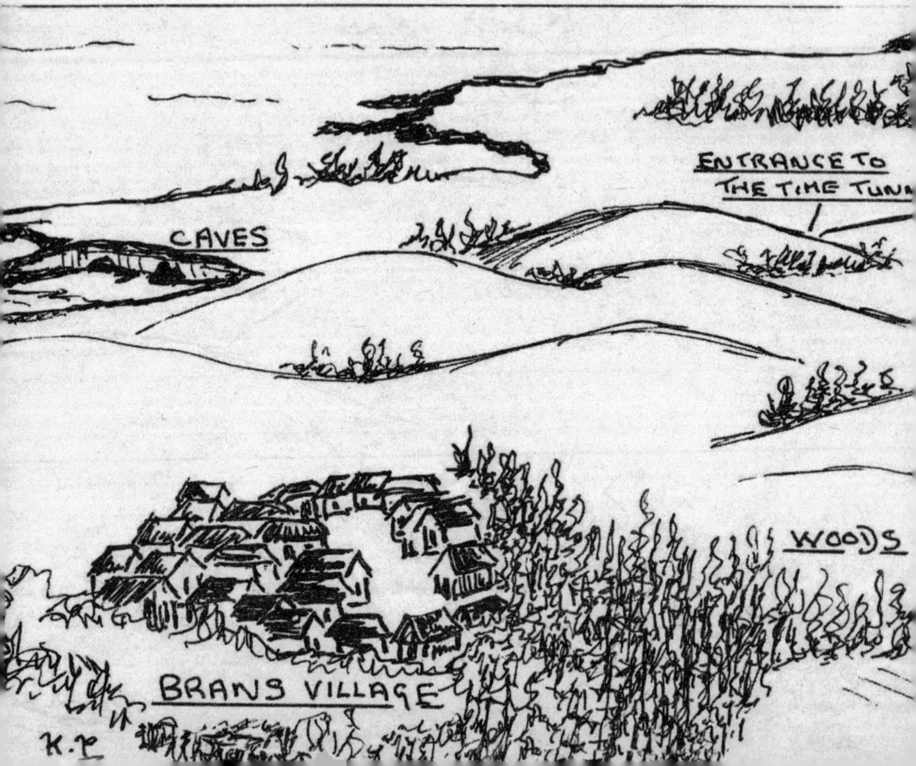

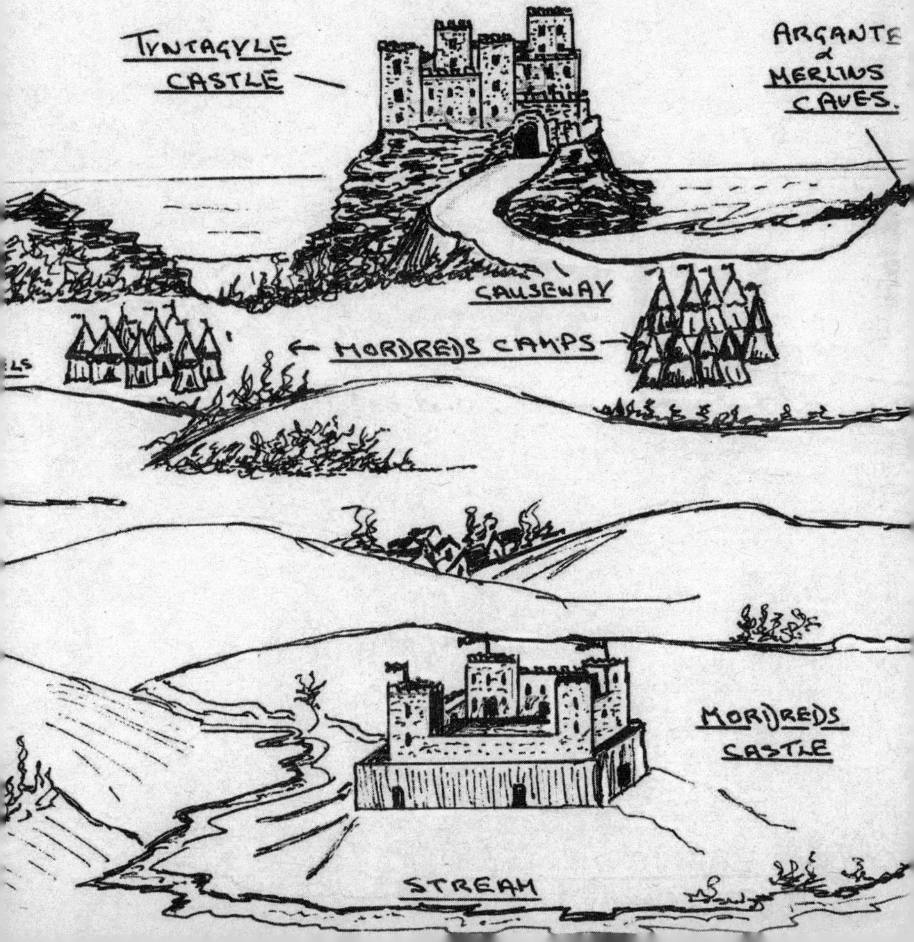
TYNTAGYLE CASTLE
ARGANTE & MERLINS CAVES.
CAUSEWAY
← MORDREDS CAMPS →
MORDREDS CASTLE
STREAM

Introduction

In the gloomy darkness of the crypt, Mordred held the torch higher as his men struggled to move the large stone carving of a majestic knight, which lay across the surface of the tomb. The torch cast an eerie glow around the catacomb, illuminating the hideous face of the old hag as she stood beside Mordred, rubbing her hands together gleefully.

There was a loud scraping noise as the men finally slid the heavy stone effigy aside to reveal a large opening in the floor, with steps leading down into a dark vault. The two men recoiled, sickened by the pungent smell of the burial chamber, and looked anxiously at Mordred. They were aware that opening the tomb was an act of desecration, and could only hope that he wasn't going to ask them to do more.

"Go on, go on!" cackled the old hag. "Go down and look for the casket!"

The men hesitated, but the old witch cursed and pointed a grimy, knobbly finger at them, sending a bolt of magic streaking through the air. It hit the floor and exploded like firecrackers around the terrified men's feet. They scuttled down the steps with the torch, not at all sure what was in store for them below, but barely a minute or so later they came back empty-handed and looked fearfully at Mordred.

"Sire, there is no casket down there. Only a large trunk. Is that what you desire?"

"Bring it up! Bring it up now, so that I may see it!" shrieked the hag, before Mordred could even answer.

The two men hurried back down the steps, and climbed back up from the tomb carrying a large wooden case between them. It was surprisingly light, and they bore its weight with ease before setting it down on the floor in front of their master.

"This cannot be it?" queried Mordred. "It is far too big, surely."

The old hag circled it, muttering, holding out her long bony arms and, smiling toothlessly in her delight. "Oh this is it, this is the prize!" she gloated. "We'll take it now, to your castle, Medraut," she said, and then turning to the men, she hissed, "Quickly!"

Terrified of her magic, they swiftly did as she instructed, and carried the wooden box out of the church and into the open, where their horses awaited them.

The men tied the trunk across two of the horses so that it was balanced as evenly as possible, and then walked on foot, leading the horses, as Mordred and the old witch rode on ahead up to the pass. When they reached the tunnel entrance they tethered their horses next to the two already there, untied the trunk and lifted it down again.

The two men reluctantly carried the chest between them, following Mordred and the old woman into the passageway. At first, carrying the trunk seemed effortless, as if it could almost have been empty, but the further the two men carried it along the tunnels, the heavier the wooden box became – and with every step, the men grew weaker. Their brown hair began to turn grey, their skin began to sag around them, and their faces grew visibly older as the seconds ticked by.

"Have you seen what is happening to them?" Mordred asked the old woman, anxiously.

"'Tis of no consequence," she replied. "Let them carry it as far as they can, although I fear they will not make it to your castle."

"There is a cave not far from here – perhaps we should take the box there," said Mordred, even more alarmed as he watched the two strong men's hair turn white before his very eyes. "I do hope you know what you are doing," he said, uneasily, to the old hag beside him.

"Of course I do! Do you doubt my powers?" she snapped back venomously.

"No, no, of course not," Mordred answered quickly. "Bring the trunk down the next tunnel, into the cave!" he called out to the men.

By the time they were half way through the tunnel, the men could no longer carry the box. The weight of it had become so extreme that, with their strength gone, all they could manage to do was drag it painfully, bit by bit, until they reached the cave. Between them, they had just managed to haul it into the centre, when suddenly one of them collapsed over the trunk, finally exhausted by his supreme effort to get it there. As his tired, weak frame slumped over the wooden box, the man's appearance started to change dramatically, as though he were simply fading away. His body disintegrated and disappeared into a cloud of dust that blew away with the strong sea breeze as it whistled through the cave.

His friend sank to his knees in horror, too weak to do anything else. Mordred and the old sorceress watched the second man in silence as he fell forwards onto the cave floor and finally drew his last breath. His body shrivelled, crumbling into a pile of bones and yellow skin, and as the wind blew forcefully again, his remains dwindled to little more than ashes that were carried away over the sea.

For a moment, no-one spoke. Even the old witch looked disturbed at what the wooden trunk seemed to have done to those who had touched it.

"Do you intend to open this crate?" asked Mordred, warily. "Do you think it wise? Perhaps we should forget this altogether."

"And have no revenge? You foolish man!" she sneered. "I will weave a spell of darkness to protect us from its powers."

"If you are sure …" started Mordred, as the old hag put her

head down and mumbled a string of incomprehensible words. She waved her hands back and forth, as though summoning something unseen from an unearthly realm. A cloud of darkness billowed through the cave like a black fog as the old witch continued with her incantations in some ancient language. As she moved towards the wooden trunk, her voice rose higher and became frighteningly shrill and manic.

The usually fearless Mordred shrank back against the wall as the cave began to shake, rocks started to crash to the ground and everything became as black as night. Even his flaming torch could not penetrate the darkness that surrounded him as the rocks continued to thud onto the floor of the cave.

Suddenly, silence fell as the blackness lifted and the cave became eerily still. The dark sorceress let out a long triumphant screech that echoed around the walls in endless ripples of discordant sound.

"'Tis done, my spell is woven, 'tis but a matter of time before everything will be ours!"

Mordred stepped forward, his eyes lighting up with the sparkle of greed and they congratulated one another, the old woman's deranged laughter reverberating around the cave. Suddenly the rocky walls shook again and there was a crack of thunder.

"What is happening now?" asked Mordred in alarm, as the rocks began to fall again.

"I do not know," said the old woman, cowering back fearfully. "I sense a powerful force surrounding us, the like of which I have never before encountered!"

There was a brilliant flash of lightning and the large metal clasps, which had been holding the trunk tightly closed, sprang upwards with a sound like a bolt being drawn. Mordred and the witch jumped back as the lid of the trunk creaked open and a bright orange light flooded out into the cavern. They backed uneasily towards the wall as the air around them filled with whispering voices.

When the lid was fully open a small golden casket rose up out of the depths of the trunk and floated in the air above it. Slowly, as though carried by unseen hands, the casket drifted across to the other side of the cavern until finally it came to rest in a small niche in the rocks. The ethereal murmurings gradually diminished until they faded away altogether, leaving an eerie stillness. On the other side of the cave, in a dark recess, the orange radiance glowed protectively around the casket, casting strange shadows over the rocks.

Mordred looked at the old hag in horror. "Whatever have you unleashed upon us?" he demanded, angrily.

Chapter One

Nightmares of another time

Everything was quiet in the Moore household in Chesterton. The last of the twins' exams were finished and Rachel had gone to her bedroom to empty out her schoolbag. She pulled out her revision books and dumped them unceremoniously in the bottom of her wardrobe, closing the door very firmly. Quietly delighted that she wouldn't have to look at them again until the new term, she flopped onto her bed to read the magazine she had picked up on the way home from school.

Her father, John Moore, put his head round the door as she was half way through a fashion article.

"Will you be all right while I pick Gareth up?"

"Yes, fine," she replied, without looking up.

"I'll pick up some fish and chips on the way home," her dad said, as he pulled the door shut behind him.

"By the way," he added, opening the door again, "if Bronwyn phones ..."

"I know, Dad, you're on your mobile. I'll get her to ring you on it," Rachel reassured him.

"Right, well, I'll get off then," he added rather awkwardly, aware that he'd disturbed her again unnecessarily, and a couple of minutes later Rachel heard the front door slam closed. She knew her father was becoming seriously concerned that they hadn't heard from Bronwyn, who had been visiting her sister Catherine, in Valonia, for over two weeks now.

Rachel went back to her magazine in the hope that the glossy pages would distract her from the circumstances that she knew were worrying her father. She tried to concentrate on the latest escapades of one of her favourite popstars but the words didn't even register. Instead thoughts of the epic holiday in Valonia that she had shared with her brother, Gareth, three years ago overtook any celebrity news that she was trying to digest.

She had spent the last three years trying to forget their experiences in Valonia and Tyntagyle, and until now it had worked. It was in Valonia they had learnt that Bronwyn was not their Aunt, as they had been led to believe, but in fact their Mother. It had taken a while for them to come to terms with this startling revelation, but Bronwyn had returned home with them, much to the delight of their father, and they had settled into a normal family life. Mr Moore seemed happier than the twins had ever seen him and Rachel loved having Bronwyn there, but now she was missing and Rachel was becoming as worried as her father.

As the memories of Tyntagyle, Merlin, and the Knights of the Round Table came rushing back to her, Rachel suddenly shuddered as she recalled the terrifying meeting that she and Gareth had had with Argante, the ethereal goddess of the lake. These were the thoughts that she had kept firmly in the back of her mind, events that none of them ever mentioned deliberately. Their trip back in time, and the legacy that Valonia had presented them with, now seemed almost unreal, even though she knew that it wasn't, and an inexplicable feeling of dread washed over her as she remembered her visions there as a seer.

It was only occasionally now that she went back there in her dreams, waking up with a start, relieved that she wasn't really back there again, and for a second she felt quite cross with Bronwyn for stirring up the memories that she had tried so hard to ignore. But Bronwyn had returned to visit Catherine in Valonia before and there had never been a problem - she was always back in Chesterton within a couple of days. This time was different though, as it had been barely a month since Bronwyn had seen Catherine. She had been noticeably edgy all week and then suddenly announced that she had to go back to see her sister again. Mr Moore hadn't been very pleased and had tried to dissuade her, but Bronwyn had been most insistent and left the next day with no real explanation as to her urgent need to return to Valonia.

Bronwyn had phoned to let them know she had arrived safely, and again a few days later from the neighbouring village post-office to say she would stay a week and be home on Saturday. Since then, however, they had heard nothing. It was almost two weeks since her last call and Rachel knew that her father was really worried, even though he tried hard to disguise it.

Rachel tossed her magazine on to the bed in exasperation and turned on the radio, in the hope that the sound of the DJ's light-hearted banter would help to drag her mind away from the uncertainties that plagued her. Determinedly she turned the volume up and tried to ignore the feelings of impending doom that had washed over her intermittently for the last seven days.

Usually Rachel would have been quite happy to have the house to herself, but today she was more than a little relieved to hear the front door open. The sound of her brother's voice drifted up the stairs, loudly recalling his fencing dual with his latest opponent.

"You should have seen it, Dad, it was so good! He was supposed to be the best the other team had, and I got him in three moves, like that, and that, and that!" Gareth exclaimed enthusiastically, no doubt re-enacting his victory with the aid of an imaginary rapier.

Rachel sighed, knowing all too well that in due course she, too, was likely to be subjected to a blow-by-blow account of her brother's victory in his fencing duel.

Gareth had decided to take up the sport a year ago. "Fencing?" Rachel and her father had both exclaimed in surprise, when Gareth had told them about this new interest.

"Yeah, I found a club on the internet – it's only two miles away, and they have tournaments against the other clubs. It sounds amazing!"

"Yes, but fencing? Why on earth would you want to do that?" queried his father. "You already play football and rugby – are you sure you've got time to do another activity?"

"But I really want to learn fencing, and it's only one night a week," Gareth had insisted, defensively. "Anyway, it's boring to do the same as everyone else; I want to do something different!"

Different or not, eventually his father had been persuaded and Gareth, who was a natural all-round athlete, had started his lessons on Fridays after school.

"These lessons have nothing to do with Argante's prediction that you will 'return to defeat Mordred with a sword' of course," Rachel said to him once, in private.

"No, of course not!" he had replied hotly. "I've told you, I just want to do something that no-one else is doing. All my mates play football!"

They both knew that this wasn't the truth, and that fencing was the only swordsmanship Gareth could possibly learn in the twentieth century, but Rachel had decided not to challenge him, as to do so would provoke a conversation about the very place and people she preferred to try and forget. So instead she had shrugged her shoulders and it wasn't mentioned again.

However, the fact that they didn't talk about Valonia, didn't mean that it wasn't there, lurking in the background, like unfinished business – leaving an unspoken bond between them. After all, however much they chose to ignore it, they were still the new Keepers of the Power, even if they had no idea what that might involve, or how it might affect their lives in the future.

Rachel went downstairs to join her father and Gareth, and found her dad busily unwrapping the fish and chips, so she hastily got three plates out of the cupboard whilst Gareth grabbed a handful of knives and forks.

"No, before you ask, there haven't been any phone calls," said Rachel, as she saw her father look at her half-expectantly. "I'm sure Bronwyn will call tomorrow," she added, seeing his face drop.

"Bound to!" agreed Gareth, attacking the steaming fish and chips and almost burning his mouth in his haste. "This is so good

– I'm starving!"

They ate their dinner quietly, each not wanting to admit to the others that they thought anything might be wrong, and their usual dinner-table conversation was subdued.

Later that evening, as Rachel emerged from the bathroom she met her brother coming out of his room.

"At last!" he said grumpily. "I was beginning to think you'd fallen down the plug hole, you've been in there that long!"

"Well I haven't," she replied crossly, "and since you're here, I could do with talking to you," she said, as she went into her own room.

"Why, what's up?" her brother asked, bouncing onto her bed. Gareth was intrigued, as he wasn't normally invited into the pink sanctity of his sister's bedroom – only her giggling friends were allowed that privilege!

"I don't know – I've just got this really bad feeling about Bronwyn," Rachel answered.

"Well, we're all a bit worried. I know Dad is, even if he isn't saying much," Gareth replied. "But you know how difficult it is to call from Valonia. Bronwyn's probably been too busy to keep trekking all the way back through the pass just to phone us. Besides, she's lived there all her life and you seem to have forgotten that we only saw her twice a year, before anyone decided to inform us she was our mother! And I don't remember her phoning then either! So I'm sure she's fine!" he continued, with a hint of anger in his voice. "Anyway, she didn't even tell any of us why she suddenly had to go, so maybe she's just decided to stay there!"

Although Rachel had been delighted to learn that Bronwyn was their mother, Gareth had found it difficult to accept, and remained slightly resentful that their parents had kept the truth from them, still blaming Bronwyn particularly.

"Bronwyn wouldn't just abandon us, not now. Even you can see how much she loves being here!" Rachel insisted. "I just have this awful hunch that there's something really wrong – it's like the feelings I used to get, before!"

"I haven't heard you say that for a long time," said Gareth, looking at her quizzically.

"Well, that's because I haven't felt like this for years. It's difficult to explain, but it's more like an instinct that's somehow connected with that place!"

"Well, I hope you're wrong," he answered, looking thoughtful. Three years ago Gareth would have taken great delight in making fun of her strange premonitions, but not now, after their experiences. "Look, you're just getting jittery because it reminds you of being there again. Don't start reading things into it – I'm sure Bronwyn's fine," he added, in an attempt to console her.

"Yes, I'm sure she is," Rachel agreed, trying to sound reassured. "It's probably after all those exams this week. Maybe I'm just suffering from stress!"

"Aren't we all!" he agreed. "That maths paper was awful today, and don't even mention the science one – how bad was that?"

"Oh, that was really dreadful! I'm sure we haven't even studied the stuff in the last part of the paper, because I didn't understand it. I had to leave the last four questions," she grimaced.

"Well, if you only left the last four, you did better than me! I dread to think what marks I'm going to get," he said, shrugging.

Rachel felt better after she had spoken to Gareth, and managed to put her worries out of her mind before she went to bed. After a couple of pages of her book she turned off her CD player, settled down and went to sleep surprisingly easily.

The next thing she knew, she was standing outside the tunnel entrance at Tyntagyle, where she and Gareth and Merlin had met the Knight Percivale on their previous visit.

This time she was completely alone. This is a dream, she thought to herself. It had to be, although it felt very real. She could feel the wind on her face, blowing her hair and making her shiver. She looked down and saw that she was in her nightdress, with bare feet, and she could feel a stone digging into the side of her foot. There were no lanterns this time, just blackness, with a small amount of moonlight shining across the open space. She stood there, not sure what she was supposed to do next. If it was a dream, shouldn't things just take on a life of their own?

As she stared across into the small patch of moonlight, she could see a figure coming towards her. It was Merlin, walking slowly, leaning on his stick heavily as though it was a great effort. He stopped and beckoned to her, so she started to run towards him, when suddenly she became aware of thundering hooves on her right and stopped in her tracks. She turned and saw a dark figure on horseback approaching rapidly. Alarmed she dashed back to the cave entrance, ducking out of sight behind a boulder as he pulled up his horse just inches away from her.

"It will not be long, old man; I told you I would have my revenge! Where is your magic now, eh?" the horseman sneered. "Useless old fool, how does it feel to know that you can do nothing?" He laughed loudly and it chilled Rachel to the bone. This was unmistakably the voice of Mordred. He seemed unaware of her presence, only interested in taunting the old wizard. He laughed again, turned the great black horse around, and galloped away into the blackness.

As soon as she was convinced that Mordred had gone Rachel ventured out towards where she had last seen Merlin. She was shivering even more now, mainly with fear at being drawn back into all this, and also of what might be about to happen if Mordred's threats were true. She peered across the plain, but there was no sign of the old wizard.

"Merlin, Merlin!" she shouted, again and again, scanning the darkness for his cloaked figure. Her voice seemed to be getting fainter and she was aware of a pulling sensation, as though she were being drawn backwards. The air rushed past her, and for a second she felt as though she was flying backwards through a tunnel at great speed.

With a jolt she realised she was in her bedroom, standing next to her bed, and she was cold: so cold that her teeth were chattering.

She climbed back into bed and pulled the covers up as far as she could until she felt the warmth coming back. What sort of a dream was that? she thought in shock. It had felt as though she was really there, and how had she ended up out of her bed? Had she sleep-walked? It took her a long time to go back to sleep, as she was almost frightened to close her eyes in case she dreamt that she was there again. Fortunately the next sound she heard was her father's voice as he opened her bedroom door.

"Are you all right? Were you up late?" he asked. "You don't normally stay in bed this long. Gareth went out ages ago – I'm surprised you didn't hear him, he's not exactly quiet in the mornings."

"Yes, I'm okay, I just had a really bad night's sleep. I had the most awful nightmare!"

"Well, I'm sure a cup of tea will sort that out," Mr Moore said, as he put the mug down on her bedside table.

"Thanks, Dad," she said gratefully, as he left the room.

She drank the tea in bed, and gradually began to feel a bit better, although she still had a throbbing headache. Finally she got up and made her way across the hall to the bathroom.

"Oh my goodness!" came her dad's voice again, from behind this time, as he reached the top of the stairs with a pile of neatly-ironed clothes. "Aren't you a sight! You look as though you've been dragged through a hedge backwards! And I thought I heard you having a bath last night!"

Rachel just nodded; to reply was just far too much of an effort at the moment.

When she returned to her room she looked in the mirror; her long golden hair was tangled and resembled a matted haystack. She looked down at her nightdress and noticed the bottom was covered in dirt, and so were her feet. There was a small cut on the side of her foot, which smarted as she rubbed it in disbelief. She went to her bed and pulled back the covers. Her crisp white sheets were brown where her feet had been and as she pushed the sheets back further, she found bits of earth and grass at the bottom. The horror that maybe she had not been dreaming after all was too much to take in, as she stared at the dirty sheets in bewilderment. She thought again about Bronwyn's mysterious departure and unexplained absence, and the feelings telling her something was wrong, that she had discounted the night before, came flooding back into her mind along with a fleeting vision of Valonia itself.

"Please tell me this isn't happening again!" she said out loud in despair.

Chapter Two

A Call from an Old Friend

Rachel couldn't wait for Gareth to get home. She was supposed to be meeting her friends in the afternoon but she rang them and cancelled. At the age of fifteen she would normally discuss most of her problems or worries with her best friends Louise and Tracy. This, however, was something they wouldn't understand as they had never spent a holiday stepping back in time to stay with the Knights of the Round Table in King Arthur's castle. This was something she could only discuss with her brother or Bronwyn. After all, who else would believe her? Even her father didn't really understand.

Eventually, at lunch-time, she heard Gareth come in and she rushed downstairs to tell him everything. "You won't believe what happened to me last night!" she said, almost colliding with him as he took off his trainers at the bottom of the stairs. "I had the most dreadful nightmare, at least that's what I thought it was, until this morning, but it wasn't! I'd really been there, back to Tintagel. I saw Merlin, and Mordred came on that huge black horse of his – it was awful! There's something really wrong, I know there is!"

"Whoa, slow down, what are you on about?" Gareth answered, as he tossed his trainers into the box underneath the coat rack.

"Oh good, I'm glad you're back," came their father's voice from the kitchen. "I thought we'd have some lunch before I go out –

what do you fancy, beans on toast or cheese?"

"Beans please, I'm starving!" grinned Gareth.

"What about you, Rachel?" Mr Moore asked.

"I'm not hungry," she answered, upset that Gareth seemed to be paying more attention to his stomach than to her latest revelation.

"Did you hear me?" she asked Gareth, annoyed with him. "Okay, whatever, beans or cheese, I don't mind," she said quickly to her father, realising he was coming out of the kitchen to deliver a lecture on eating regularly, since she had missed breakfast.

"Yes, I did hear you," answered Gareth, "but you're not making much sense."

"Go and wash up, Gareth – lunch won't be long," interrupted their dad again. "You've got half the football pitch all over you! Rachel, would you set the table, please?"

Irritated by this intervention, Rachel sighed in frustration, and put the place-mats on the table, followed by the cutlery. By the time Gareth came back downstairs, their lunch was ready and they all sat down to eat, denying Rachel any opportunity to continue her conversation with her brother.

"Oh, I forgot to tell you, there was a phone call yesterday while you were at school, from someone called John," said Mr Moore, valiantly trying to think of something to say to lighten the mood that his daughter seemed to have brought with her to the table.

"For me or Rachel?" asked Gareth, with his mouth full.

"I'm not sure, he asked for either of you, as I remember."

"John?" the twins answered, puzzled, almost in unison. They looked at each other and shrugged their shoulders.

"Can't be for me, I haven't given our number to anyone called John," said Gareth. "Got a new boyfriend then, sis?"

"No, I have not!" was Rachel's indignant reply.

"Well, he did say he'd ring back today," said Mr Moore.

Lunch finally over, Rachel seized the opportunity to tell her brother about the dream as soon as their father had left the room.

"Look, I'm not surprised you had a nightmare," was Gareth's unsympathetic reply. "You were working yourself up about Bronwyn not phoning before you went to bed. I'm sure that's what caused it!"

"No, it wasn't a dream, it was more than that – I was there, really there! You saw me coming out of the bathroom last night; you even complained I'd been in there too long! If it was only a dream, come and explain this, then!" she said angrily, dragging him upstairs to her room where she shoved her muddied nightdress into his hands. "How did this get so dirty? And look, the sheets are covered in dirt, too!" she exclaimed, throwing back her bedcovers and revealing the bits of grass still on her sheets. "I even hurt my foot on a stone," she continued, removing her slipper and pointing to the small jagged cut, while Gareth looked on speechless. "Well?" she persisted. "What do you think?"

"I have absolutely no idea!" was all he could manage. "Maybe you sort of transported yourself there by mistake. I don't know!"

"Transported myself, and how in the world did I manage that then?" retorted Rachel.

"I don't know – I'm just trying to make suggestions!" Gareth answered helplessly.

Before they could deliberate any more, they were interrupted by the phone ringing downstairs.

"It's for you!" called Mr Moore. "It's that chap Johnny again."

Gareth ran down and took the phone from him, with his sister close behind, in time to hear her brother say, "Johnny – I'm sorry, Dad said you'd called but we didn't realise it was you, how are you? It's Johnny from the farm in Valonia!" Gareth whispered to Rachel, as their father put his jacket on and motioned to them that he was going out. As soon as he had gone Gareth pressed the conference button so that she could hear the call.

"I'm fine," Johnny continued, "but I'm so glad I've got you this time, there are things I need to tell you."

"What things?" asked Rachel.

"Hello, Rachel, gosh, can you both talk at once on your phone? That's really clever!"

"Yes, we can. What's the matter?" she asked him.

"There's something really strange going on here. I don't really know how to explain it, but it's as though things are changing. The people are changing."

"How do you mean?" asked Gareth.

"It's as though they have gone back in time, they don't remember anything that's happened over the last few years. For instance, my family don't remember anything about my accident. My Mum even asked me how I got the scar on my forehead. I seem to be the only one in the village that isn't different."

"What about Bronwyn and Catherine?" asked Rachel, increasingly worried now.

"Well, that's another thing. I know Bronwyn was here last week because I saw her – but the other day when I asked Catherine where she was, she said Bronwyn was away at university!"

"What?" the twins exclaimed in unison.

"That's impossible," said Gareth. "That's where she met Dad, before they got married, before we were even born!"

"That's what I mean," said Johnny. It's as though they've all gone back years in their minds, apart from me. Although I have to say I feel much better than I did. I used to have trouble speaking, after my accident. I knew what I wanted to say, but it just wouldn't come out. That's all gone now and I'm back delivering the post from the village again, just like I used to! That's how I can ring you from the post office."

"But where's Bronwyn?" asked Rachel, almost beside herself with worry.

"Well, that's why I thought I'd better ring you, because Catherine doesn't even seem to remember her being here last week. Isn't she with you?"

"No, and we haven't heard from her for a couple of weeks either!" replied Gareth, now as concerned as Rachel.

"You have to come back – you have to put it right," declared Johnny.

"Us, how can we put it right? We don't even know what's going on there!" Rachel protested in horror.

"You're the Keepers of the Power. You have to!" answered Johnny resolutely. "You're the only ones that can do anything. That's why I had to speak to you."

"Look, Johnny, I don't know how we can help," started Gareth.

"There's a train that comes in tomorrow at four o'clock – I'll wait for you in the pass with the horse and buggy. You have to come, you have to come and help! Look I've got to go now, people are coming into the shop and I don't want them to hear this. I'll see you on Sunday," Johnny finished, and there was a click of finality, as they were cut off.

"He's gone," stated Gareth, looking at the silent receiver in his hand. "He's put the phone down!"

The twins looked at each other blankly, not sure what to make of the conversation at all. They went back upstairs to Gareth's room, and sat down on his bed, both of them stunned by what Johnny had said.

"What on earth are we going to do?" asked Rachel.

"Well, normally I'd say nothing, since Johnny wasn't really the full ticket last time we saw him, but this time he sounded completely different. I know it's an unkind thing to say, but did you notice he wasn't talking in the strange child-like way that he did before?"

"Yes, I did notice – he was almost like a different person compared to the last time we spoke to him!" Rachel agreed.

"If there was anything really wrong there though, surely Merlin would do something about it?" said Gareth.

"Of course he would," she agreed, "but when I saw him last night he looked different, as though there was something wrong with him. He looked older and weaker; he was beckoning to me, as though he wanted to tell me something. Maybe he's ill; maybe whatever it is that's affecting everyone else is affecting him as well!"

There was a pause whilst they both stared at one another, trying to make sense of what had happened.

"I hate to say this," said Gareth, eventually, "but we're going to have to tell Dad."

"How much of it, though?" she asked.

"All of it, I think!"

"He'll have a fit!" replied Rachel.

They waited anxiously for Mr Moore's return, and they were not looking forward to updating him on what had happened. It was an hour before they eventually heard his key in the front door, and both took a deep breath before going down to tell him everything. They found him in the kitchen grumbling about how long the queues were at the supermarket as he unloaded two shopping bags. Rachel helped him put away the groceries to speed up the process and Gareth told him that they needed to talk. Slightly intrigued he followed them into the lounge as it was not often that both of his children wanted his advice on something at the same time.

He sat quietly; listening carefully, as they unburdened their story. Starting with Rachel's experience the night before, to the end of the phone call with Johnny, by which time the normally good-natured man looked fit to explode.

"That damn place! That damn, damn place! If Bronwyn's missing, I need to phone the police!" he shouted, jumping up, white-faced. "Are you quite sure this lad's right? It's a bit of a tall story!"

"I don't know, but we haven't heard from Bronwyn, and Johnny said there's something strange going on there," answered Rachel, as she and Gareth glanced nervously at each other. They had never seen their father like this before, as he paced up and down, still cursing Valonia under his breath.

"Well, that's it, I'll have to go down there, and find out for myself, with the police if necessary. They'll soon sort this lot out!" he finished angrily.

The twins looked at each other even more apprehensively – this was not going well at all! They had automatically turned to their father to help them, but suddenly realised now how little he must know about the place. They had assumed he understood all of the complications of Valonia and their heritage, given that he had helped their mother to conceal her true identity, but after his comments about the police it dawned on them that he actually knew very little about Valonia at all.

"Look Dad," said Rachel gently, "I know you don't want to hear this, but the police won't be able to do anything there. We need to find out exactly what has happened. Gareth and I will have to go."

"Good heavens, I'm not having you two disappearing off down

there! I'd probably never see either of you again! No, I'm going, and that's that!" His voice had a tone of finality, and Rachel looked at her brother uncertainly.

"Dad, if you want to go, that's fine, but Rachel's right, we need to be there. We need to come with you," insisted Gareth as his father looked about to explode again.

"Dad, believe me, I don't want to go back there again," said Rachel quickly, "but if there's something strange happening there, you wouldn't be able to stop it. Gareth and I might be able to get Merlin to help us."

"That damn place!" he repeated. "Merlin, magic, ancient powers! I can't believe I'm having this conversation again. I really thought we'd seen the last of all this!"

He sighed heavily and flopped back into the chair. "All right, we'll all go, then!" he conceded, against his better judgment.

He knew he was beaten, and if the truth were known, he didn't have the faintest idea of what he could do when he got there. He was well aware that Valonia was a law unto itself, a place where strange things went on that he didn't understand, nor ever wanted to. His wife and children were part of some heritage that no ordinary person could even comprehend – but like any husband or parent, he was prepared to try to protect his family in any way he could. Even if he had absolutely no idea how he was going to do it!

The next day, all three of them hurriedly packed a few basic essentials, and caught the train to Cornwall. As they sat looking out of the window, Rachel remembered how excited they had been the last time they made this journey with Bronwyn. Although she had made a silent vow three years ago, never to go to Valonia again, she had an even stronger feeling now that they had made the right decision to return.

Gareth, deep in his own thoughts, couldn't help feeling a bit excited. He, too, had often thought about their holiday in Valonia, and although he hadn't dared tell his sister, he had often wished he could have another glimpse of the castle, and listen to more of Merlin's tales. Despite there having been elements that were a bit frightening at the time, Gareth had found the experience there rather exhilarating. It was every boy's dream come true, to be surrounded by heroes from the past.

Mr Moore, on the other hand, was deeply troubled. He had been very quiet since their conversation last night, and was really wishing that he hadn't been persuaded to let the twins travel with him back to Valonia. He'd spent years keeping them safely away from the blasted place, at Bronwyn's insistence, and now here he was, taking them back there again and possibly into danger. He'd had enough difficulty coming to terms with their stories of magic and time-travelling the last time they'd visited, and now he was frankly out of his depth, with no clue as to how to put any of this right.

John Moore felt a moment's anger at Bronwyn for going back to Valonia and causing them to be in this situation. Admittedly she belonged there and understood the place, but he had really hoped they could make a life together, a very long way away from it. What on earth was he going to do if they couldn't find her? he thought miserably, as he glanced at his children.

"It'll be all right, Dad – don't worry, I'm sure we'll sort it out when we get there," said Rachel, noticing her father's strained expression.

He nodded, deciding to make a conscious effort to pull himself together. After all, wasn't he the one that should be reassuring them?

"We're nearly there – I'm sure it's the next stop," said Gareth, trying not to sound excited.

They got off at the pretty little station and walked up the hill, along the hidden pathway and on to the pass where Johnny was waiting, as he said he would be, with Rufus and the cart. Even Rachel couldn't help being pleased to see the big black horse. He nuzzled her gently, as though even he understood that something was wrong.

The cart made its way out of the pass, and at the top of the hill they caught sight of Valonia, innocent and sleepy-looking, exactly as they remembered it.

Johnny had been filling them in on the details of what had happened, as they were travelling. He had watched Catherine's house for a few days after she had announced that Bronwyn was at university, and there had been no sign of the twins' mother at all.

"I did a rather bad thing, then," confessed Johnny. "I waited until Catherine went out and then I climbed in through the window at the back and had a look around. All Bronwyn's things were there. Her case, her clothes – even her brush and comb were on the dressing table in the bedroom at the front. I found her address book there as well – that's where I got your phone number from."

"You did the right thing, calling us," said Mr Moore. "I'm sure we'll get to the bottom of it," he asserted, sounding a lot more confident than he felt. Johnny looked unconvinced; after all, this man was an outsider. What could he do against a powerful magic that could alter peoples' minds? No, Johnny was still pinning his hopes on Rachel and Gareth, and he smiled at them, knowingly.

"Catherine's expecting you, I told her you were coming," he said politely to Mr Moore, as he turned back to face him.

They climbed down outside the pretty cottage and Mr Moore thanked Johnny before walking up the path with their bags. The twins said goodbye, and as they left, Johnny caught Rachel's sleeve. "Your dad's very nice, but I don't think he'll be much use here. He doesn't understand our ways – he's not one of us. Not like you two."

Rachel smiled at him, as he said earnestly, "Listen, I'll help you – anything you need, just let me know, anything at all!"

"I know," she whispered back. "Thanks, Johnny, you're a good friend."

Johnny was positively beaming at this as he clicked his tongue at Rufus, who had been nibbling at the hedgerow whilst they were talking, and the cart trundled off. By the time Rachel joined them, Catherine had opened the door.

"John!" she cried as she hugged her brother-in-law. "It's lovely to see you! Is Bronwyn with you?"

"No – we thought she was with you," he answered cautiously.

"Oh, well I am sure she will be, when she knows you're here," Catherine answered, unconcerned. "Now then, who do we have here?" She looked past him, towards the twins.

“Hello Catherine, it’s us, Gareth and Rachel, we stayed with you last time with Bronwyn, remember?” asked Gareth. Catherine looked at him blankly.

“You must remember us? We stayed with you three years ago,” tried Rachel.

“No, I don’t think so, dear.” She turned to Mr Moore again, looking confused. “I’m sorry, John, who did you say they were?”

“She doesn’t remember us at all!” said Rachel, under her breath.

“Umm,” John said helplessly, as he looked from Catherine to his children, realising this was a difficult situation and that he had to handle it carefully. “They’re my niece and nephew,” he announced, immediately wondering why on earth he had complicated things even more.

“Oh, well, why didn’t you say so? Come in, come in,” Catherine said, ushering them in with a large beam on her face. “Go into the kitchen – you know where it is, John – and I’ll make you all a nice cup of tea.”

“Great,” said Gareth, as he followed his dad. “Demoted again! Why is it that whenever we come here, we’re always someone’s niece and nephew?”

“I’m sorry,” said their father, under his breath. “I just didn’t know what else to say. She has no idea who you are!”

“Sit yourselves down, now,” directed Catherine, as she filled the enormous old kettle. “I can’t understand why Bronwyn didn’t come with you. Is she meeting you here? I don’t know, her head is so full of wedding plans these days, I don’t think she knows what she is doing.”

“Wedding plans?” asked Mr Moore, looking stupefied.

“Oh, now, don’t tell me you two have had an argument!” admonished Catherine. “Is that why she’s not with you? Don’t tell me the wedding’s off!”

“Off?” Mr Moore looked at her, even more aghast. “Wedding?”

“She means your wedding to Bronwyn!” hissed Rachel.

“Err, no, no. Look Catherine, there seems to be some confusion here. Bronwyn came to stay with you; she seems to have gone missing," said Mr Moore, valiantly trying to drag the conversation back into some sort of sensible order.

"No John, she hasn't been here since she left for her term at university – she would be with you, not me! I don't understand – are you saying you don't know where she is?" Catherine asked, looking puzzled.

"Err, well, no, we don't. In fact, I was hoping you would know!" This wasn't going well at all, Mr Moore thought, uncomfortably.

"Well, she hasn't been here! Not for ... well, I can't exactly remember." A look of panic crossed Catherine's face; the tea forgotten, she sat down, looking as worried as they did. "Oh no, that's both of them, then!"

"Both of them?" enquired John.

"Yes, I don't know where Geraint is, either."

"Geraint!" they all said together, in horror.

"But he's ..." Gareth started, silenced immediately by a heavy kick on the leg and a frown from Rachel.

'Dead,' was the word he was about to say, and Rachel knew that. Geraint was Bronwyn's twin brother who had been lured to his death by Mordred when Bronwyn was living with them in Chesterton, when the twins were very young. His death, as Bronwyn's fellow Keeper, was the reason she had returned alone to Valonia and kept her own children a secret, to stop them from being Mordred's next target.

"I don't know where he is," Catherine continued, looking distraught. "I think he went on his usual fishing trip, but the truth is, I can't remember! This is awful! My mind has been in a complete fog lately. I can't remember where he went, or even when he went. Now you say Bronwyn should be here, as well? This is dreadful!"

"Don't worry, Catherine, we're here now. We'll all sort it out together," Mr Moore said reassuringly, patting her hand. "I'm sure there's a reasonable explanation for all of this."

"Yes, of course there is. I'm being silly. Oh, I am so glad you're here!" she answered, looking relieved that there was someone else to take charge. "Oh look, I've even forgotten the tea. I'll make it now."

The twins and their father sighed, and exchanged worried looks, as Catherine went back to her teapot.

Chapter Three

The Missing Graves

If their arrival had been uncomfortable, the evening was even worse, as Catherine alternated between remembering and forgetting why they were there. As the night wore on it became abundantly clear to Mr Moore that Catherine was becoming more and more confused by their very presence, and he and the twins were all quite relieved when the time came to go to bed.

The morning proved no better, for Catherine hadn't the vaguest idea who Gareth and Rachel were when they walked into her kitchen. They told her they were John Moore's niece and nephew, and were only too relieved when their father joined them. Catherine busied herself with a cooked breakfast, and as she put the plates down on the table, she stunned them all again by saying,

"So when did you say Bronwyn was getting here?"

"Oh, soon, I hope," muttered John Moore, tired of explaining.

"Oh good, Geraint will be so pleased to see her. He missed her last visit, you know."

She was interrupted by Gareth choking loudly on his bacon at the mention of Bronwyn's dead twin-brother again.

"I think we may go for a walk after breakfast, Catherine. Get some sea air," interjected Mr Moore, deliberately steering the conversation away. "The twins are anxious to look around again."

As soon as he saw her surprised look, he realised his mistake.

"Really?" Catherine asked, with a frown. "Have they been here before?"

"This is a lovely breakfast, Catherine," Mr Moore said, charmingly, deliberately avoiding her question. "I bet if we go down to the beach now, we might catch the fishing boats coming in. We could get you some nice fish for dinner."

"Oh yes," she answered immediately. "If you go now, you'll probably meet Geraint's boat coming in."

With that, they needed no further prompting, and all three of them hurriedly finished the remains of their breakfast in record time. Within a few minutes they had picked up their jackets and left the cottage.

"That was hard work!" commented Mr Moore, as he closed the gate behind them. "I'm sure I shall have indigestion later, I don't think I have ever eaten anything that quickly.

"Dad, what are we going to do?" asked Rachel, as they turned into the lane.

"Well, we aren't going to get any sense out of Catherine, that's for sure," answered their father dryly. "I think we need to go down to the village. I'm hoping that it might just be her: maybe we'll get some sense out of the others."

They walked towards the village and saw a cluster of people around the fishermen who had pulled their boats up onto the beach. Several people recognised Mr Moore and asked if Bronwyn was with him. Both Gareth and Rachel remembered some of them from their last visit, but it was quite apparent when they asked him who the twins were that, like Catherine, they had no memory of having seen them before.

John Moore, Gareth and Rachel walked further along, to the shops which were now just opening, and saw Mr Dregarney creating a stack of big metal buckets outside his hardware shop.

"He'll know who we are, Dad!" said Gareth. "He's the one who gave us the bikes last time we were here," he said delightedly, rushing towards the stout man before his dad or Rachel could stop him.

"Hello Mr Dregarney, I bet you remember us! It's Gareth and Rachel, Bronwyn's children – you lent us bikes to ride last time we came to stay. You do remember us – don't you?" he finished, changing tack as he saw the man's stunned look.

Mr Dregarney dropped the buckets with a clatter and stared at them for a moment. "Bikes? I don't have bikes here. The only bikes I have are the ones my two are riding. Are you playing a prank on me, young man?" he asked, straightening the lopsided tower of buckets. "Bronwyn's children, indeed!" he laughed. "Why, she can't be that much older than you are!" he said to Gareth, whose expression had now changed from hopeful to rather glum.

Mr Dregarney's gaze turned to their father. "Ah, it's John, isn't it – Bronwyn's fiancé? Nice to see you again! He's a bit of a lad, isn't he, this one here? Young scallywag, pulling my leg like that! He had me going as well, for a moment. Bronwyn's children, indeed!" he said, his big belly still shaking with laughter as he held out his hand. John Moore shook it, uncomfortably.

Mr Dregarney seemed quite oblivious to the fact that he had just made no sense at all. His daughter was behind the counter in the shop – they could see her quite clearly, and she was definitely far too old to be riding a child's bike. Mr Dregarney also seemed unaware of his own confusion over Bronwyn's age – he'd said she was not much older than Gareth, and yet he was apparently quite happy to talk to her 'fiancé'! This hadn't gone unnoticed by John Moore, and he shifted even more awkwardly.

"Big day soon, I hear – wedding bells, eh?" smiled the jolly man. "She's a good lass, Bronwyn – she'll make a good wife, make no mistake of that. In fact, I'd marry her myself, if I was thirty years younger. But don't tell Mrs. Dregarney, eh?" He shook with laughter again, and after another brief, stilted conversation they were glad to move on.

"This is going from bad to worse – what on earth is the matter with all of them?" said John Moore, irritably, as they made their escape.

"They don't remember us at all!" said Rachel, visibly troubled.

"Well, it was three years ago, and you've both grown up quite a bit since then," replied Mr Moore, logically.

"Dad, if you'd seen the drama that went on in the cavern with Mordred when we were here last time, you'd understand why they would remember us," said Rachel, earnestly. "The whole village was there! Merlin told everyone that we were the new Keepers of the Power. Of course they'd remember that – after all, it's the most important thing in Valonia. No-one seems the least bit concerned that we're twins, either. Last time, that was all they talked about."

The twins looked at Mr Moore expectantly, as though waiting for his answer, but he hadn't a clue how to reply, and said nothing. 'Keepers of the Power?' he thought, frantically. He had absolutely no idea what his children were talking about, and in truth he didn't like the sound of it at all. He wondered for a moment what sort of nonsense Bronwyn had been filling their heads with.

"Dad, exactly how much do you know about this place?" asked Gareth suddenly, noticing the bewildered look on his father's face.

"Umm ... not a great deal really," John Moore answered, stiffly.

"But you must do," stated Gareth, flatly. "You've been here – everyone clearly knows who you are. Besides, you lied to us for years, telling us our mother had died, and that Bronwyn was our aunt. Why would you do that unless you knew all about Valonia and why we had to be protected?"

They had walked away from Mr Dregarney's shop and back towards the beach whilst talking and Mr Moore sat down on the nearest wall, feeling totally inadequate. He looked at his children and inwardly fumed at his wife who, in short, had been completely different to anyone he had ever met, but he had loved her so much that he had willingly accepted that her background and the place she came from were distinctly unusual.

"I've only ever been here once, and it was before Bronwyn and I were married," he replied, in a tired voice. "I thought it most strange that Bronwyn didn't want her family to come to our wedding, so I insisted that we came to Valonia so that I could at least meet them. I have to admit that their way of life here came as a bit of a shock, but there are isolated cults like this all over the world, where people shut themselves off and insist on ignoring anything modern, keeping to their old traditions. Besides, Bronwyn was keen to leave it all behind her."

"Yes, but it's a bit more than that here," prompted Rachel, visibly unhappy with her father's explanation. "It's not a cult, Dad, and you must know all about it – otherwise why would you have gone along with what Bronwyn asked, and told us she was dead?"

"I shouldn't have done that. I've regretted it ever since," said Mr Moore, shaking his head. "I just didn't know what else to do."

"Well, telling the truth would have been good. Isn't that what you're always telling us to do?" said Gareth.

"I know," replied Mr Moore, "but it wasn't that simple. When Bronwyn came back from her brother's funeral she was hysterical. She told me that there was a maniac in Valonia, killing all the twins. She said he had killed her brother and that you wouldn't be safe if he found out about you. Well, naturally I told her to inform the police, but she said they couldn't stop it. She was so distressed she swore me to secrecy and insisted on coming back here alone, leaving the three of us."

"So why couldn't you tell us the truth?" asked Gareth.

"How?" asked their father. "How could I tell you both that your mother deserted you because of some ridiculous fantasy, based in a strange village that wasn't even in touch with the real world? She also insisted on being able to visit you, occasionally, and it was easier to go along with her being an aunt, otherwise you would have been devastated every time she left. I hoped that she would get over it and tell you she was your mother, but time passed, you started to grow up and I suppose I had always hoped that she would come back to us," he finished miserably.

There was silence for a moment and a glance passed between Rachel and Gareth as this confirmed that their father didn't know as much about their heritage as they had thought.

Rachel sat down next to Mr Moore and gave him a hug. "It's not your fault, Dad," she said, feeling quite sorry for him. "You're still the best Dad in the world."

Mr Moore smiled at his daughter's words and resolved to try and pull himself together. After all, he was the adult here! Coming back again to the very place that had caused so many problems for his family, had caused him to feel guilty and dispirited.

"Right, come on, let's get to the bottom of all this!" he said determinedly, getting up.

They walked back towards the shops again, hoping to find someone who could shed some light on the whole situation. However they were to be disappointed, for the village seemed unchanged. Even the villagers looked the same, physically, but something had definitely changed as the things they said made no logical sense, and none of them remembered the twins either. Johnny hadn't been exaggerating; something had affected all of them.

They reached the post office at the end of the row of shops, where they saw Johnny coming out of the door with the postbag over his shoulder.

"How are you getting on? What have you found out?" he asked expectantly, directing this more at the twins than Mr Moore.

"Nothing, yet," said Rachel, glumly.

"It's just like you said – Catherine doesn't remember us, she doesn't remember Bronwyn being here and she thinks Geraint's still alive!" chipped in Gareth.

"That doesn't surprise me," commented Johnny. "Some days my mum can't remember who my sisters and brothers are!"

"Whatever do you mean?" asked Mr Moore, horrified.

"She gets really confused. She knows who the older ones are, but some days she forgets who the younger ones are. My dad's as bad – yesterday he asked Hannah who she was."

It was Rachel's turn to look shocked, as she remembered his little sister with the pigtails who had taken a shy liking to her.

"They told Abigail she was going to be late for school this morning," Johnny continued. "She even went upstairs to get ready, but she couldn't remember what she had to wear. Not surprising really – she left school years ago!"

"So what on earth did she do then?" asked Rachel. They had both got on really well with his twin sister Abigail, who had spent so much time teaching them to ride.

"Well, the really strange thing was that by the time she'd come back downstairs, they'd all forgotten about it. She went out to the horses, the same as she always does, and started to groom them as though nothing had happened! You have no idea how peculiar it is to watch all this, when you seem to be the only one who knows exactly what's going on around you!"

"Oh, I think we're getting the picture," said Mr Moore. "Something must have happened that's affected everyone's mind. It must be some sort of illness that's resulted in memory loss."

"Is that what you think?" said Johnny scornfully. "You think it's just the people, don't you?"

"Well, yes, of course," answered Mr Moore. "What else could it be? It has to be an illness of some sort. A virus, maybe?"

"No, you don't understand. It's not just the people," said Johnny, irritated by Mr Moore's rational explanation. "It's the place!"

Mr Moore looked at Johnny even more blankly; statements like this made no sense and didn't seem to merit a response. How could it be the place? This was all completely beyond him.

"What do you mean?" asked Gareth, annoyed at his father's reluctance to grasp that this was something out of the ordinary.

"Right, come with me and I'll show you," said Johnny, marching off towards the beach.

"Where are we going?" asked Rachel, breaking into a trot to keep up with Johnny as they passed the slipway where the boats were.

"You'll see!" he answered, looking determinedly at Mr Moore.

Johnny led them up the lane to the churchyard, and up the small path that wound around the side of the church. He went right to the back, where there was only grass, bordering a few old gravestones.

"Can you remember where Geraint's grave is?" he asked them.

"Yes, it's at the back somewhere. I remember we saw Bronwyn putting flowers on it," offered Rachel.

"Try and find it, then!" challenged Johnny, looking defiantly at Mr Moore. They looked around, reading every single inscription on the graves at the back of the church.

"It's not here. I don't understand!" cried Rachel, after they had exhausted their supply of gravestones to look at. "Bronwyn was definitely at the back here, by the fence, when she visited the grave before. So, where is Geraint's grave, then?"

"It was here!" Johnny said flatly, pointing to a large patch of grass behind them. "And now it's gone!"

"There must be some mistake," ventured Mr Moore, not liking any of this at all.

"No, it was there, Dad, I remember," countered Rachel, and Gareth nodded in agreement.

Mr Moore sighed again; his worst fears were becoming realised. Things he didn't understand and had no explanation for. 'Damn place!' he thought to himself again, as they all started back down the path in an uncomfortable silence.

"For what it's worth, the grave of Mordred's sister Celia has gone as well. She was buried right here at the front, with the rest of their family. All the old graves are here, but none of the more recent ones – they've all disappeared!" said Johnny, breaking the silence. "Do you want to see? I'll show you where it was, if you like."

"No, no, that won't be necessary," said Mr Moore, sounding deflated. More graves having disappeared was something he simply couldn't get his head around.

"Have you seen Mordred lately, Johnny?" asked Rachel, abruptly.

"No, not since you were here last," Johnny replied, glancing at Mr Moore before pulling Rachel to one side. In a low voice he said to her, "You won't find out anything while he's with you. I don't mean to be rude, but he's an outsider."

"We need to find Merlin – he'll know what's going on," Rachel answered softly, her voice barely audible. "We need to get to the cavern and go through the tunnels to Merlin."

"I can take you there. I'll come round to the cottage with the buggy this afternoon - but you'll have to get rid of him!" Johnny told her, inclining his head towards the unfortunate Mr Moore.

"Oh, we wouldn't take Dad, anyway, not to meet Merlin! No, we'll be alone, don't worry. We'll wait for you to pick us up," she reassured him.

When they got back to the cottage, Catherine had left a table full of food and a note to say she wouldn't be back until later that evening. Her absence was something of a relief, and Mr Moore was profoundly grateful she wasn't there, although he didn't say so. Another awkward afternoon, with Catherine talking about her dead brother, or Bronwyn's wedding, was more than he felt he could cope with after the extraordinary revelations in the churchyard. His head throbbed and as he had expected he had been suffering with dreadful indigestion all morning after eating breakfast at a record pace earlier on.

John Moore was used to dealing with facts and figures. His life was orderly and he liked it that way. He knew about Valonia, of course, and he had listened to some of the twins' fanciful stories after their visit three years ago, dismissing them as simply excitement about the legends of Tintagel Castle. Bronwyn had returned to him and life had become normal, exactly the way he had always wanted it – but just when he'd thought he had seen the back of Bronwyn's strange past, here it was again. Worse than ever, now, because seemingly he was going to have to get involved and find some way to solve the problems this blasted place was presenting him with. Problems that he didn't even understand, like missing graves, and a whole village full of people who seemed to have lost several years in their minds! He had absolutely no idea how to put any of this right, and if he hadn't been so very worried about Bronwyn, he would have been more than happy to get on the next train home with his children and leave them all to it.

"Dad, Johnny's coming to pick us up in a while. We're going to have a ride round to see if we can find Merlin – he'll be able to tell us what's going on here," said Rachel, interrupting her father's dismal train of thought.

"I'll come with you, then," Mr Moore answered unenthusiastically, not wanting to let them out of his sight.

"We'll be safe with Johnny, Dad," Rachel assured him, firmly. "Anyway, I think it would be a good idea if you have a good look round the cottage while Catherine's out – perhaps you might find some clue as to where Bronwyn is."

Gareth nodded, impressed at his sister's diplomacy.

"Well, I suppose I could search the place," Mr Moore conceded reluctantly.

"Yeah, you see what you can find here," said Gareth, "and we'll see if we can find Merlin. That's Johnny now – come on Rach – good luck, Dad, we'll see you later," he finished quickly as they picked up their jackets and sped towards the door before their father could stop them.

Mr Moore sighed heavily as they shut the door. There had always been something really strange about Valonia he thought, as he recalled how uneasy his brief visit with Bronwyn, years ago had left him. Initially Bronwyn's home had come as quite a shock to him, but there was also something oddly familiar about it. It was almost as though it had been quite natural for him to be there, and he had returned home with an uncomfortable feeling that he couldn't explain. He had deliberately tried to ignore anything to do with Valonia since then, blocking it out of his mind, but now that same, strange feeling of knowing something and yet not knowing it was back again, making him even more disturbed.

He made his way upstairs to search the bedrooms for anything he could find. His mind kept returning to how quickly he had fitted into Valonia last time and he remembered his first riding lesson with Bronwyn – when he had found that he had perfect control of the horse, even though he had never ridden one before! He had even proved to be a better rider than any of them. He couldn't help but agree with Johnny's words, that it was 'the place'. It appeared to him now that maybe 'the place', had always had some strange effect on people.

But that was completely irrational, he thought, and reminded himself that he was normally a very rational person! No, the quicker they left here, the better, he decided with a shudder, and tried to distract himself by embarking on a practical search, pushing the unsettling thoughts firmly to the back of his mind.

The twins ran up the path and clambered in haste into the buggy. "Quick, before he changes his mind!" said Gareth, and Johnny clicked his tongue at Rufus, who moved off obligingly at a trot.

"Where to then – the pass?" asked Johnny.

"Yes, up to the top, where the entrance to the cavern is," confirmed Gareth.

Black clouds were gathering ominously above the range of hills in front of them, and the buggy rocked and swayed as they drove quickly up to the pass. When they reached the top, by the two big stone rocks, they asked Johnny to stop, and climbed down from the buggy.

However they found that the large rocks at the top of the pass looked different to how they remembered them. The two enormous stones were there, but the entrance they had crept into last time was nowhere to be seen. The stones were much closer together, and looked as though they might actually be blocking the entrance which had previously given access to the cavern.

"We are in the right place, aren't we?" asked Gareth, doubtfully.

"Of course we are," replied Johnny, looking surprised that he had even asked.

"It looks different, there's no opening here," Gareth said, puzzled, examining the huge rocks.

"Well of course there isn't – the rocks seal off the entrance until someone opens it!" Johnny answered, with a frown.

"But you'd have to move these stones, and I can't see how anyone could do that – they're enormous!" queried Gareth.

"Maybe there's a secret lever, or something," Rachel ventured, running her hands around the edge of the stones.

"Who normally opens it?" asked Gareth.

"I dunno – the Keepers of the Power, I suppose, or Merlin," Johnny shrugged.

They carried on searching for some time, looking for anything that could possibly move the huge stones. Johnny watched them, looking decidedly unimpressed.

"Oh, this is useless, I can't find anything!" said Rachel.

"Me neither!" agreed Gareth, despondently.

"You're the Keepers – aren't you supposed to know how to move the stones to open up the tunnel?" asked Johnny.

"Probably, but we don't really know anything about being a Keeper," Rachel said apologetically.

"Don't you have some sort of magic that does things like that?" Johnny asked, still finding it difficult to comprehend that they genuinely didn't know what to do.

"Well, if we have, we don't know about it," answered Rachel flatly.

"Short of using 'Open Sesame!', which obviously doesn't work," said Gareth dryly, as he waved his arms and shouted at the rocks. "We have absolutely no idea how to shift them! In fact this is all pretty useless; we might as well go back. We'll have to come back when we've figured out how to get in there. The other Keepers must have known something that we don't," he finished, as they climbed back into the buggy rather despondently.

Johnny dropped them off outside the cottage, and it was agreed that they would meet up again the following afternoon, hopefully after they had found a way of getting into the cavern. The sun was starting to go down as they knocked on the heavy door, and their father let them in, looking relieved to see them.

"Did you find anything?" asked Gareth.

"No, I didn't – shh, mind what you say, Catherine's back," he answered, putting his finger to his lips.

After another uncomfortable meal, Catherine joined them in the cosy lounge at the back of the cottage. Mr Moore had lit the fire, which was now crackling merrily in the grate, casting a warm glow around the room as Catherine brought in mugs of cocoa and biscuits. The room was cheerful and homely, but their spirits were low and the conversation was as stilted as before.

"Catherine, who are the Keepers of the Power, at the moment?" asked Rachel suddenly, almost causing her aunt to drop her cocoa.

"Well, Bronwyn and Geraint are, of course – but how do you know about such things? You're not from here," she said accusingly, looking suspiciously at John Moore. "Who told you?"

"Bronwyn told us," Rachel ploughed on, ignoring her father's discomfort and Catherine's shocked expression. "So when they become Keepers, how do they know what to do?"

"Good Heavens, what a question!" Catherine protested, looking even more horrified.

"So how do they know? Who tells them?" Rachel carried on, insistently.

"They just do. The information is handed down through the

generations. I really don't think I should be discussing this with you, and why did Bronwyn tell you? None of us ever discuss our ways with anyone from outside the village!"

"Well, she did, and all I want is the answer to one more question. If there were new Keepers and there was no one left to tell them what to do, how would they find out?"

"That would never happen!" said Catherine adamantly, although a fleeting look of concern crossed her face.

"What if it did?" quizzed Rachel, still determined to get an answer.

"Well, there are manuscripts, but that would never happen, it's unthinkable! Why are you asking me all these questions?" Catherine asked, looking flustered. "Has something happened to Bronwyn or Geraint?"

"No, no, of course not!" interjected Mr Moore quickly, glaring at his daughter.

"Where is Geraint, then? And when is Bronwyn coming?" Catherine asked, her voice starting to sound slightly hysterical. "Why does this girl know about all of this, why would Bronwyn tell her, and who is she, anyway?"

"Do calm yourself, Catherine – here, drink your cocoa, it's getting cold," Mr Moore said soothingly, passing her the mug. She took it absent-mindedly, without even looking at it.

"I don't understand, John – yet I feel as though I should. Do you know something I don't?"

"No, no, of course we don't," Mr Moore reassured her. He turned to glare at Rachel warning her not to launch into any more questions that might make Catherine even more hysterical than she already was.

"It's been a long day for all of us, I think we should go to bed. I'll see to the fire for you," he said firmly.

"But John …" began Catherine.

"Gareth and Rachel will take the mugs out, won't you?" he continued, ignoring her. "Say goodnight to Catherine, and take the tray into the kitchen," he added, clattering the mugs quickly onto the tray and thrusting it into Gareth's rather unwilling hands.

"But we …" Gareth started.

"Enough! Bed! Say goodnight to Catherine!" he said firmly, wanting nothing more than to end this conversation and get Catherine off to her bedroom.

Realising that they weren't going to get anywhere, Rachel and Gareth gave up and said goodnight, leaving their father to deal with their distraught aunt. They took the mugs into the kitchen, and as soon as they were out of earshot, Gareth said, "Wow, I can't believe you did that, badgering her like you did! Quick, let's go back and listen – they'll think we've gone to bed."

Rachel followed him and they both listened, through the small opening in the doorway, to their harassed father trying to get Catherine to calm down,

"Where's Geraint?" Catherine asked again. "He should have been back ages ago!"

"I'm sure he'll be back soon," the twins heard their father lie, rather unconvincingly.

"Why did that girl want to know about the Keepers? She asked some strange questions. Why would she want to know things like that?"

"Oh, you know what youngsters are like, all questions," he said noncommittally, and the twins could hear him frantically raking the fire to put it out as quickly as possible.

"But why did she want to know how the knowledge is passed down? We aren't stupid here – of course we have records and books which contain the knowledge, just in case – but why was she asking, has something happened?"

"No, I think she was just being nosey, that's all," he answered, in a rather tired voice. "Goodness me, is that the time? Come on now, Catherine, I really must go to bed. The fire's out, and everything will look better tomorrow!" he finished confidently.

Catherine must have accepted this, for the twins heard footsteps coming towards them and fled upstairs, retreating quickly into Gareth's room and closing the door quietly behind them.

"Well, I have to hand it to you, you surprised me, down there," her brother said, with rare admiration. "What on earth made you keep on at Catherine like that? It's not like you, at all!"

"I'm just sick to death of all this cloak-and-dagger stuff. It's no different from when we were here last time – secrets upon secrets, and no-one will tell you anything. I just thought if I kept on, she'd let something slip, but she didn't really give much away. I don't think she's very happy with me, either," Rachel said ruefully.

"Who cares? She won't remember any of it in the morning, anyway. Don't forget that she did actually say that there are manuscripts! We didn't know that before."

"Great. So all we have to do now is to find them," Rachel answered, glumly. "We don't have a clue how to do that either!"

"Not necessarily – I've got an idea," said Gareth, excitedly. "Remember those books in the attic, with Bronwyn and Geraint's names inside? The old books, that had K.O.P. on the cover? I know Bronwyn and Catherine moved them last time, because they didn't want us to read them, but if Johnny's right and the village has gone back in time, they'll still be in the attic!"

Rachel wasn't entirely convinced. "It's worth a look, I suppose, but not now, in the dark."

"No, I'll get them in the morning," Gareth answered, and they stopped talking as they heard their father coming up the stairs. John Moore opened the door and gave vent to his disapproval of Rachel's indiscreet questions.

"Rachel, what on earth possessed you to start all that downstairs? For heavens sake, we're having enough trouble with Catherine as it is, without you making her worse!" he said exasperatedly. "Anyway, I've decided that enough is enough. If there's no news of Bronwyn by lunchtime tomorrow, I'm going to the police. They can sort this out. Bronwyn is a missing person, and it's their job to deal with that, not ours! I'll get that lad to take us back through the pass to the village by the train station – there's bound to be a police station there! Now, for goodness sake, go to bed, Rachel!" he said crossly as he left.

"That's bad news, looks like we don't have long to get some answers then," whispered Gareth, before Rachel headed for her bedroom.

Chapter Four

The She-devil's Rescue

"Wake up, wake up, I've got them!" Gareth whispered, shaking his sleeping sister. He dropped two heavy books on her bed. "Hang on to them, while I go and get dressed."

Rachel sat up, rubbing her eyes and groaning as she looked at her watch. It wasn't even six o'clock yet. This was early even by Gareth's standards. She decided to throw on her sweater and jeans quickly, as she knew he wouldn't give her a moment's peace once he was back.

She was right. Gareth arrived back with two drinks and a bag of Catherine's home-made biscuits, and immediately said, "Right, come on then, let's get stuck in. You start on this one!" He thrust a big, dusty black book at her. "And I'll have a go at this monster!"

He rammed a large biscuit into his mouth and opened his book. Rachel slowly opened the curtains and sat down next to him on the bed, still half asleep.

"This is heavy stuff. I can't understand half of it," he said, after a few minutes of trying to make sense of the old-fashioned writing and language. "You got anything yet?"

"I don't know. This volume does seem to have some sort of explanations in it, as though it was meant for the Keepers," she said, hesitantly. She flicked through the old yellow pages. "Wait a minute, listen to this." Gareth sat up with interest as she read out a passage haltingly, deciphering the strange writing as she went along.

And Argante, the green goddess spake.

His body shall be laid in a place between two worlds.
A place that none shall know of, where he may lay undisturbed.
This place shall be named Avalon.
A place where none shall go, save the chosen few.
The place of Avalon shall be sealed in a time different to all others.
The line of the chosen few will remain with it always to keep the ways.
Here the Power and the Chalice shall remain with our last Great King
In a place of safety that can never be found.
None shall lay claim to them, save two appointed Keepers.
This done, the gateways shall be closed forever.
Access to the old world shall only be gained by the hearts and minds of the guardians.

"She's talking about Arthur!" said Gareth, in wonder. "He must be buried there!"

"Yes, but she also refers to the Power and a Chalice – what do you reckon that is? It must be something important," pondered Rachel, reading it again, silently. "It also says they're in Avalon – but it must be the same Power, there can't be two, surely!"

"I just don't know; that is a bit strange," answered Gareth. "She does mention two appointed Keepers though – wouldn't that be us, now?"

"Maybe, but we're not in Avalon and the bit about 'access through the hearts and minds' isn't much help, either!" said Rachel, despondently.

Frustrated, they both returned to their reading.

"I'm getting fed up with this one," Gareth said, standing up. "There are pages with strange passages on them. They're all elaborately decorated as though they're important, but they don't make much sense. Here, look at this one, for instance – it's got really weird-looking emblems that form a border that goes all around the writing."

Rachel glanced at the page briefly, before Gareth lifted up the book and read it out loud to her.

As soon as Gareth started narrating, Rachel found his voice becoming distant. The room slipped away and visions of the castle, the knights and the horsemen with lances and shields drifted in and out of her thoughts, accompanied by a strange feeling of falling backwards. She could hear Merlin's voice somewhere, and she tried hard to concentrate on his words.

"Are you listening to me?" Gareth stopped, noticing the vacant expression on Rachel's face.

"Rachel, Rachel!" he said, prodding her, slightly annoyed that she didn't appear to be responding.

She felt a strong pulling sensation as though she was rushing forwards. The images stopped, and the room became clear again. She was aware of her brother staring at her, and she blinked, several times.

"That's it!" she cried. "Did you feel something happen then?"

"Like what?" Gareth asked disdainfully.

"Something was happening while you were reading that!" Rachel exclaimed, excitedly. "It was similar to the night I went back there; it was the same sort of feeling."

"Well, I didn't feel anything," shrugged Gareth, sounding rather put out that it was always his sister that these things happened to.

"I know what we have to do. It's in our minds! That's what the other book said." Rachel grabbed the book out of his hands and read the passage. "Look, you were asking to go back!"

"Well, I didn't go anywhere – I didn't move at all," he replied, flatly.

"Don't you see? The other book was telling us that we have to think our way back – and ask permission, by the sound of it! Hold on to me tightly, and read it again."

Gareth looked doubtful, but he did as he was told. He linked his arm round Rachel's back and they both held the book in front of them, and he began to read the passage again.

"By all that remains sacred and true, we ask.
May the Great ones grant entry to the world beyond that of which we know?
To the Tombs below us: yea, to the very bowels of the earth.
To a place in time, where none but a few may venture.
We ask only in the necessity to uphold the duties entrusted to us.
We ask in the names of the great ones before us.
To protect and serve in the name of Chivalry and Honour as are our duties.
We ask to gain entry to the place that none but the true shall enter."

Gareth's words became dim and distant again as the spiralling sensation started. Rachel closed her eyes and said over and over in her mind, 'Take us to Merlin! Take us to Merlin, Take us to Tyntagyle!'

Images flashed quickly past them of the cavern and the tunnels of time as they fell backwards in a whirling cloud that engulfed them in smoky subdued colours. It wrapped itself around them as though it were transporting them in a swirling tornado. They clung tightly to each other as the air rushed around them, sucking them deeper and deeper into the unknown. Together they spun through the whirling cloudy vortex until finally the cloudiness disappeared and was instantly replaced by a falling sensation into a deep, black void, as though it had just let go and dropped them.

Suddenly it stopped and they both landed on a hard surface, the force of the impact breaking their grip on one another, and they rolled apart, stunned, both of them blinking as the daylight stung their eyes.

"Ow!" shouted Gareth, as, dizzily, he tried to get up. In trying to regain his balance, he immediately fell backwards again over a boulder.

"We've done it! Look, we're right at the entrance on the other side of the tunnel. We're back at Tyntagyle! We've gone back in time!" exclaimed Rachel, wincing slightly as she picked herself up.

Gareth looked out across the open space towards the castle.

"Blimey! So we are, we've done it! Woo hoo!" he shouted, punching the air. "That was so amazing! I can't believe it!"

"I know – we're really here! We can go straight to Merlin now!" Rachel said delightedly.

Their excitement was to be short-lived. It ended abruptly as soon as they ventured out of the tunnel entrance, and were seized roughly by several men, who dragged them away from the rocks and into the open. Rachel and Gareth found themselves surrounded by a surly band of men holding lances and hatchets. They were rough-looking and wore the rounded helmets and tunics of their time; their clothes were dirty and their hair long and tangled.

"Bring them forward. Let us see clearly the persons dropped from the sky!" growled a deep voice.

Gareth struggled and tried to kick the man behind him who was forcing his arms backwards in a vice-like grip. His kick made contact with the man's legs but did nothing to make him loosen his hold, instead he pulled Gareth's arms back even further until he winced with pain. Rachel was pushed forward and thrown against her brother, almost knocking him over as the man behind him let go of Gareth's arms. Gareth turned to kick him again, but stopped as two lances immediately came up against their throats.

"What trickery is this?" demanded the owner of the deep voice. "Why, 'tis naught but two young boys! No, no 'tis not," he exclaimed, looking closely at Rachel. "'Tis a boy, and a wench in knave's clothing!"

"'Tis a she-devil!" exclaimed a thin, rough-looking man, with a long beard.

"Aye, 'tis sorcery! 'Tis a she-devil, sent by Medraut and that witch Morgana, I'll be bound," said another.

The men stared at Rachel with open hostility.

"If 'tis a she-devil she be, we must burn her at the stake!"

"Aye, aye, we shall burn the she-devil!" more rough voices joined in, each as unsavoury as the last, pushing them from one to another.

"Take them back to the camp!" one man shouted as the men moved closer to them.

"Nay, take the witch to the camp, and we shall be cursed forever. I say burn her now, before she can weave her jinxes and hexes," another shouted superstitiously. Gradually the others joined in, shouting in agreement, poking their lances forward if either of the twins made so much as a move. The men were getting more and more menacing, and Rachel was close to tears. She shook with terror as she hung on to her brother. Several men reached forward and gingerly touched her bright pink sweatshirt, retreating quickly as though burnt. Their voices were almost chanting now, shouting for Rachel to be killed, convincing each other that she was a witch sent by Medraut.

"Stop!" shouted a commanding voice. "Make way!"

A dark figure on a pure white horse with a silvery mane came towards them. The men fell silent, instantly lowered their lances and parted for the horse to come through.

"What goes on here?" asked the figure, as he drew his horse nearer.

"'Tis sorcery, Sire! 'Tis a boy and a she-devil dropped from the sky! Conjured up by Medraut and his witch!" explained the gruff voice.

"Aye! Aye!" the others joined in.

"Silence!" commanded the dark haired man, pulling his horse up right next to them. He looked directly at Gareth. "So, young knave, what have you to say for yourself?"

"Galahad!" breathed Rachel, as she recognised the dark features and wavy hair.

"Sir, we've come to see Merlin – we need his help. We're nothing to do with Mordred, he's our enemy as well," Gareth answered, his voice shaking.

The knight said nothing, but scrutinised him carefully.

"Sir, we need to get to Tyntagyle and Merlin. We need his help to find Bronwyn – we don't know where she is and there are some really strange things going on. He's the only one that can help us," Gareth finished, aware that he had been gabbling, his words tumbling out in fear. The knight appeared not to be listening; instead he was looking carefully at Rachel.

"You know my name?" he questioned, ignoring her brother.

"Yes," answered Rachel. "We met you when we came to the castle with Merlin, some time ago. There was a feast; the other knights were there as well, and Merlin introduced us to you. Our names are Gareth and Rachel. Please take us to Merlin, he'll confirm who we are."

Galahad leant forwards, looking steadily at her. "Rachel? Rachel?" he said thoughtfully. "Yes, I believe I have met you before." A smile crossed his face then, and he sat back in his saddle and laughed. "I believe I do remember. 'Tis the goose girl, with the golden hair!"

Rachel felt her cheeks getting hotter and she knew she was going red, as she remembered with embarrassment how Galahad had rescued her from the goose that had pecked at her in the castle courtyard. Everyone had found it very amusing, apart from her! 'Trust him to remember that!' she thought, glaring at him.

"Stand aside, these are friends of Merlin and you will treat them with respect," Galahad commanded, and the men quickly stepped away. "I shall escort them to the castle myself to ensure their safety," he said with authority. "You, and you," he continued, pointing at two of the men, "you shall accompany us. Get your horses." The selected men obediently went to the group of horses to their left, untied them quickly and mounted, returning to join Galahad's pale, silvery stallion.

"Gareth, you shall ride with Owain." Galahad motioned to a large man on an equally-large brown horse, who immediately held out his hand and heaved Gareth up behind him.

"Rachel, you shall ride with me, but first you will put this on," said Galahad. He untied his cloak and handed it to her.

"I'm not cold," she answered frostily, ignoring the cloak he held out to her.

"You may not be cold," answered the young knight, the impudent grin crossing his face again, "but I will take no maiden to the castle in that unseemly attire."

Rachel glared at him again. 'Unseemly attire', indeed! She met his gaze steadily, deliberately disdainful as he threw the cloak round her shoulders.

"Put it on!" he said more firmly.

Rachel pulled the cloak around her and tied it at the front. Her lips were pursed, and she stared back at him haughtily. He held out his hand to help her onto the horse.

"I'm fine walking, thank you," she announced, and Gareth stared at her in amazement.

"Rachel, get on the horse, will you!" he said impatiently. What was wrong with her?

Galahad laughed openly. "I think you might find it a long walk, my lady!"

"Rachel, for goodness sake, just get on the horse!" repeated Gareth, incredulously.

"Are you going to ride, or would you prefer to stay with my men?" asked Galahad patiently, still grinning.

Rachel turned slightly and glanced at the band of uncivilised looking men behind her, and although the thought of having to ride with the teasing, arrogant young knight annoyed her, the prospect of being left with the mob behind them, or even of having to ride with the other man, whom she was sure she could smell even from a distance, made her finally deign to take Galahad's hand, and he pulled her up effortlessly onto the horse. She was forced to put her hands round his waist as the horses moved off. Unfortunately this didn't go unnoticed, as Galahad looked over his shoulder at her and laughed again at her discomfort. She treated him to another frosty look.

Gareth was still staring at her, trying to work out why his

usually mild-tempered sister was behaving so rudely towards the man who had just rescued them. He for one was distinctly relieved at being removed from a potentially dangerous situation, and felt nothing but heartfelt gratitude. Yet Rachel was acting unbelievably haughtily, and displaying the type of disdainful behaviour she usually reserved exclusively for Gareth's friends, when she would sniff and look down her nose at them like a disapproving parent. Gareth shook his head, and resigned himself to the fact that he would never understand girls.

The horses made their way across the open grassland in the direction the twins remembered, towards the castle at Tyntagyle, and Gareth couldn't help feeling more and more excited with every step. Rachel remained silent, sitting rigidly behind Galahad, still feeling awkward and embarrassed by this young knight who seemed to enjoy making fun of her.

"Your brother said you have travelled here to find someone?" asked Galahad, over his shoulder.

"Yes, we've come to ask Merlin to help us," Rachel answered stiffly.

"You have travelled a long way for this," Galahad commented.

"You could say that," she replied, not wanting to say too much. "How do you know?"

"Your clothes," he answered simply. "'Tis obvious that you are not from here! This person, she must be important to you, to take so much trouble?"

"She is. Bronwyn's our mother," Rachel answered, and Galahad turned sharply, giving her a brief look of understanding.

"You think she is here?"

"I don't know, but I have a strong suspicion that Mordred may have had something to do with her disappearance."

"Mordred, Medraut! Curse the very name! We have reason to believe that there is something afoot. He has set up an encampment outside the castle. My men have been watching it."

"It's not just her disappearance; it's a lot more complicated than that," said Rachel. "There are other things we need help with, things concerning where we come from," she said, aware that she probably wasn't making any sense to him, but the knight didn't question her. Instead he nodded gravely, accepting her half-hearted explanation without question, and gave her another look of sympathy.

Soon the great castle came into view, and they made their way, in single file, up the grassy causeway towards the castle entry, where the men, having recognised Galahad, had already begun heaving open the huge, solid wooden gate. The two horses walked sedately through the gateway and into the busy courtyards, and the knight led the way to the inner gate in front of the main courtyard, where they would dismount.

Galahad swung his leg over the neck of the beautiful white horse and jumped down, in one easy movement. He turned and put his hands around Rachel's waist to lift her down. For a moment she found herself looking straight at him, with her hands on his shoulders. Immediately, the awful scenes she had seen in her dream, the last time she had been at the castle, came straight into her mind as vividly as though they had never gone. For a moment, she was back there, standing on the hill with him, looking at the burning village, hearing the screams of the villagers. She felt the same deep sadness and bitter, helpless rage that she had experienced before; feelings that she knew were his.

Galahad almost pushed her away, and stepped back quickly. His roguish smile was replaced by a brief look of fear that flickered across his tanned face. The vision left as quickly as it came, and Rachel, too, stepped back, her cheeks bright pink with embarrassment.

Galahad looked at her curiously for a moment. "You are a seer, aren't you?" he asked quietly.

"Yes," she replied, looking at the floor, and he nodded, slowly.

"Come. I shall take you to Merlin."

As Galahad strode towards Owain and Gareth, Rachel saw that they had already dismounted and were waiting for them. Gareth's eyebrows were raised, and he looked at her with a puzzled expression.

"So what was all that about then?" Gareth asked.

"What was all what about?" she returned. "I was just getting off the horse, that's all!"

"Right, so one minute you're refusing to get on his horse, as though he's got the plague – and the next minute you're standing gazing up at him. So that was all in my imagination, was it?"

"Well, it certainly wasn't like you're making it sound!" she hissed, pushing past him angrily.

She waited by the turret door for Galahad and Gareth to catch up. Owain led the horses away and Galahad took the twins up the winding stone steps to Merlin's rooms. When they reached the top, Gareth knocked on the door, and they heard Merlin's familiar voice.

"Come in, come in," he said, and Gareth opened the door, bounding in first.

Just as Rachel was about to follow him, Galahad caught her arm, and she turned to look at him. "This Bronwyn, your mother. If she is here, I will help you to find her," he stated, a serious look in his brown eyes.

"Thank you," she answered and for the first time, she managed a smile. However irritating and flippant he appeared, she suddenly felt a great strength and compassion exude from him and she knew without a doubt that he was someone they could trust, with their lives if need be.

Chapter Five

The Orb of Resolution

Merlin welcomed them into his turret quarters and the twins felt instantly more at ease as soon as they entered the sanctity of the mystical room. It was exactly as they remembered with its piles of cluttered parchments and magical objects adorning every surface. It was all so comforting and familiar but, to their surprise, Merlin was not the man they remembered. He was lying on one of his long settles with a blanket over him. He looked pale and almost fragile, his rosy complexion gone. His long white hair framed a face that was much more lined than they remembered. There was a roaring log fire in the grate even though it wasn't cold.

"Rachel, Gareth and Galahad of course!" he said, nodding to the knight. "Forgive me not getting up. I am pleased to see you. Yes, very pleased indeed."

"Merlin, are you alright? You look ill!" cried Rachel, rushing over to him in concern.

"Yes, yes my child," the elderly wizard replied, waving his hand dismissively. "This is such a very pleasant surprise, most pleasant indeed!" he smiled at the twins. "And Galahad, what brings you back so soon?"

"I was on my way back to join my men, when I met up with your friends; I escorted them to the castle. I believe they have business with you, so I will detain you no longer," the knight answered with a bow.

"Galahad, I am indebted to you for overseeing the safe passage of my two young friends," said Merlin.

"Think nothing of it," Galahad replied, courteously.

"Oh, your cloak," said Rachel, as she untied it and handed it back to him. "Thank you," she added politely, not wanting to admit that she had been grateful she was wearing it when they got to the castle. She had forgotten how conspicuous she would have been.

"Think nothing of it," he repeated, with a mischievous smile, making Rachel's face turn red again. "I have pledged to help your friends," Galahad said to Merlin as he reached the door. "They come in search of a woman. I will send riders to the other encampments to find out if anyone has seen her. I will return tomorrow if I have news."

Merlin thanked him again and he left.

"Well now, well now," Merlin pondered turning his attention back to the twins. "I think maybe we all have tales to tell. What is this about you searching for someone? Sit down and tell me what brings you here."

Gareth told him about Johnny's phone call, Rachel's dream, the strange happenings in Valonia and finally Bronwyn's disappearance and Merlin shook his head. "This is worse than I feared," he said, with a worried frown.

"We thought you'd know about all of this. I thought you were calling us back. I saw you when I came back in my dream and you beckoned to me as though you wanted to tell me something," said Rachel.

"No I did not," said Merlin, shaking his head again.

"But you did, I saw you!" said Rachel adamantly.

"I don't doubt that, but that was not a vision conjured up by me. I fear this was the work of Morgana, to lure you back. In fact you are the last people I would have wanted to come back at the moment," answered Merlin gravely.

"I don't understand," Gareth said confused. "Who's this Morgana?"

They were interrupted by a shy young servant girl who brought in a tray of food and drinks, which she almost dropped as the mention of Morgana's name. Once she had left, Merlin motioned for them to eat and he continued.

"Morgana is Mordred's younger sister, renowned as a sorceress and a shape shifter, better known as Morgan Le Fey or the Black Goddess, as some like to call her. She joined him in his camp several weeks ago."

"A shape shifter, what on earth is that?" asked Rachel, looking afraid already.

"Someone who can change their form at will. She can delude people into seeing her as something completely different. She once spent two days in one of her enemy's encampments listening to all of their battle plans, and all they saw was a stray black dog!"

"Wow, I wish I could do that!" said Gareth, impressed.

"I still don't understand, Mordred hasn't got the Power back has he?" asked Rachel, ignoring her brothers last remark.

"No, no, the Power has been quite safe with its Keepers far away!"

"Oh, no, that's us and we've come back!" said Rachel. "Is that what he wanted?"

"Yes, I fear so, Mordred has always wanted the Power, as you know, but I fear now that he has his sights set on even greater things – the arrival of his sister proves that, for they have been near enough enemies for a long time. And even worse news: I have since heard that they have been joined by Morgause their mother, a powerful, dark sorceress, whose strength comes from pure evil. She is very much a force to be concerned about!"

"But surely they wouldn't be a match for you, with all of your magic?" Gareth said confidently.

"Morgause is one of the most feared sorceresses in the land. Her daughter, Morgana, although not as powerful, has a different kind of magic. The combination of these powers could conjure up the sort of dark magic that would be difficult to counteract. Mother and daughter working together, however terrible their magic could be, is something I would never have even considered possible, as they have always had such a deep hatred of each other."

"Sounds like a really nice family!" said Gareth, sarcastically, "but I still don't think they'd be a match for you!"

"Alas, they are, or were. They have already worked their magic on me. I was caught unawares and the two sorceresses have somehow worked a spell that has left me weak and powerless."

The twins glanced at each other in horror. They'd come back automatically expecting the old wizard to be able to put everything right. Instead this was all starting to sound even worse than they could ever have imagined.

"Can't you do something to break it? How could they have done this to you?" asked Gareth, still unconvinced that anyone could harm Merlin in any way.

"I believe that Mordred has something very special and very powerful in his possession. Something the two sorceresses are using to create spells that wouldn't normally be possible, even with their combined powers!" He shook his head sadly, "I fear that Mordred has committed a great desecration, and he has stolen the Chalice!"

The twins sat to attention immediately, they looked at each other, remembering the reference to a Chalice in the ancient books they had been reading back at the cottage.

"They are somehow using the Chalice to alter time. They are changing events of the past; which in turn will alter the events of the future," Merlin continued.

"Is that what's been affecting everyone in Valonia?" asked Gareth.

"Yes, Valonia would be affected first, and it could in fact have dire consequences for the village."

"What do mean, dire?" asked Rachel.

"Valonia is in its own time, it shouldn't really exist. It was created by us, not only to house the Power with its Keepers, but also to hide the Chalice. If Mordred alters enough things in the past, Valonia could disappear altogether, along with all the people in it!" Merlin said.

"That's dreadful!" exclaimed Gareth in horror. "What about us, would it affect us?"

"It would affect the whole of the future eventually, but since you are Keepers living in a different time, you were beyond his grasp," he replied.

"That's why he's tricked us into coming back, isn't it?" asked Rachel.

"I fear that it is. It would be much easier for them to get rid of you in this time, one which theoretically you shouldn't even be in. It all disturbs the balance of time, and that is a dangerous thing!" he answered, shaking his head sorrowfully again.

"So what about Bronwyn, do you think he's got something to do with her disappearance?" asked Rachel, remembering the reason that brought them there in the first place.

"I suspect that he has. I think that Bronwyn is being used as bait, to lure you here!"

"You mean that Mordred might have her?" asked Gareth.

"I think that this is something we must consider. It would make sense; it would be his best opportunity to entice you back. He knows that you would come to me for help to find her!" answered Merlin. "He has succeeded in altering time in Valonia already, but you two weren't living in that time, so he needed to bring you back here, to destroy one or both of you, for his plans to work. This puts you both in great danger I am afraid!"

"So, we've fallen into his trap, we've done exactly what he wanted!" said Rachel looking frightened.

"Yes, I fear so," said Merlin slowly, nodding thoughtfully. "But all is not lost. They may have bound my powers, but my wisdom is not something that even their magic can curtail! Besides, you must remember that you are the chosen Keepers of the Power," he said, brightening up considerably and displaying a satisfied smile as though he were secretly pleased that they were there. "The fact that you have come back here shows your true connection to the Power and it will help you put things right, stop Mordred, restore the balance of time, and equally important, you will be able to return the Chalice to its rightful place."

Rachel and Gareth exchanged worried glances again. Gareth was about to ask more questions about the Chalice, when Merlin waved his hand and said, "I must think, I will need to draw my strength from the wisdom of centuries, and my druid ancestors.

Leave now, take my cloak Rachel. Take a walk both of you, clear your heads, we will meet later for supper, and tonight we will find a way to end Mordred's plans. I will call upon the powers I had long before he was born: powers from my heritage and together we will avenge him!" he said, almost triumphantly.

The colour started returning back to the previously white, lined face, Merlin's eyes took on a vivid emerald green and his strength seemed to be returning as he spoke. He threw back his blanket and went to his desk, rummaging through the clutter as though searching for something. The twins, realizing they had just been dismissed, did as they were instructed and left. They climbed back down the stone stairs and turned, not towards the busy courtyard but to their left along the great stone walls that protected the castle on the seaward side. There were less people this way and they climbed up the steps, walking along the battlements to the highest point, passing only the odd lone sentry on duty. There was a sheer drop beyond the safety of the walls down to the jagged coastline, where the crashing waves permanently surrounded the black rocks. The wind blew strongly against them as they leant against the stone parapets looking out to sea.

"I have a nasty suspicion," said Gareth, when he was sure they were out of earshot, "that we're the ones who are going to have to put all of this right!"

"I can't see how, this is going from bad to worse!"

"I know, but Johnny automatically came to us for help because we're the Keepers, and now Merlin's got no powers to help, who else is going to do it? Ok, he's going to come up with a plan, but I've got a horrible feeling that it's going to involve us."

"Surely not!" said Rachel, worried. "It was bad enough thinking that Mordred was behind this, but now we've got two sorceresses to deal with as well! What on earth can we do against them?"

"I have a bad feeling that we're about to find out later," answered Gareth dryly.

The two despondent twins continued on their way around the battlements. Rachel, remembering the looks she had received earlier over her pink sweatshirt, hugged Merlin's cloak tightly whenever they passed anyone, so they wouldn't look too closely at her clothing. They reached the furthest point that jutted out into the sea. The wind was even stronger here and the noise of the waves battering the rocks below was quite loud. The air was damp with their spray even at the great height of the castle. Two sentries were standing talking, their bows leaning against the stone wall. They picked them up as the twins approached, but as they drew nearer, they lowered them again and nodding almost respectfully.

"'Twas you that arrived earlier with Galahad - Merlin's friends," stated one of the men.

"Err … yes," answered Gareth, not sure if he was asking a question or not.

"Heard tell there is great sorcery around," the man continued, raising his eyes almost fearfully. News obviously travelled fast here, and they wondered if the sentries had heard the men's account of them 'dropping from the sky'.

"Well we don't know anything about that," answered Gareth lamely. The men were both looking him up and down now, curiously.

"So do you have to guard here all the time?" asked Rachel coming to her brother's rescue by changing the subject. "I wouldn't have thought anyone could attack the castle from here," she said, looking over at the sea battering the rocks.

"No, and probably never will, but see over yonder," the sentry pointed to the left below them, where the rocks formed an impenetrable looking steep cliff that rose towards the castle.

"If that cliff were to be scaled, it could be a weak point; 'tis our job to guard against the enemy at every corner," he said proudly.

"Aye," his fellow sentry agreed. "So what is the news of Medraut? We have heard tell, that he has set up an encampment to the left of the causeway. Why? Well, no- one knows the answer to that, save him!"

"Aye, 'tis a mystery," agreed his comrade.

They looked at the twins expectantly, hoping to glean some knowledge as to why their enemy had set up a camp by the castle.

"I'm afraid we don't know anything about that either," answered Gareth.

"Aye, his men have been here for three days, and there is talk of two witches that accompany him!"

"Aye, Morgan Le Fey, a witch and a siren, if ever there was one!" the men nodded to each other and looked at the twins again as though hoping they would be able to give them more information on this subject.

"Well, we don't know anything about witches either," said Rachel hastily. "In fact we really ought to go now. Merlin will be waiting for us."

At this the two men nodded and the twins returned the way they had come.

"What's a siren?" asked Gareth, when they were a safe distance away.

"A woman who is irresistible to men and draws them to their deaths, I think. Don't you remember that in Greek mythology? The Greeks had loads of sirens, apparently!"

"Vaguely," answered Gareth, who was hastily racking his brains, guilty of not learning a great deal at all in that particular subject at school.

When they arrived back at the turret room there was no sign of Merlin, only the young girl Isolde, whom they remembered from their last visit. She immediately bobbed her customary curtsey as they went in.

"Merlin has asked me to tell you that he will join you anon, and he has instructed me to leave some clothes in yon room, I hope they will be to your liking miss." She curtseyed again and left, looking shy and awkward.

"Oh no, I'd forgotten about the clothes! Great, dress up time again!" said Gareth who had hated the clothes he had to wear last time.

"Well it's better than everyone staring at us as though we're from another planet. Anyway you won't need to wear them until tomorrow," answered Rachel.

At this moment Merlin entered the room followed by two girls with trays of food.

They were relieved to see that he was looking much more like his old self. He had dressed in long flowing orange robes decorated with gold braiding and his face had resumed its normal healthy pink glow. The girls quickly left after depositing two great bowls with steam escaping from under their lids, chunks of bread and a pitcher full of a strange looking brown beverage.

"Ah, now, let's eat and plan, my children," said Merlin picking up a ladle and spooning out a thick broth into bowls for them. He looked flushed and excited. His usual exuberance seemed to have returned tenfold.

Gareth was dying to ask a million questions but he managed to contain himself until they had almost finished a large bowl full of the thick, tasty stew.

"Merlin, there's an awful lot we need to know," he started.

"Ask away my boy," Merlin answered, as he patted his long beard with a thick napkin.

"Well, let's start with this Chalice, what exactly is it? It was mentioned in the old book we found in Valonia, the one we read the passage from that got us here." Merlin looked up quickly when he heard this.

"You didn't come through the cavern?" he asked in surprise.

"No we couldn't get in. The stones were blocking the entrance. We read a passage from an old book and we arrived outside the tunnel entrance, that's where Galahad's men found us," said Rachel.

"Well done, well done!" Merlin answered excitedly. "Oh, I am so pleased you're starting to use your powers! The book, do you have it here with you?"

"Oh no, we forgot about it!" exclaimed Rachel. "It must still be in the tunnel, we let go of it when we landed."

"We need to get it back then, before it falls into anyone else's hands," Merlin interjected. "That book could prove invaluable to you!"

"What about the Chalice though? You still haven't answered my question," insisted Gareth.

"The Chalice is a powerful holy object; it was brought to us for safe keeping. It is not something meant for mankind to have. Men in your time have sought it for centuries. It was buried along with Arthur so that it would never be found. It is said to have great powers, healing powers, and the power of immortality. It holds another part of the power left by the creator, the same type of power that you are so carefully guarding for us."

"You think that Mordred has it?" asked Rachel.

"Yes, I am certain they have stolen it from Arthur's tomb!" he said gravely. "But, I am still at a loss to know how. Anyone who touches the Chalice to use it for their own gain will instantly crumble into dust. I can't understand how they have managed it, but somehow they have. I am sure that this is what Morgause is tapping into in order to make her spells stronger, strong enough to bind and weaken me despite my resources. I fear that this is how they have managed to change the events in the past, something that no ordinary sorcerer would be able to do. The balance of time is something to be protected above all. To actually alter events that have gone before goes against all the laws of nature! We have to get the Chalice back at all costs; this is only a measure of what could be done with it in the wrong hands! We have to return it to Arthur's grave to put this right," Merlin finished determinedly.

"So, what exactly is this Chalice? You're making it sound very much like something I've read about, but it was called the Holy Grail," Gareth asked, his tone slightly incredulous.

"If you want to give it a name then that's what it shall be. Men have fought crusades to find this holy relic and some have even lost their lives in pursuit of it! Many have travelled far and wide and would journey to the ends of the earth to gain this trophy, because it is not of mortal making. We have to get it back!"

"So it is the Holy Grail then?" asked Gareth in amazement.

"If that is the name by which you want to call it, then yes, it is," answered Merlin.

"So while everyone has been looking for it for hundreds of years, it's been buried in Avalon with Arthur?" asked Gareth.

"That's what the book said," exclaimed Rachel, "in a place between two worlds."

Merlin nodded. "It has been a well kept secret, safe in Arthur's tomb in Valonia. I have no idea how Mordred found out about it."

"You just said 'in Valonia'," questioned Rachel, "The book said the Chalice was in Avalon."

"Do you not remember my telling you before that Avalon, and Valonia are one and the same," answered Merlin. "The only thing that is different is the time, Avalon was Arthurs resting place and years later the spelling altered and it became Valonia."

"So Valonia is really the Avalon that everyone has been trying to find for hundreds of years as well," Gareth mused. "But the book also said it was a place in-between two worlds where 'none can go'. What did it mean by that?"

"They are both in entirely different times, balancing between times natural course, rendering it impossible for anyone else to go there."

"But Dad's in Valonia now and he's been there once before with Bronwyn, before they were married. He's not from there, so how does that work then?" asked Gareth, still puzzled.

"I had no idea your father had been to Valonia," answered Merlin in surprise. "And he is there now? That's most unusual, as he is not from the line."

"So other people don't go there at all then?" asked Rachel.

"No, no they don't, they wouldn't find it, because in your time it isn't there," replied Merlin. "Maybe your father was allowed in because he was brought there by the Keepers, Bronwyn or yourselves. There can be no other explanation."

"So how on earth are we going to put all of this right?" asked Gareth, doubtfully.

"Ah that will be simple!" said Merlin confidently. "You will find the Chalice and return it to Arthur's grave. In doing that, you will also find Bronwyn, as I am fairly sure that Mordred is holding them both and the problems you have told me about will all stop!"

There was a silence in the room as the twins stared at Merlin.

"We have to find it?" asked Rachel, glancing at her brother, who was nodding silently with an expression that said 'I told you so'.

"Yes of course," answered Merlin. "You are the ones sent to do this task and the Power will help you, after all you are its Keepers!"

"That's all very well Merlin, but how are we meant to do that?

We can't stop Mordred on our own! You want us to not only rescue Bronwyn, assuming we can find her, but we've also got to take the Chalice away from Mordred and two sorceresses! We came here for help and now you're telling us we've got to do this all this on our own!" Rachel said jumping to her feet, unaware that tears of exasperation were rolling down her cheeks.

"I know this might all seem a bit daunting, but you are not on your own, my child," said Merlin, only slightly sympathetically. "The Power is with you and you are the seer, you will know what to do, it will guide you. After all, this is why you came here, to put things right and to find Bronwyn, did you not?"

The absurdity of Merlin's statement did nothing to calm Rachel. In fact it had the opposite effect and her tears rolled down even faster as she realised that the old wizard was quite confidently expecting them to sort everything out themselves. Leaving them with a situation that was much worse than the one they had originally come to enlist his help on.

"You keep saying I am a seer, but I'm not, I don't see anything!" she said, miserably.

"Yes you do, my dear!" Merlin insisted.

"No I don't!" she exclaimed.

"That is because you choose not to, and you close your mind to it. Come, come over here." Merlin got up and went to his desk. He pushed aside a clutter of parchments, clearing a space in the middle, and went to one of the cabinets behind him. He opened up the leaded glass doors and took out a strange looking object, placing it in the middle of the desk.

"Come," he beckoned to Rachel again, and the twins joined him at the desk, looking curiously at the odd, antiquated article placed in the middle of Merlin's jumble of papers. It was a huge, round ball made of a smooth glass or crystal, which appeared to float inside a metal criss-crossed, cage-like frame on a stand. "Gareth, I would like you to go first, look at the ball inside and tell me what you see, describe it to me."

"Well, it's a metal frame, a bit like a bird cage, one of those old fashioned ones. Except there's a small dragon on the ring at the top," said Gareth as he inspected it carefully.

"Yes, yes, never mind the frame. Look inside it, what do you see?" replied Merlin impatiently.

"There's a glass ball, it's a bit like the one that the gypsy had at the fair," continued Gareth, bending down to look closer. "Now that's weird, because it's not actually sitting on the frame, it's sort of suspended in the middle. What on earth is it?"

"This is the Orb of Resolution: it's very rare, in fact it may be the only one left in existence," answered Merlin knowledgably. "Now Rachel, come and tell me what you see."

She did as instructed and examined it, the same as her brother had.

"It's exactly what Gareth said," she replied.

"Look closer at the ball, is it like the gypsies crystal?"

"No it isn't," she said, as she inspected it again. "It's nothing like it, this one's completely different - it's almost like a big drop of water, waiting to splash."

"It's not solid then?" asked Merlin quietly.

"No, it's moving inside, rippling just like water, and it's going round. It looks as though it's floating in the middle of the frame."

She was fascinated now, as she watched the orb rotating gently, every moment looking as though the invisible skin would burst and its contents flood over Merlin's cluttered desk.

"Now, clear your mind and concentrate on the orb. Ask it to show you what you need to know," Merlin said softly.

Rachel gazed at the moving orb, the watery movement within it was quite strange and she felt her thoughts starting to drift. She couldn't help but look deeper into it as she saw tiny threads of colour emerging deep within the fluid substance. They began to move together until a picture was forming.

"What can you see?" asked Merlin, his voice barely audible.

"I can see a woman," answered Rachel, fascinated, as a figure began to materialize deep within the ball. "She's really beautiful and she has long blonde hair, she's wearing a long green dress and there's a big pendant round her neck." She leant closer to see clearer, totally absorbed.

"It's a strange metal pendant; it's got red stones in it, set in a sort of C shape, and there are leaves raised up in the metal curling round the stones."

"That's interesting," Merlin nodded and stroked his long beard. "What else do you see?"

"Riders, horses," she answered, as the woman disappeared and a new vision appeared, deep within the ball. "No, it's Gareth and me, we're riding with them. Galahad's white horse is leading, and we're heading towards a group of big tents with black flags flying from their tops. There are lots of men dressed in black and silver tunics. The silver bits are metal, like strips of armour! We're riding straight past them out towards the sea. Oh it's gone!" she finished as the picture disappeared. She looked back at Merlin in surprise, to see him nodding and smiling in satisfaction.

"There you are my dear, I think you have just proved to yourself that you are a seer!" he said, as he scooped up the strange object and locked it safely away in his cabinet.

"Have I?" she asked, still unconvinced. "But how do you know?"

"Because only a seer can use the Orb of Resolution!" he announced firmly. "It didn't work for your brother, all he saw was a solid glass ball, but you saw things in it that only a seer would be allowed to see!"

"But what I saw wasn't any help, it didn't mean anything," Rachel answered.

"Well you are a novice, but I can assure you that anything you saw will mean something. Something that will, no doubt, become apparent in time."

Rachel looked at Gareth and shrugged her shoulders. Merlin seemed quite happy with her performance.

"Now, we will retire!" the old wizard announced. "Tomorrow will be a big day and a good night's sleep is in order now, so that we may prepare ourselves!"

"Prepare ourselves for what?" asked Gareth dubiously.

"Well, for whatever tomorrow may bring, of course," replied Merlin unperturbed. "Your room is ready upstairs and there are clothes for you to put on in the morning. I bid you good night! Sleep well, for you will need all your strength tomorrow," he finished with a wave of his hand towards the other room. The twins found themselves automatically heading up the narrow staircase towards the small bedchamber without even bothering to protest, slightly confused, deflated and, strangely enough, extremely tired.

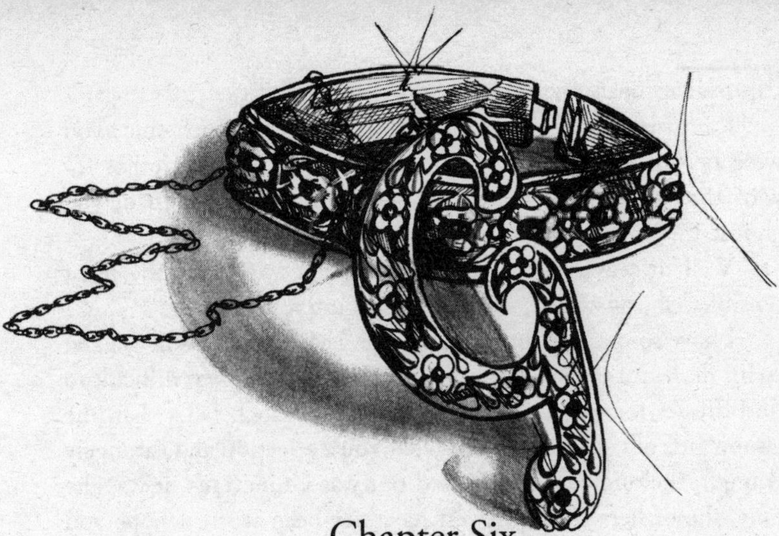

Chapter Six
Guinevere's Gift

Gareth opened his eyes and found that Rachel was already up and dressed. She was busy brushing her hair.

"Blimey, you look different!" he said sitting up. He had fortunately missed her trying each dress on in turn until she had finally picked a simple, long, dark green one. They had slept in the large bed, something neither of them had been impressed with, used to their separate bedrooms and privacy at home.

Gareth rubbed his eyes. "Great plan of Merlin's, last night!" he said sarcastically, remembering last night's events.

"Tell me about it!" his sister answered. "I'm dreading what's going to happen today!"

Gareth smiled wryly and got out of bed to inspect the clothes left for him. Rachel left him to it, not wishing to hear his complaints. She went down into the turret room which was empty apart from some more trays of food and drink, which she helped herself to and looked idly at Merlin's desk.

"This outfit's not as bad as the tights last time," remarked Gareth, to her surprise, as he joined her. "At least its baggy trousers and a shirt, like Galahad wears," he continued. "I can put up with that!"

At this moment they were joined by Merlin, who nodded his

approval at their appearance.

"I am so glad they fit, you've both grown so much since you were here last; it was more difficult to find suitable clothes for you! That is an interesting choice of dress Rachel, what made you choose it?"

"Well, it was the plainest; I thought it would be the most sensible," she answered, surprised at his interest.

"I have something for you, my dear," Merlin said as he walked to his desk and picked up a small wooden box. "It was difficult to find dresses for you this time as you are so much taller than the young girls of your age here. So I left you a selection and, strangely enough, the one you have picked out was Guinevere's, it was the only one of hers there, the rest have not been worn. I hope you don't mind."

"No, no, not at all," she answered, stroking the dress reverently. This made it even more special. Merlin opened the wooden box and handed a piece of jewellery to Rachel.

"It's the pendant I saw last night in the orb!" she exclaimed as she held it in her hand, admiring it. "It's not a C, it's a G, I didn't see the small bit on the end, I was too busy looking at the leaves and the stones!"

"You described it exactly last night, and this morning you have picked out Guinevere's dress, so there must be some reason to this," Merlin said, as Rachel examined the necklace. "This pendant was a gift to Guinevere from Lancelot. As you probably know she was married to King Arthur and this was a forbidden relationship. But they loved each other none-the-less and because of this she left it with me for safe keeping. She was never to return for it!" he nodded sadly remembering the events of the past. "It has been in my cabinet ever since."

Before Rachel could answer there was a knock at the door and Galahad entered, giving Merlin a deep bow.

"I have news," he stated.

"Galahad, come, take some refreshment while you enlighten us!" Merlin answered. Galahad nodded towards Rachel and Gareth before he accepted a plate of food from Merlin and sat down.

"My riders tell me that Mordred was seen several days ago, travelling with two women and a wolf following behind them. One of the women was old and dressed in black. They recognized her as Morgause. The other woman they said was younger and very pale skinned with golden hair," he said with a glance at Rachel's thick hair, which was the same colour as Bronwyn's. "They could not get close as the wolf was circling them and their horses became nervous, but they called out to them and Mordred ordered them away," continued Galahad. "They said that the golden haired woman neither turned her head, nor acknowledged their presence. She stared in front of her, like a person bewitched. My men are soldiers; I trust what they say, they are not generally given to being fanciful."

"We trust your judgment, Galahad, pray do go on," Merlin urged him.

"Mordred and his companions were travelling away from his encampments towards the headland and they were on their own."

"Mmm," pondered Merlin in response, tugging at his beard thoughtfully. "It is unlike Mordred to travel without his men."

"Most unlike him!" agreed Galahad, "especially since he was travelling with women! I have never seen him travel anywhere without guards. He has set up an encampment by the causeway, and there is word that he intends to set up another. This bodes ill, my friend! This must mean he has more men on the way. I cannot think of any reason for this, unless he is intending to make an attack on the castle."

"Surely not!" answered Merlin. "Mordred doesn't have enough men to do that, and if this was his intention, he would be in the camp with his men, preparing them for battle!"

"Then I hope I am wrong, my friend, but 'tis still a strange affair."

Gareth and Rachel listened intently to the two men's conversation; Rachel was still holding the pendant, stroking its metal leaves absentmindedly. Suddenly the room and people in front of her disappeared and were replaced by a cloudy vision of galloping horses, with riders holding banners, lances and crossbows. She looked across the room and stared at them all with a glazed expression.

"There are many men coming. They're riding over the hills, I can see them!" she stated, as they all turned to look at her, surprised by her sudden intervention. "They're Mordred's men! He's not with them though, he's in a cave by the sea," she continued as the vision changed. "It's surrounded by rocks and high cliffs, Bronwyn's there with him. We're meant to go there, we're meant to stop him!" she said, as she unknowingly placed the pendant on the table. The room drifted back into place again and she was conscious of their surprised faces.

"You can trust what she says," Merlin said, noticing the stunned look on Galahads face.

"I know that," the knight answered, still looking at Rachel.

"If this is the case, and you are to go to Mordred, you will need to go quickly, while there is still a way through," said Merlin to the twins. "And Galahad, you must send out a warning!"

"I will send riders to the others," he answered immediately. "I will summon the other knights to gather their men from the villages, so they may bring up their forces from behind to surround them. We need to put the castle on alert, my friend. If there is to be a battle, we will need to prepare."

"But what are we going to do when we get to Mordred? We can't go on our own, we don't even know where this cave is," said Gareth.

"I shall take you," said Galahad standing up. "They will be safe in my care," he added towards Merlin.

"I have no doubt of that!" answered the old wizard.

"I will go now to alert Kay, Bors and Percivale. I will meet you both in the courtyard with the horses," he finished, and bowed before heading for the door.

"Thank you, Galahad, and may God protect you," said Merlin, with his customary nod of the head.

The door closing brought Rachel back to her senses. She was vaguely aware of what she had said, although it had been as though someone else had been speaking.

Gareth and Merlin joined her at the desk, where Merlin picked up the pendant.

"Put it on," he instructed. "I want you to wear it at all times, for some reason this pendant is helping you to unleash your powers," he said, ignoring her horrified look and fastening it round her neck.

"Did I just dream that we are going to go after Mordred?" she asked, the full meaning of the conversation suddenly sinking in.

"You most certainly are!" Merlin answered proudly. "Such a vision, my dear, and I do believe that Guinevere is helping you, through the pendant."

"Why would she want to help us?" Rachel asked.

"Guinevere would have enough reason to want Mordred dead," Merlin answered.

"Why?" joined in Gareth, as inquisitive as his sister.

"'Twas Mordred that told Arthur that Guinevere was in love with Lancelot: a secret that would have come out eventually, but a secret that he took great pleasure in telling, because he knew what the consequences would be."

"And what were they?" asked Gareth.

"They had done wrong, and for that they both died, Lancelot as a traitor to the King, and Guinevere on the stake as an adulteress!"

"That's awful!" said Rachel, touching the pendant on her neck in sympathy.

"Awful it is, yes, but we all have to take the consequences of our actions. Lancelot knew she was Arthur's wife and Guinevere was guilty of loving two men. Sometimes we cannot help who we fall in love with: that is something, as mere mortals, we have no control over!" said Merlin.

"That's so sad!" said Rachel. "I'm surprised that you can forgive her though, since Arthur meant so much to you."

"Guinevere was very young, and it is a huge honour to be betrothed to the king. In turn she grew to respect and love Arthur. I know that! But Lancelot was probably the true love of her life, maybe the person she should have married, had things been different!" he said sympathetically. "Anyway, I have something else

I want you to take with you." He produced a small silver dagger in a sheath studded with sparkling red jewels and held it out to Rachel. "This was Guinevere's too, hide it on your person and let no-one know you have it."

Rachel took it solemnly and put it in one of the deep pockets in the dress where it would be concealed by the folds.

"Now then, young man, come with me," Merlin instructed Gareth, who dutifully followed him to the other end of the room where the wizard opened up a large wooden trunk. After much rummaging he produced some chain mail and a leather helmet, which he thrust at Gareth, before going over to one of his many cabinets. He unlocked it with a key taken from a large bunch that he pulled out from under his robes. The cabinet door swung open to reveal a collection of swords, standing neatly in a wooden rack.

"Hmm … now to find one that suits - always difficult!" Merlin said, as he pulled out one after another, looked at Gareth, and put them back in turn. Eventually he took out the lightest sword he could find, and handed it to him. "I think this one might serve your purpose," he said, as Gareth gingerly took the sword from him. It felt nothing like the thin rapiers that Gareth was used to duelling with in his fencing lessons. It may have been the thinnest sword that Merlin had, but it was still much heavier than any of the swords he was used to handling. His face paled as he held the sword awkwardly in his hand and the thought that he might actually have to use it against someone was even more unsettling. In his lessons no-one got hurt, the swords were pulled back before they made contact with the body: and he looked at Merlin despairingly.

"No one will be expecting you to use this in battle," said the old man kindly, as though he could read his thoughts. "But best to have it anyway, just in case you need it."

They wrapped up the rest of the food in a large cloth and went to join Galahad downstairs. As they left, Merlin whispered to Rachel, "Remember, trust your instincts!"

Rachel nodded and hugged him. They made their way down and into the courtyard. Bors and Kay had joined Galahad with several other men, their horses saddled and ready to go, and the twins joined them nervously.

"We will ride to my camp first and pick up an extra horse for you," said Galahad. "The others will ride on to collect support from their villages; we will leave them and continue to the headland to find Mordred. There are many caves there, I am sure we will find him in one of them."

The twins nodded silently in reply.

"Gareth, we have a horse for you." Galahad indicated a spirited chestnut mare, its reigns held tightly by Kay. "Rachel, you will ride with me."

"I can ride with my brother," said Rachel, as Galahad once again held out his hand to pull her up onto his horse.

"You will not," he said firmly as he caught her hand and pulled her upwards. "Your brother will have enough trouble with the horse, never mind defending himself if need be! No, you will ride with me where you will be safe."

Rachel looked hopefully at Gareth, who was valiantly struggling to control the large spirited horse that was dancing backwards, tossing its head, instantly recognizing an inexperienced rider. With a sigh she gave in and decided not to argue.

Mounted and ready for their mission, they made their way out through the gate and onto the grassy causeway, where the horses followed each other in single file.

"I'm sorry, but we need to go back to the tunnel entrance, where you met us," said Rachel. "We've left something really important there. Merlin said we had to get it back."

"Then we shall stop there first," answered Galahad, not even asking for an explanation.

They reached the tunnel quite quickly. The men pulled up their horses and waited, while Rachel, Gareth and Galahad dismounted and went into the entrance. Galahad, raised his eyebrows when they told him that they were looking for the old book, but politely said nothing and helped them search. It was Gareth who eventually found it further inside the tunnel, wedged in-between two boulders.

"Stop, listen!" said Galahad, silencing them as they picked up the book, trying to straighten out the pages. They stopped in their tracks and listened to an eerie sound, coming from deep within the tunnel.

"What is it?" whispered Rachel as the strange, echoing, clopping noise got louder.

"Horses, if I am not mistaken!" answered the knight. "Quickly, hide behind those rocks!"

Galahad pushed the twins out of the tunnel, and indicated to the other men who quickly positioned themselves either side of the entrance with swords drawn. The twins did as he instructed and ducked down out of sight. The noise got louder, until even they could tell it was the sound of horse's hooves.

"There are only two horses!" said Galahad listening intently. "Take the men as they come out!"

His men stood poised and Gareth and Rachel held their breath as a figure emerged from the entrance leading two horses and Galahad's men leapt out, their swords in front of them.

"Don't hurt me!" came a frightened voice. "Please don't hurt me!"

"Johnny! It's Johnny!" shouted Gareth standing up. The men lowered their swords slightly and looked first at Gareth and then back at their frightened victim.

"Gareth!" said Johnny relieved.

"You know this person?" asked Galahad.

"Yes, it's Johnny!" said Rachel, following her brother out from behind the rocks. "Oh, you've brought Rufus!" she exclaimed, as she saw the big black horse Johnny was leading.

"Rufus?" questioned Galahad.

"Yes, he's brought me Rufus; he's the horse I normally ride."

"He's our friend, he's been helping us," joined in Gareth, as Johnny took in the sight of the knights, looking from one to another in open admiration.

"Hmm, you look a strong enough lad," said Galahad, eying Johnny up and down. "Can you fight?"

"I … I'll … have a go, sir," stuttered Johnny, his eyes shining in wonderment.

"If he is their friend, then he is with us, and we could do with one more. Give him a sword!" said Galahad, and Bors tossed a heavy sword to Johnny, who caught it deftly.

"This alters our plans; we have an extra man and an extra horse. Kay, Bors, you can travel on without me to alert the others. Go to my camp first and alert my men, send riders to Caerwise and Alturnun. We need to form a considerable army behind Medraut's camp. I have an ill feeling that we may need all the men we can muster," Galahad instructed the others, and they nodded in agreement. "We will ride on to find Medraut," he finished.

With that, the men mounted their horses and rode off at great speed. They briefly watched them go and Rachel climbed up onto Rufus's broad back.

"Come we will ride we will need to make haste as the tide can be fickle on the headland," said Galahad, and they all followed him, galloping off in the opposite direction to his men.

"Where are we going?" asked Johnny, his face flushed with excitement.

"To find Mordred! I'll fill you in on the details as we ride," answered Gareth. Johnny drew his horse up next to Gareth's, listening carefully to the events that had happened so far and about the Chalice.

"That's unbelievable!" said the young farm boy, his eyes as round as saucers. "And that's really Galahad, the Knight? Lancelot's son Galahad! That's so ...!" For a moment he was speechless. To be a part of this was more than he could ever have hoped for, even in his wildest dreams. "I won't let you down," he said solemnly. "I will do anything, anything at all!"

"We know. You've helped already by bringing me Rufus," smiled Rachel as she drew level with them, comfortable now riding the solid black horse who responded to her as though he read her thoughts. "I don't understand how you got here though," she finished.

"Well, I took the horses to meet you, like I said I would. Remember?" he started, and they nodded, recalling their last conversation with him. “But when I got there your Dad said he didn’t know where you were, and that you had gone out early. So I thought you must have gone back to the cavern, and when I got there the rocks had moved and the entrance was open, so I thought I would follow you and bring the horses.”

Rachel and Gareth exchanged a puzzled look, each wondering how or why the entrance was open and how Johnny had been able to enter the long tunnel that had subsequently allowed him to travel back in time. Neither of them told Johnny about how they had got there themselves!

“I have heard of this place, but I never thought I would ever see it,” finished Johnny, still in awe of the position he found himself in.

They followed Galahad down a steep overgrown track until they reached a small shingle beach surrounded by high, rugged cliffs that jutted out towards the sea. The tide was out and a wet sandy beach was left beyond the rocks. The sand was dark with deep rivulets left by the waves that had been pounding against the rocks earlier that day.

“We will tether the horses over there and continue on foot,” instructed Galahad as he dismounted and led his horse back into the shrubbery behind some trees. “It is too rocky further round for the horses; no-one will see them here.”

They all dismounted and followed Galahad, looping the reins over the branches.

“Is it safe, to walk on the beach? It’s very wet?” asked Rachel, remembering the stories of quicksand when they were in Valonia.

“When the tide is out this part is safe, although I believe there is quicksand further on round the next headland. The tide is the thing to watch here, it comes in fast and will cut off the way back if we are out there too long,” Galahad replied. “Do not worry,” he grinned at Rachel’s horrified look. “If need be there are many caves all along here that the tide doesn’t reach. Merlin has entrusted you into my care and I will not let you drown.”

She didn’t answer, annoyed again by his almost patronizing manner, which made her feel so awkward. He didn’t speak to her brother like that, or if he did, it obviously didn't bother him. In fact both Gareth and Johnny seemed eager to please him.

They followed Galahad again onto the beach climbing over the stretches of rocks interspersed with stretches of wet sand, along the rocky coastline. Much to her annoyance Galahad took her arm on several occasions and helped her over the slippery rocks, which she was finding so difficult to scale. She was hampered by her long trailing skirts, which were now wet and heavy. Johnny and Gareth, oblivious to her predicament, were scrambling ahead much faster, holding on to their swords which were slung in leather straps hung from their waists to prevent them catching on the rocks as they leapt from one to another with ease. As the boys climbed over a larger set of rocks and jumped down on to the sand they stopped in their tracks as they saw a large cave with an equally large wolf standing in the entrance.

The wolf saw them and hunched forward into an attacking position, baring its teeth, and snarling, as it fixed its gaze steadily upon them. Galahad and Rachel jumped down behind them as Gareth immediately put out his arm to stop them.

"Keep still!" he hissed. "There's a wolf, and it's ready to come at us at any minute!"

"Wolf? What wolf?" asked Rachel in surprise, looking down the beach.

"The one in the cave entrance, that's about to attack us! Are you blind?" Gareth replied, as he drew his sword and pointed it in front of him. Johnny and Galahad did the same, all their eyes steadily fixed on the snarling wolf.

"I can't see any wolf," stated Rachel, fearfully looking around the rocks. "There's a woman in the cave entrance, but there's no wolf!"

She looked in the same direction as the rest of her motionless companions and her gaze was met by the steely black eyes of a beautiful young woman dressed in black with strings of heavy black jewellery adorning her milky white skin. Her long, straight, jet black hair hung in a heavy curtain down past her waist, and she stared, unflinchingly at Rachel who immediately felt a chill go through her as she met the hard black eyes.

"Are you telling me you can't see it?" asked Gareth again, incredulously. "It's growling at us, as we speak!"

"No, I can't see any wolves, but there's definitely a woman in the entrance," answered Rachel. "And she doesn't look too happy to see us!"

Chapter Seven

The Golden Casket

They stayed motionless with swords drawn, all eyes on the wolf as it snarled again. Rachel in turn stared at the hostile lady in the entrance.

"You see a woman?" questioned Galahad, not taking his eyes of the wolf. "Describe her."

Rachel described the young woman, who was quite beautiful in a cold, hard way, her haughty gaze still meeting Rachel's with a look of sheer malice.

Galahad gave a short laugh and dropped his sword slightly. "Stay there, I think I know who you can see, Rachel." He took several paces forward and Johnny and Gareth, seeing this, raised their swords even more nervously.

"Is he mad?" said Gareth, amazed at Galahads audacity.

"Morgana, I take it that this is your latest guise," said Galahad as he stepped forward to face the wolf. "You must be coming up in the world, the last I heard; it was that of a mere stray dog!"

Johnny and Gareth both gasped and stepped back in fear as they watched the shape of the wolf grow bigger, twisting and writhing, finally distorting hideously until it was replaced by the form of a beautiful, slender, black-haired woman now looking intently at Galahad. Rachel, however, saw none of this and looked incredulously at the two boys, watching their mouths drop open in awe, at the transformation they were witnessing. They hurriedly scrambled back onto the rocks in fear, as Galahad calmly walked towards the black-haired woman.

"What's the matter with you?" Rachel asked them.

"Didn't you see that? It was horrible! That wolf has just stretched, and stretched until it turned into her," said Gareth, pointing towards the woman that Rachel had been looking at all along. She stared at him blankly, not understanding any of his garbled explanation.

"So I was obviously right," said Galahad laughing casually, even though the woman he now conversed with had, a few seconds ago been a wolf!

"This is indeed a pleasure, Galahad, as always my favourite knight. Pray tell me what brings you to seek me out?" came a low sultry voice in reply.

She smiled at the knight and held out her hand, her eyes never leaving his face. Galahad responded by taking the offered white, shapely hand, and kissed it.

"The pleasure is mine Morgana," he said with a bow. Her dark red lips formed a perfect smile and the long dark lashes fluttered almost coyly around the black steely eyes. Morgana tossed the long curtain of jet black hair, smoothing it gracefully around her shoulders. Rachel looked on in disgust at this display of mock affection.

"So, Galahad, pleasant that it is to dally with you, you have not answered my question. What brings you here?" she asked, her tone sharpening slightly, the smile never leaving her bewitching, pale face.

"Though 'tis a treat to behold such beauty again, I seek an audience with your brother. I believe you travel with him?"

"My brother?" she asked inquiringly. "You are well informed as always, but why would you still seek my brother when you now have me?" The lashes fluttered again as she caught Galahad's arm, affectionately stroking it, looking steadily up at him alluringly and with a certain familiarity.

Rachel glared at the woman now, as the two boys stepped forward to join her.

"I have matters to attend to with him," stated Galahad pleasantly, still looking at the dark-haired woman.

"I think I'm going to be sick in a minute, if I have to watch much more of this!" said Rachel under her breath.

"And who is this, that you bring with you?" Morgana asked, the hard, steely eyes turning sharply towards Rachel, unconcerned with her two companions.

"She is naught but a young wench from the castle; she travels with her brother and a friend. I am merely overseeing their safe passage," answered Galahad dismissively.

'Wench?' thought Rachel angrily. 'How dare he, wench indeed!'

"I think not, sir," said Morgana sharply. "A wench she may be, but a wench that can see through the guise of a shape shifter? I think not! I think you try to deceive me, sir! I ask you again, who do you bring?"

"I bring you someone that your brother will want to meet," Galahad answered glibly, the pleasant bantering tone never leaving his voice.

"That's better, so you have come to deliver this person and her companions to my brother?" she retorted, her voice pleasantly sultry again. She flicked back the long curtain of black hair again, never taking her eyes of Galahad. "So deliver the wench and her peasant friends, and you shall be free of them. My brother will deal with them, leaving you only the pleasant task of entertaining me. What say you to this? Is this not a good idea?"

"Whatever you wish, my lady," smiled Galahad.

"These are my wishes; I trust you will fulfill them?"

"Most certainly, Morgana, how could I resist?"

Rachel was almost bursting with anger at this point. It was bad enough being referred to as a wench, but what was he playing at? Whose side was he on? He certainly hadn't given any of them a second glance since he had encountered the dark beauty before them! She said as much angrily under her breath to Gareth, who shrugged his shoulders, as puzzled as she was.

"He did volunteer very quickly to come with us, and he did seem to know exactly where they were I suppose," he answered reluctantly, not wanting to think badly of the knight who had been more than helpful so far.

"Yes, and he might very well be turning us over to them, and we're just following on blindly, straight into a trap probably. He seems to know this woman very well!" stated Rachel, as Morgana's hard, cold gaze turned to her again.

"Follow, if it be your will," said Morgana nastily over her shoulder to them, as she led Galahad into the cave, her long black dress swishing gracefully as she walked.

They glanced nervously at each other and followed behind. The cave was large, and very dark. It took a few minutes for their eyes to adjust before they could make out two figures at the back of the cave and an orange glow shining from a recess in the rocks to their left. A small, stooped woman draped in black was coming forward towards them, silhouetted by the orange glow behind her. Morgana and Galahad stepped aside to let her pass with Morgana whispering something to her as she passed them.

As she came closer they could see she was old. The face underneath the dark cowl was almost skeletal, its brown skin creased with deep lines stretched over jutting, angular bones. Her sunken dark eyes glinted malevolently at them out of deep, dark sockets, as piercing and intent as those of Morgana, but containing a look of sheer evil. As her powerful gaze fell on each of them in turn, they shuddered involuntarily, as though someone had just doused them in cold water.

The ancient woman's bony frame was swathed in a long, black hooded outfit, hanging in ragged points tinged with greens and dark blues. She stopped in front of them, her deep-set, black eyes looking intently from one to another, and finally resting on Rachel.

"A child of the light!" the old hag murmured sarcastically in a cracked voice as she looked hard at Rachel, who stepped back, recoiling from the stench emitting from the old woman. Suddenly a long bony hand shot out from under a tattered sleeve towards Rachel, and she jumped back even quicker to get away from the dreadful, old witch, colliding heavily with Johnny.

"A child of the light wearing a dead woman's jewellery and a dead woman's clothes no less!" she cackled again. This time her laugh was low and evil, and echoed round the cave. "The clothes of a harlot!" she continued, as she looked at Rachel. "But this child of the light is no ordinary child! Oh no! No ordinary child would see through the guise of a shape shifter. No, there are not many with that perception," she said, pacing slowly round Rachel, inspecting her closely.

The old sorceress turned her attention to Gareth, standing silently beside Rachel. She looked him up and down slowly and carefully as though assessing him. Johnny, hovering behind them, was treated to a brief look before her interest turned back to Rachel again. Swirling round unexpectedly her scrawny hand shot out towards the pendant Rachel was wearing and Rachel instinctively put her hand over it to protect it from the vile old woman.

"Get away from me!" Rachel shouted, her voice surprisingly commanding.

The old woman retracted quickly as though burnt. She stepped back several paces and stared hard at Rachel, with a look of guarded fury and resentment. Much to Johnny and the twins relief she finally turned away, walking back with a dismissive toss of her hand, as she spoke to a figure in the shadows at the back of the cave.

"The girl has powers but she knows not how to use them, she is a threat none-the-less, as she could use them involuntarily. They surround her, but she is not in control of them! The boy has limited powers, they are not yet unleashed and he has no idea of how to use them, he needs the girl. Separate them and the boy is useless! The other one is naught but a peasant, not even worth a second glance. If these are your Keepers, I say kill them now, for they are of no use to us, they are no threat and certainly no match for my powers! In fact I am surprised you would even concern yourself with them. Kill them and be done with it!"

The tall dark figure stepped forward slightly and as the light caught him the twins recognized him as Mordred. Rachel and Gareth moved forward slightly to see better into the gloom at the back of the cave where Mordred and his mother were whispering. The orange glow on the other side was casting shadows, making it difficult to see.

"None-the-less I still have a use for them before we kill them!" stated Mordred's unmistakable voice.

Gareth moved forward again, straining to see behind Mordred, as a limp, lifeless looking figure caught his attention at the back of the cave.

"Look!" he shouted, pulling at Rachel's arm. "That's Bronwyn; she's lying over there on the rocks at the back. What have you done to her?" he shouted angrily at Mordred.

Gareth rushed forward to get to Bronwyn, but was intercepted by Morgause who moved forward quickly, blocking his way. She raised her arm, and a long gnarled finger pointed towards him out of the ragged sleeve. She muttered something incomprehensible and a green spark that looked surprisingly like lightening, shot towards him.

The bolt of magic hit Gareth squarely on the chest, halting him temporarily as though stunned. He shook his head, regained his balance and faced her defiantly before rushing forward again.

"Leave me alone you old hag, I want to see Bronwyn!" he shouted angrily.

This time Morgause let out a bloodcurdling screech that filled the cave, and she delivered a second, sizzling emerald spell, so fierce that it threw all of them back. Rachel fell backwards against Johnny, who managed to catch her as he stumbled back himself. Gareth took the full brunt of the green magic and was knocked completely off his feet, landing heavily on his back on the cave floor with his sword spinning away from him.

Morgause's triumphant laugh filled the cave, bouncing off the rocks, echoing all around them.

"Now, maybe you will see sense and do as you are told," said Mordred, moving out of the shadows. "Morgause wants nothing more than to kill you all, where you stand! I, however, am much more reasonable! I have a task for you; do it and you can have your Bronwyn and go back to wherever you have come from!"

"No, I want to see if Bronwyn's all right first, she could be dead for all we know!" Gareth shouted angrily, struggling to his feet. "What have you done to her?"

Johnny picked up Gareth's sword and silently handed it back to him, as they all looked towards the motionless figure lying on a rocky shelf at the back of the cave. Even after all the previous noise, Bronwyn still lay stiff and pale, unaware of the commotion that had been going on around her.

"I have told you," said Mordred, his patience waning. "You will do something for me first and then you shall have her."

"No!" said Gareth firmly. "We're not doing anything for you, until I know what's wrong with her. I want to see her now!" he shouted, moving towards them, this time with Johnny and Rachel joining him.

"Stop, don't move, stay where you are!" shouted Galahad, much to Morgana's annoyance. "Do what they say!"

"Oh, like you are, you mean?" snapped Rachel. "You traitor!"

"Stop, I implore you, do as they say! You have no idea what you are dealing with," shouted Galahad again. "You have no idea what kind of black magic she can conjure!"

Ignoring him completely, the three of them continued to move slowly forward. Morgause pushed Mordred out of her way, muttering insanely, moving her arms in wide semi-circles looking up at the cavern ceiling, jabbering frantically in a language they had never heard before. The rhythmic droning of her strange words invaded their thoughts, and as hard as they tried not to listen to it, and had no idea as to its meaning, it gradually became a strong pulsating, relentless wave. It filled their minds until their limbs became stiff and all movement became difficult. Any thoughts of why they were there were rapidly disappearing.

The pulsing sensation became so strong that Rachel felt as though her head would burst. She was vaguely aware of her brother shouting 'Nooooo ...' somewhere beside her and involuntarily found herself grabbing the pendant round her neck with both hands.

She closed her eyes as everything apart from the relentless chanting began to drift away from her. She felt the metal leaves of the pendant digging into her palm and suddenly she found that the reverberations in her head were growing weaker and her own thoughts began to flood back in a jumbled rush. She opened her eyes, reeling with shock as she realised what was happening to them.

Next to her, Gareth was holding his hands over his ears, his face distorted by pain, with a motionless Johnny beside him, his eyes staring blankly ahead. None of them noticed Morgana touch Galahad's forehead and place herself in front of him protectively as his eyes closed.

The ancient old sorceress chanted even more frantically, glaring at Rachel, whom she realised was escaping her spell.

"Gareth, Gareth!" Rachel shouted, frantically shaking his arm, still holding the pendant with the other hand. He didn't respond, his eyes were shut and he appeared oblivious to her, as she gripped his arm even harder. “Gareth, look at me! You have to fight it! Don’t listen to it! Don’t let her get the better of you!” she shouted in panic.

She felt him move the arm she was holding on to and gradually, as though he were emerging from sleep, he finally turned and looked at her. The blank expression started to go and he let go of his head.

“The pendant is helping me, I can feel it! We have to stand up to her! The spell is losing its effect on me and it will with you, hold on to me, and it can help you as well. We need to get over to Bronwyn!”

Gareth nodded, still appearing slightly dazed, but he hung on to her arm tightly and they turned to face Morgause, walking slowly forward again.

As they drew nearer, Morgause directed all of her spell towards Rachel, looking her steadily in the eyes as she mumbled her strange words. Rachel felt an extreme force against her but she stood firmly, facing the evil old woman, determined that she was not going to get the better of her.

“Go to Bronwyn, quickly! She’s not bothering about you. I’ll try and hold her here,” she whispered to Gareth, who struggled to walk to the back of the cave where Bronwyn’s motionless figure lay.

Morgause, clearly furious now, faced Rachel with a look of pure, angry malice. She chanted harder and faster, almost in a frenzy. Rachel stared back at her, keeping hold of the pendant firmly with both hands, locked in a determined battle of wills. Mordred watched, surprised that his mother’s powers weren’t working against Rachel.

“She’s breathing! I think she is all right,” shouted Gareth from the back of the cave. He shook the limp Bronwyn several times but got no response. Her eyes were open but she neither looked at him nor made any movement at all.

Morgause let out an angry screech and immediately the pulsing stopped. Morgana whispered something in Galahad’s ear and he opened his eyes, looking slightly dazed.

“So she is no match for you then?” Mordred asked the old woman sarcastically as he moved forwards.

“The girl is stronger than I thought,” answered Morgause, now beside herself with rage. "But I can finish her!" she raised her hand again, pointing towards Rachel.

"Stop, stop!" said Mordred. "You had your chance a moment ago."

"What have you done to Bronwyn?" asked an angry Gareth, coming back with his sword pointed at Mordred.

"Put that down," Mordred answered as the tip came up towards him. "If you use that, Morgause will kill all of you including Bronwyn. Now do as I say and lower your sword. One simple task is all I ask. Bronwyn shall be restored, and you will all be on your way."

Gareth looked at his sister and she nodded resignedly.

"What is it you want us to do?" she asked, as Gareth withdrew his sword and moved back.

"That's better," said Mordred calmly. "I want you to go and get a casket for me from over there," he motioned vaguely towards the orange hue on the other side of the cave, "and put it into a pannier on my horse."

"A casket, is that all?" asked Gareth dubiously.

"Yes, that's all, and you shall have your Bronwyn."

"What's the catch?" questioned Gareth mistrustfully; this was all sounding too easy.

"There is nothing untoward if that is what you mean. The task is quite simple."

"Where is this casket?" asked Rachel.

"Over there, on a shelf in the rocks," Mordred answered, pointing towards the orange glow. "I will get the horse; it's in the next cavern beyond, while you get my casket."

"Over where? I can't see any casket!" said Gareth, as Mordred returned leading his jet black horse into the cave.

"Haven't you gone yet? It's over there, I have told you several times already!" he answered impatiently, producing a large piece of sackcloth and a heavy wooden box with metal strips and clasps. "I want you to wrap it in the cloth and place it in this."

Gareth and Rachel looked at each other, puzzled; it was all sounding too simple.

"Why do you want us to do it, why can't you put it in there yourself?" asked Gareth suspiciously.

"Do I have to repeat myself again? Just do as you are asked," retorted an angry Mordred, who was used to being obeyed without question. These children were trying his patience now and he was finding it very difficult not to lose his temper completely with them.

Gareth sighed and started to walk towards the orange light.

"No, the girl shall go!" Morgause said, stepping in to block his path again.

"Oh for heavens sake, I do not care who goes, what difference does it make?" questioned Mordred, his patience exhausted now that even his mother was opposing him. "Just get my casket!" he shouted, his temper boiling over.

"Fool," she answered with her evil laugh ringing out again. "If it is to destroy anyone, let it destroy the girl, let her bones lie with the others. The boy is no threat without her, and you have lost nothing!"

"What do you mean destroy me?" asked Rachel, worried now, "and whose bones?"

"Three good men have tried to lift it, you'll find their bones in the three piles of ashes next to it!" answered Morgause with an unpleasant smile. "Burnt to a cinder before they even got close enough to touch it, and with the help of the Gods yours will be the fourth pile! Let us see how strong your magic is against this!"

Suddenly Rachel knew what was in the casket; she glanced at her brother and knew he was thinking the same. It had to be the Chalice!

"I can do this," she whispered to him. He looked doubtful and shook his head.

"No, it's alright. I know it won't hurt me!" she reassured him, confidently.

"Rachel, you must not attempt this, there is powerful sorcery here!" came Galahad's voice, as he tried to pull his arm away from Morgana's grip. He wrenched himself free and came to Rachel's side. "I will go!"

"Galahad!" screeched Morgana, her put-on soft, sultry tones disappearing in an instant. "Leave her be! What does it matter if the wench perishes?" She lowered her voice again, beguilingly, as she reached his side, "Come, we shall leave them to whatever befalls them. All of them."

"Stand aside woman!" said Galahad pushing her back.

"I thought you were taking care of him!" Morgause said sharply to her daughter. "It looks as though your great charms aren't working either!"

Morgana glared at her mother and Rachel in turn.

"What do I care!" she answered sulkily, walking back.

"Rachel, I will do it!" repeated Galahad. Morgana placed a hand on his arm and spoke softly to him, her voice taking on its velvety sultriness again as she attempted to entrance him with her magic as a siren. He ignored her completely and her magic appeared to have no effect on him at all.

"No," Rachel answered firmly. "It has to be me; I know I am the only one out of us all that can do it!" With that she started to walk across the cave towards the orange glow.

As she got nearer to it she felt a tingling sensation, like pins and needles all over. She approached the glow, with the prickling feeling becoming stronger, and then she heard whispering voices. They appeared to be all around her, the empty air seemed to be full of them, and she had the sensation of brushing against something invisible, like cobwebs that touched her lightly as she passed. She shuddered as she stepped past three mounds of blackened bones sticking out of piles of dust, and tried hard not to look at them. The light was getting brighter and brighter as she reached the small alcove where the radiance was coming from.

"I'm sorry," she whispered to the invisible owners of the voices, feeling that she ought to for some reason. "I have to do this, I have to help Bronwyn, but afterwards I promise we'll take it back to safety."

She had almost reached the glowing alcove in the rock, where the soft orange light appeared from nowhere. She stepped forward shakily and saw the golden casket sitting on a small flat surface as though it had been hewn out of the rock especially for it. The orange hue emitting from it didn't appear to be coming from the casket, but from the very rocks around it.

She stood looking at the illuminated box, not moving or daring to reach out to it, although strangely enough she didn't feel that frightened, she was more in awe of it. Although the casket shone quite brightly, it was small and apart from having some intricate carvings on it, it was difficult to imagine that this box could be so powerful. It looked almost insignificant. But she knew that it wasn't!

Her attention was drawn to the flickering movements in the light that surrounded the casket. She looked up and intermingled with the shadows was the ghostly translucent face of a woman, hovering above it, moving in and out of the glow with a silvery light. Was it a woman? Rachel wasn't even sure. She hesitated and murmured "I'm really sorry; I know I'm not supposed to take this. I know the Chalice is inside and it's some sort of holy object, but I don't know what else to do. If I don't take it to Mordred, Morgause will probably kill all of us!"

The face smiled a kindly, gentle smile. "We know this, and because of your dilemma, you may take the casket but you must keep it in your possession. You must not give it to the Black Knight."

"But I'll have to, or he'll kill us," answered Rachel fearfully.

"He will not kill you, or any of your friends that help you. You have our word on that, the powers of the Chalice will be with you and you may use them in your quest," answered the ghostly apparition.

"But what about Bronwyn? He won't let us have her back!"

"The woman Bronwyn will have the same protection, no harm will come to her, but under no circumstances must you let the Black Knight take possession of the Chalice again."

Rachel nodded. "All right, I'll do what you say, I won't let him have it, but you will help us won't you?"

"Do not worry, my child, you may pick up the casket and go with our protection. You will have the help you need. We ask only one thing, that the casket be returned to safety."

"We will, as soon as we have sorted out this mess, we will take it back to where it came from, I promise!" answered Rachel.

The face smiled again and nodded in approval and understanding towards Rachel, so very gingerly she reached out and gently lifted the casket out of its rocky protection. As she did so the light flickered, faded, and disappeared completely, along with the apparition. Alone again, she turned and walked back, clutching the golden casket firmly to her chest.

As Rachel drew nearer, everyone looked stunned by the apparent ease with which she had completed the task. Her brother let out a big sigh of relief, and Morgause and Morgana stared at her with a hatred she could almost feel as she walked past them. She ignored the cloth and box that Mordred had ready for her and walked past them, joining her brother instead. She turned to face them still clutching the casket firmly.

Mordred rubbed his hands together, his eyes glinting in triumph.

"Come, wrap it for me and put it in the box," he said.

"No!" said Rachel.

"No? No? What do you mean no?" thundered Mordred. "Give me the casket now!"

"No!" answered Rachel again, aware of the looks from her brother and Galahad.

"I can't believe you did that, are you all right?" said Gareth with relief, ignoring Mordred who looked fit to burst a blood vessel in his fury at any moment.

"Yes I'm all right," she answered, looking around, suddenly realising someone was missing. "Where's Johnny?" she asked.

"He's … oh no, we've forgotten all about him!" answered Gareth, as they both looked back, to see the lone figure of Johnny standing motionless, eyes blank and staring, totally unaware of anything that had been going on around him since Morgause had cast her spell.

Chapter Eight

The Power of the Chalice

Gareth ran back to the motionless Johnny and shook him, trying to get a response.

"Johnny! Johnny? Look at me! Please look at me!" he shouted at the farm boy, shaking him again and again, to no avail. There was not so much as a flicker of recognition in his eyes.

"Never mind him! Do as I tell you and put the casket away!" roared Mordred.

"He looks as though he's in the same sort of a trance as Bronwyn," Gareth told his sister, as she rushed to join him.

"She has bewitched him with that spell," said Galahad. "I have heard tell of this, although I have never seen it for myself. You were lucky; it could have been all of you."

"Poor Johnny, I feel so awful, we forgot all about him," said Rachel. "I didn't even look to see if he was still with us!"

"I am waiting! The casket!" Mordred bellowed even louder, red in the face and furious that his demands were being ignored. "Give me the casket, now!"

Rachel came forward, still holding it in front of her, and noticing that Mordred and Morgause immediately stepped back several paces.

"They're frightened of it; they don't even want to get near it!

They can't touch it themselves and they know it! That's why they wanted me to do it," exclaimed Rachel, as quietly as she could to Gareth.

"The casket's here, take it if you want it so badly!" she said, moving towards them again. It immediately started to glow slightly and she could feel the warmth spreading into her hands, as though it were a warning. Morgause and her son moved back even quicker this time.

"Wrap it in the cloth and put it in the box as I asked," repeated Mordred, in an attempt to sound patient.

"No!" said Rachel confidently. "If you want it you're going to have to take it from me!"

"What? How dare you oppose me, you stupid girl!" exploded Mordred, unable to contain his rage any more. "Do as I say, or you will never see Bronwyn again! Morgause. Get the woman! Get her now!"

The old woman scuttled off to the back of the cave as he shouted nastily at her. "You stupid old hag, I never should have listened to you. And you!" he directed at his sister Morgana, still sulking behind them. "You've proved yourself to be little more than useless! Call yourself a temptress? The knight is more interested in a silly young girl than in you!"

Morgause commanded Bronwyn to stand, and she obeyed unblinkingly, her pale form rising slowly off the stone shelf. The old witch grabbed her arm and pushed her towards Mordred.

Morgana rejoined Galahad again, still determined to prove herself. Her face was pale and hard, and her eyes glistened like steel. She took his arm again, looking up at him with a sultry gaze, intending to lock the young knight into her power.

"You underestimate me, brother, he is not interested in the girl: not while I am here," she said, and Galahad glanced at her briefly, which she took as a sign that he was agreeing with her and under her enchantment.

Ignoring her, Mordred roughly grabbed Bronwyn's limp, expressionless form from Morgause, and holding her tightly in front of him, he drew his sword and placed it across her throat.

"Now, you will do as I tell you, or I will kill her!" he said with a sneer.

"If you kill Bronwyn, you'll never have this casket or its contents," announced Gareth boldly. "We'll take it back to Merlin and use it against you, all of your family and anyone that fights with you, until there is no-one left to help you! And if you let your old hag of a mother harm her in any way, we'll kill all of you anyway!"

He drew his own sword in defiance and stood firmly, calling the older man's bluff, secretly praying that he wasn't making things even worse! He faced Mordred with his sword pointed towards him, while the tension built as the Black Knight grew redder and redder, until he looked as though he might actually kill Bronwyn out of sheer frustration and rage.

"Remember, we've got the Chalice, Mordred!" joined in Rachel. "Remember what it can do. After all, that's why you want it, isn't it?"

"Get the horse. Get the horse!" screamed Mordred, unsure of himself now, he withdrew his sword from Bronwyn's throat. "Put her on it!" he shouted, bundling Bronwyn into Morgause's arms and pushing them both toward the black horse.

"If I don't have the casket, you don't have her!" he shouted as Morgause tried in vain to get the limp Bronwyn to mount the horse.

"Don't just stand there, you useless female, help her!" he screamed at Morgana. Reluctant to leave Galahad's side, Morgana clicked her fingers, and Bronwyn's feet rose off the floor as she was propelled upwards towards the saddle. Morgause gave Bronwyn a final push and she slumped over the horse's back.

"No!" shouted Gareth, running at Mordred with his sword outstretched. "You're not taking her anywhere!"

Mordred swung to face him, his sword drawn in an instance, raised in defense. He swiped quickly with one swift movement, immediately knocking the light sword out of Gareth's hand, sending it spinning across the cave. He followed it through in one easy move, positioning himself to strike Gareth's chest. As he delivered his final blow, his sword was met in a clash of steel as Galahad leapt forward and counteracted the blow.

Albeit surprised, Mordred met Galahad's blow with another hefty strike, and the two men ferociously clashed swords again and again. Mordred was a good swordsman with years of experience and he forced Galahad back. Undeterred and agile, the young knight jumped on to a rock and went for the tall dark man from another angle. Again Mordred met the thrust.

A furious battle commenced between the two men, with Galahad proving himself to be quick and nimble, the great heavy sword in his hands looking as light as one of Gareth's rapiers as he met Mordred's thrusts again and again with mighty clashes.

However expert with a sword Mordred may have been, it was easy to see he was tiring much more quickly than his young opponent, as Galahad rained heavy blows in a fast assault.

Mordred met the mighty swipes of Galahad's sword deftly until the young knight eventually swung one last heavy blow that caught him off balance, sending Mordred's sword crashing to the floor. Mordred fell backwards from the force of the blow and Galahad brought the tip of his sword up against his opponent's throat, where one final thrust would finish their dual.

This time Rachel saw Morgana's transformation as she distorted and twisted, changing back again into the huge wolf. She hunched forward, snarling, ready to pounce and Rachel screamed as she saw the wolf spring with all its force, launching itself towards Galahad.

"Galahad, look out!" Rachel shouted, too late, as the wolf knocked him sideways, sinking its fangs into him. Galahad regained his balance and tried to wrestle the large grey beast off. The skin tore on his arm as the wolf shook it brutally like a rag. For a second it released its powerful grip and withdrew for a second, only to snarl and launch its full weight on him again. This time Galahad fell backwards onto the floor where the ferocious animal placed its front paws on his chest pinning him down firmly before sinking its teeth viciously into his neck.

The knight struggled to hold it off as the wolf tore into him savagely, undeterred and unwilling to release its victim.

Rachel put her hands over her eyes and screamed, not seeing her brother leap forward and drive his sword into the side of the wolf. It temporarily dropped its victim, howling in pain, as Gareth withdrew his sword, covered in blood. It shook itself and fixed its eyes firmly on Gareth, baring its teeth and snarling, hunching itself for another attack. As the wolf sprang towards him, Gareth brought his sword up, impaling it as it landed on him, the force knocking them both to the ground. He rolled away quickly and pulled his sword back as the great animal landed on the hard floor, a steady stream of blood surrounding it.

Rachel stared as the dying wolf slowly transformed back, leaving the pale, dark form of Morgana lying on the cave floor in a pool of blood, her mouth smeared red from her attack on Galahad. For a moment Rachel and Gareth clutched each other in silence, recovering from the shock of the last few minutes events.

"Galahad, are you all right?" shouted Rachel, rushing towards him once she was sure that Morgana was dead. He was struggling to get up, his wounds looking ragged and nasty. Gareth joined her and they helped him up into a sitting position against a rock.

Nearby, Johnny was still standing rigid and unblinking, completely unaware that anything untoward had happened.

"Oh no, Mordred's gone," shouted Gareth, as he looked up to find the rest of the cave empty. "They've taken Bronwyn with them!"

"Oh, this is such a mess. Mordred's still got Bronwyn and look at Galahad! Look at Johnny! What on earth are we going to do with them?" cried Rachel.

"We need to get them back to the castle along with the casket!" Gareth said. "I don't like the look of Galahad's injuries, and we can't exactly call an ambulance here!"

"Someone must follow Mordred!" said Galahad, easing himself against the rock, wincing as the pain took his breath away. "You must go after them, Gareth! Don't do anything; just find out where they are going. Rachel and I can get Johnny back to the castle."

"You don't look fit to travel anywhere!" answered Gareth.

"I have survived worse. I will get them back!" he replied, gasping in pain as he tried to pull himself into a more comfortable position.

"You're too badly hurt, we've got to get you and Johnny back to the castle and Gareth can't follow Mordred on his own," replied Rachel, horrified by the suggestion.

"Galahad's right. I have to, or we'll lose them completely. We've got to find out where he's taking Bronwyn! But if I do go, will you be able to get these two back on your own? That wound on Galahad's neck is really bad, the wolf's torn quite a chunk out! He looks as though he's losing a lot of blood, do you think he can make it back to the castle?" he said quietly.

"God, I hope so! But what about you, I don't want you to go on your own, what would happen if they discover you're following them? It's too dangerous, we should all go back together!" she said. "Besides, aren't we supposed to stay together as the Keepers?"

"You're wasting time, they are getting away. You must go now!" said Galahad.

Gareth nodded, "I'll be all right," he said bravely to his sister. "We're just going to have to take a risk on being separated; anyway you've got the Chalice so you should be all right."

"Yes, but what about you? Maybe you should take the pendant with you," said Rachel, unclasping it from round her neck. "Maybe it'll help you! Just hold it firmly in your hand and concentrate hard: that was how I held off Morgause."

Gareth looked at the pendant doubtfully as she handed it to him, but he put it in his pocket anyway, partly to keep her happy. He picked up his sword and headed towards the back of the cave. Briefly, he looked back towards his sister, the wounded knight and his bewitched friend wondering if he was doing the right thing.

"Go! Godspeed!" said Galahad, as he would to his fellow knights. Gareth smiled bravely, waved his sword at them and disappeared into the blackness at the back of the cave.

Rachel turned her attention back to the two men she was left with, and was not quite sure where to start. She decided to attend to Galahad first. The wound on his neck looked worse than she had imagined and he seemed to have lost the use of his left arm.

With shaking hands, she pulled out the silver dagger that Merlin had given her and quickly tore some strips of fabric from the petticoat she wore under her long dress. She folded them into two pads which she placed over the dreadful wounds on Galahad's neck and arm. She hacked at the petticoat again until she had several long pieces which she used to secure the pads, bandaging his arm as best she could. She cut another piece to make a rough sling to hold Galahad's useless arm across his chest.

Satisfied that she had stopped the bleeding from his wounds and done what she could, she left Galahad to rest, while she went over to Johnny who appeared to be as unresponsive as before. She remembered how Morgause had spoken in a command to Bronwyn and decided to try it.

"Johnny, look at me!" she said. Nothing happened! She tried again, and again, but there was still no response, and she felt like crying.

"We need to go or the tide will be upon us," said Galahad, using the rock to lever himself up into a standing position.

"I can't leave Johnny here; he's got to come with us," said Rachel.

"We may have to if you can't get him to move, or we will all be stuck here for the night, until the tide goes far enough out again to get back," Galahad answered.

She knew he was right, they would be safe in the cave from the water, but she knew that Galahad wouldn't last the night there, with wounds as bad as his. She looked at Johnny in desperation and spotted the casket on the floor. She picked it up and said silently, 'Please help me,' before placing Johnny's hand on it. He withdrew it quickly and looked at her vacantly.

"Johnny, we're going now, you have to come with us. Do you understand?"

He didn't answer, but shuffled a couple of paces.

"Come, we must go," said Galahad. Rachel nodded and they moved towards the cave entrance. To her surprise and relief Johnny followed with trudging footsteps, still staring silently ahead.

They climbed over the rocks with Rachel helping Galahad by putting his arm round her neck, lacing hers round his back to help support him. She tucked the casket under her other arm. Johnny stumbled along behind. They made slow progress and by the time they rounded the headland back to the small beach, Galahad was leaning heavily against her, his face was ashen and the waves were lapping round their feet. She left him with Johnny at the top of the beach where it was still dry and ran ahead to get the horses.

Galahad swung slowly into the saddle saying nothing, but the pain on his face was quite evident as he pulled himself up.

Johnny was the next problem. Rachel handed him the reins but he just stood there.

"Johnny, get on the horse and follow us!" she commanded. It was really quite tiring having to instruct his every step. Again Johnny did as he was told and their small party moved off slowly, up the narrow path and back in the direction of the castle.

"Stop," said Galahad, pulling up his horse sharply as they came out of the bushy undergrowth. "Those are Mordred's men in the distance; I would recognize those tents anywhere. He has set up his second camp on this side of the causeway as we feared he might. This means we can't get to the castle without passing them! The causeway is cut off. We cannot go this way."

"Oh no," said Rachel dismally. This had to be the last straw. "How are we going to get back?"

"There is another way in through the south wall, but it is a fair climb I'm afraid."

"Well, if that's the only way in, we'll have to go that way," said Rachel, feeling very tired and despondent now. They turned the horses back and shortly came to a small gap in the hedgerows. They followed Galahad down a steep pathway so narrow that the branches and thicket caught their legs and the horses stumbled on the uneven ground.

The black slate rocks grew higher and higher around them, until at last they found themselves looking up at the castle, perched high on steep rocks to their right, with the sea dashing unmercifully against the rocks in front.

"I remember looking down on this with Gareth," exclaimed Rachel. "The sentry said it was a weak point and they had to keep watch over it. But how on earth do we get up there?"

"We climb!" said Galahad, stumbling as he dismounting and led his horse into the thick shrubbery. Rachel instructed Johnny to get off his horse and taking the reins from him, she led the horses into the foliage, tethering them all together onto a small tree. Galahad and Johnny had both flopped down against some boulders next to a small stream that trickled down off the black rocks towering above.

"I need to gather some strength before we attempt the climb!" said Galahad, slumping down further against the rocks. It was only then, that Rachel noticed his sleeve was completely soaked in blood. She bent down to look closer and she could see that, not only were the dark green sling and pad soaked, but the blood was slowly dripping down his hand. She was horrified to see how much blood the young knight was losing.

"I am growing weak," Galahad stated, as he leant his head back. "I fear I am letting you down badly."

"Oh, no, don't say that. You saved my brother's life," said Rachel the tears welling up in her eyes. "You haven't let us down!"

"Rachel, listen to me. I fear I may not be able to make it up there. You must carry on without me. No, listen," he said, as she was about to interrupt. "The climb is not as bad as it looks from here. There are small holds hewn into the rock that you can hold on to, the shelves are thin but they are not impassable. Follow them and they will lead you up, underneath the castle wall. There is a trap door there and a metal grill. You must bang three times on the door and shout, ''tis a fellow of the Order' through the grill. This is a password, they will ask who you are and let you in."

"Suppose there is no-one there? That part of the castle is normally deserted."

"Not with Mordred's men in sight. The castle will be on full alert. There will be plenty there to hear you, have no fear about that, there will be sentries watching every wall of the castle," he replied, his voice sounding weak.

“I can’t leave you here like this,” she said in dismay.

“You have to; it’s your only chance.” His face was now deathly pale and his eyes fluttered and closed, as he passed out against the rock.

Rachel tried in vain to wake him and turned to Johnny, the tears running down her cheeks. Johnny was still in a dream, not really aware of what was going on, and she looked up at the rock face fearfully, wondering if she would even be able to get him up there. She trembled at the thought of climbing on her own - she didn’t like heights at the best of times.

Rachel sat down next to them feeling very alone. She knew she was going to have to do something, but what? Her tearful gaze fell on the casket that she had discarded hastily to see to Galahad. She picked it up and said angrily. “You said you would help us, you said we were protected. So what am I supposed to do now?” A tear dripped and fell on the casket as she held it. For a moment she thought she saw the ghostly face again and she thought she heard the whispering voices saying, “Use the Chalice. Open the casket and use the Chalice!”

She blinked, and looked around, there was no-one there, but the voices still lingered in her head as she stared at the casket. Then Merlin’s words came to mind. ‘The Chalice has great healing powers.’ She stared at it, her heart beating faster. Dare she open it? Why not, what else could happen that could possibly be any worse than this? So she took a deep breath and opened it.

The box was lined in a rich, thick, silky fabric, its folds padded against a very ordinary looking, chunky earthenware goblet. She lifted it out, almost disappointed, and turned it round in her hands. The rim and stem were dark and there was some strange patterning on the lighter part. She studied it and decided that it could even be writing. It looked a bit like the Egyptian hieroglyphics they had studied at school, although she knew it wasn’t. She felt nothing unusual as she held it, and nothing strange happened.

“So what am I supposed to do with you?” she asked it, out loud. There was no apparition and no answer. She continued looking at it and out of the corner of her eye, she noticed the clear water running down off the rocks, forming a small trickle of a stream running down towards the sea. An idea crossed her mind, and she went over to it, placing the chalice under the water. It splashed into the goblet and when it was almost full she took it over to Johnny.

"Drink this, it's water," she said to him, holding the goblet to his lips. Johnny obeyed, the water dribbling off his chin as he drank thirstily. Slowly the blank look disappeared from his eyes as she took the Chalice away.

"Where are we?" he asked her, looking around in confusion. "How did we get here? I don't remember this place."

"Oh Johnny, it worked! It worked!" she said hugging him, relief flooding over her.

"But where are we?" he repeated, looking utterly bewildered.

"Do you remember anything at all?" she asked.

"I'm not sure," he answered, shaking his head, desperately trying to gather his thoughts. "Yes I do! We went over the rocks and there was a wolf. It turned into a woman and we went into a cave, that's the last I remember, apart from some other people there. There was a witch I think!"

"That was Morgause, she put a spell on you, that's why you can't remember any more. Look, I haven't got time to explain all of it because Galahad's been badly hurt. I need to help him now, just stay there while I go and see to him."

She left Johnny sitting back against the rocks, gazing around still slightly dazed, looking up at the castle, while she went back to the small stream to refill the Chalice.

"Oh, thank you, thank you," she muttered to the Chalice, as the water trickled into it again. "Now please, please help me with Galahad."

Johnny looked on even more confused, listening to her talking to the goblet.

"Wow, he looks really bad, is he going to be all right?" said Johnny in horror as he noticed Galahad for the first time. Rachel knelt down and held the chalice to Galahad's lips, but the knight was beyond drinking and nothing happened.

"Oh no, you have to help him, please, what do I do now?" she asked the Chalice again in despair, looking at his white face, noticing he was barely breathing. She carefully put the chalice down and loosened the pad from his neck, revealing a jagged, deep open wound on his neck where the wolf had bitten deeply. It was bleeding profusely.

She steeled herself, picked up the Chalice again and carefully poured a few drops of water onto the wound. Galahad's eyelids fluttered and he let out an involuntary scream of pain as the water sizzled on the wound, like fat on a fire.

"What are you doing to him?" asked Johnny, scrambling to his feet. He watched in awe with her as the gaping wound closed over and sealed, leaving a livid red mark in the shape of the wolf's teeth, raised like that of newly formed scar tissue.

"Help me with his sleeve, he's got another bad wound on his arm, we need to do the same with that!" she said to Johnny, handing him the dagger out of her pocket.

The farm boy said nothing, and set to work carefully slicing through the remainder of Galahad's chewed sleeve, pulling it open to reveal a half chewed arm.

"Oh no, this is awful, it's really bad, I don't want to disturb the sleeve anymore, it's holding it together by the look of it. What on earth happened to him?"

"I'll tell you all about it later, this will heal it," she said confidently, pouring some more drops of water from the chalice onto the hideous wound. The same thing happened; the wound sizzled and began to repair itself, while Galahad screamed with pain again.

Rachel hastily dried the Chalice on her skirt and returned it to the box, with a silent 'thank you'.

By the time she returned, the colour had begun to creep slowly back into Galahad's face and his ragged, shallow breathing had evened out. He opened his eyes and Rachel gave a great sigh of relief.

"Oh, thank God, you're all right too!" she cried. The tears ran freely down her face now in relief, as Galahad looked at her, just as stunned as Johnny had been. Slowly he stretched his arm that had been hanging useless in the sling and moved his hand incredulously when he felt no pain. He looked at the strange scarring on his arm beneath the torn sleeve and put his hand up to his neck, where he could feel the strange raised scars. He did remember what had happened though, before he had passed out, and looked questioningly at Rachel.

"How did you do this?" he asked, removing the blood-soaked sling and touching the scar on his neck again.

"Never mind that, you're all right, that's the main thing! And you can both work on getting your strength back, because there's no way I'm going up there on my own!" she answered, laughing and crying at the same time.

They sat for a while longer, and Rachel told Johnny about the events in the cave. His eyes grew wider and wider. "Oh no, if it hadn't been for that spell I could have gone with Gareth. I could have helped him!" he said finally, in disbelief that all of this had happened and he hadn't even known anything about it.

"Well, don't feel too bad, because you're going to have to help me get Galahad up there instead!" she replied.

Once Galahad looked well enough to attempt the climb, they made their way through the heavy undergrowth towards the jagged cliff face. Rachel insisted that they took the casket and the old black book that had been in her saddle bag, intent on carrying them herself, until Johnny took the heavy book from her, stuffing it inside the front of his loose jacket and buttoning it up tightly. Galahad held out his hand for the casket.

"You're not strong enough yet, and I don't know whether it will allow you to hold it," she said. The last thing she wanted to see after all this was Galahad reduced to a pile of ashes like the ones in the cave.

"And you will have enough trouble scaling that cliff in a those long skirts, without carrying anything. I have done this climb many times before, put the casket in the sling and tie it round me," he said, with authority.

Reluctantly she did as he suggested, tying it in a bundle in the sling and looping it round his neck, holding her breath to see if it had any adverse effects on him. It didn't, in fact it appeared to help his strength as they started the climb up the black rock face. Galahad led, stopping every now and then to help Rachel on to the next bit. He had been right when he had said that the climb looked worse than it was from the ground. The sharp, flat layers of rock formed narrow platforms, a sort of layered pathway with a sheer drop beyond! Each shelf gave them several steps before they moved up on to the next one, holding on to the small grooves interspersed at regular intervals in the rocks. Slowly they made their way up the cliff. Rachel tried hard not to look down, and although the rocky shelves were by no means as narrow as they had looked from below, the sheer drop as they got higher was unnerving and one stumble could have sent them straight over the edge and on to the rocks below.

"Don't look down!" instructed Galahad, as he held out his hand to help a terrified Rachel on to the next shelf. She was seriously hampered by her long skirts, the wind catching them in gusts as they climbed further. Her heart was hammering, she felt sick and dizzy, and if it hadn't been for Galahad's help and Johnny's words of encouragement from behind, she wouldn't have moved another inch.

Finally, her ordeal was over when they reached a large flat rock that stretched completely under the castle wall, wide and safe. Galahad banged on the trap door above them as he had previously instructed Rachel to do, and the guards answered straight away, recognizing Galahad's voice through the grill. The trap door was pulled open and to her relief, strong arms pulled them up into the safety of the castle.

Chapter Nine

Campfire Capers

Gareth made his way to the back of the cave and as he turned the corner he found himself enveloped in blackness. "Oh no!" he said out loud. "I can't see a damn thing! How can I follow them if I can't see anything?" He took a few paces back towards the light and his foot caught something. He picked it up and found it was a heavy conical torch that they had obviously discarded in their haste to escape.

"Yes!" he said delightedly, picking it up. But how do you light it? There were no switches. He fumbled around to see if there was anything else on the floor he could use to light it with, but there wasn't. He toyed with the idea of rubbing two stones together; the only option he could think of, and not a particularly good one, since he had no idea how to do it! Then he remembered how Merlin had waved his hand and the torches on the walls had burst into light. He tried that, flapping his hands frantically at the unresponsive torch. Nothing happened. He was just no good at this magic, which his sister seemed to be mastering so easily.

Morgause's words sprang to mind when she had said 'the boy has powers but they are not unleashed yet.' What did she mean? Maybe he could do it as well? He tried to remember what Rachel had done. In the end he decided to try his own version. He clutched the torch in one hand and the pendant in the other and closed his eyes.

"Please light the torch. I need to follow Mordred!" he said.

Gareth opened his eyes, disappointed to find that he was still in darkness. He looked at the conical object in his hand, willing it to light, and to his astonishment a slow glow emitted from the ancient torch. It wasn't very bright, but it was enough for him to see several paces in front of him. He could still faintly hear the horse's hooves echoing through the passageways, and he dashed off quickly, holding the dim torch out in front of him.

The tunnel narrowed in places and widened in others, and although it twisted and turned, it was still one main passageway. The hooves were sounding louder now, so he must be catching them up. He listened carefully and was fairly sure that there was only one horse, so he decided that Mordred and Morgause must be on foot.

Gareth stopped for a moment and listened again, as he thought he heard a noise behind him. Convinced that it must be an echo, he carried on again and thought no more about it until he heard it again. This time he didn't stop but quickened his pace instead, his heart beating faster, listening intently to what he now thought sounded like footsteps behind him. He reached another tunnel almost like a T junction at a road, and he was now positive that there were footsteps echoing behind him, so he went to the left and halted. He leant back against the wall next to the entrance, his heart hammering in his chest, and drew his sword, waiting intrepidly for whoever it was that followed him to show themselves.

Eventually a slight figure emerged and Gareth leapt out, finding his sword was aimed at the throat of a boy probably only a few years younger than himself.

"Who are you and why are you following me?" he said to the frightened boy.

"I am Bran, sire, and I was not following you. I was following Medraut."

"Why?" asked Gareth, surprised by his answer.

"Because he is a murderer, and I need to avenge the deaths of my brother and father!"

"He killed them?" asked Gareth rather stupidly, dropping his sword slightly.

"He caused their deaths! I am the only son left, 'tis my duty to avenge this!" the boy answered determinedly.

Gareth looked closely at him; he was dressed in a long straw-coloured tunic over rough trousers. He had no sword, no helmet and no armour.

"How do you intend to do that?" asked Gareth, feeling slightly sorry for him.

"I will bide my time. I will steal a dagger or sword as soon as I have the opportunity and I will kill him!" the boy answered passionately.

"Something I'd rather like to do myself!" answered Gareth, putting his sword back in its scabbard.

"You are a knight, sir! You ride with Galahad, son of Lancelot, I saw you with him in the cave. I beg of you, please help me to avenge their deaths!" pleaded Bran.

Gareth was taken aback as the boy fell to his knees, clutching the hem of his tunic. He realised suddenly that the boy thought he was a real knight due to his clothing.

"There's no need for that, do get up," he answered, embarrassed. "Maybe we can help each other."

"That would be an honour, sire," stated the boy, bowing humbly.

Gareth ignored him for a moment, listening for the sound of the horse's hooves he had been following and realising they were distant again. Had no idea which direction they had gone.

"Damn!" Gareth said, in frustration. "We've lost them!"

"Oh no, sire, I know where they are going."

"How do you know that?" asked Gareth suspiciously.

"I was hiding at the back of the cave when they put the woman with the golden hair on the horse and I heard them talking! Medraut said he was going to his camp first to see his men and then they would take the woman back to his castle. I know the way!"

"Why do you want to help me?" asked Gareth, still suspicious.

"Because, sire, we follow the same cause, and you appear to want Medraut dead as much as me! You are a knight: if I help you, I would ask your protection for our village."

"Your village?" questioned Gareth, realising he was starting to get rather out of his depth. This simple boy was under the impression he had much more power than he actually did!

"Yes, our village is next to Medraut's castle. In the time of Arthur, we had the protection of his armies against the Saxons, and Medraut would not have dared hurt us. All of the villages had the protection of the knights and Medraut pretended to ride side by side with them. Now Arthur has gone, and we are at his mercy! He is a cruel man, he cares naught for our villagers, we give our crops to the castle and he takes our men; they have to do his bidding. His soldiers have first pick of our women, they have no say, and they are taken to the castle. I fear for my sisters and my mother, if they can't give crops or money to the castle they will become servants or worse!"

"But the knights are still here, surely they can help?" said Gareth.

"There are many small villages like ours and there are not enough knights left to help everyone. There were many that fell in battle along with Arthur. They do not have the same power as they did when he was alive. If I ride with you will you help us?"

"I'll see what I can do!" said Gareth, now feeling, with a strong certainty, that he could trust this young lad who had so much at stake.

"Then I will pledge my allegiance. Come, we go this way!" said the boy, setting off determinedly.

They could see daylight in the distance now and they travelled in silence. Gareth thought that this passageway looked remarkably like the one he and Rachel had used to get to the castle with Merlin. As they got nearer the entrance he realised it was the same one. They could hear men's voices and Bran stopped Gareth from going any further.

"That will be Medraut's men; they are camped not far from the entrance. You cannot go out there as they will recognise you as a knight straight away. Stay here and hide, I will get you some different clothes," he whispered and strode off confidently.

Gareth stayed well back out of sight and waited. Bran was gone a long time and he started to worry. Suppose the boy was really on Mordred's side! Had he trusted him too easily? He could lead them straight to him!

Eventually he spotted a figure heading towards him, so he ducked down behind a boulder nervously. He couldn't see who it was, as the figure was a silhouette against the light. He breathed a big sigh of relief as he recognised Bran carrying a small bundle which he thrust at Gareth.

"I am sorry that I was gone so long, I had to bide my time before I could steal these," said Bran.

"Where did you get them?" asked Gareth, opening out the rough bundle and revealing a long straw-like tunic similar to Bran's.

"I sneaked into one of the tents by the encampment. Put it over your clothes and hide your sword underneath. There is a hood, pull it up and follow me, the men are busy eating at the moment - they will pay us no heed if we look as though we are going about our business. We will pretend to be collecting firewood."

Gareth followed the boy out in his new rough, stolen clothes. Bran immediately ferreted about in the bushes, collecting the broken branches as he went. Gareth rather nervously did the same, glancing up every now and again, terrified that they would be noticed. By the time the men did see them, Bran and Gareth were both carrying armfuls of branches and Mordred's men paid no attention to them at all. The two boys made their way past them and carried on following the shrubbery still collecting wood.

"You're good at this aren't you?" said Gareth, impressed.

"I have to be!" answered the boy. "The trick is to blend in."

They were now level with the encampment of tents that clustered in a circle around a main area. The conical straw-coloured tents all bore a black flag with a red symbol fluttering in the breeze on their pointed tops. Gareth kept his head firmly down as there were many men in black tunics and silver chain mail, going about their own business. Many were grouped in the main area in the middle, and were a surly looking bunch. Every now and then Gareth stole glances at them, trying to calculate how many men Mordred had there. He decided there were too many to count, but suffice to say, there was a substantial amount!

"You there, stop!" a loud, gruff voice shouted, and the two boys both immediately froze. "You there, come hither!"

"Now what?" said Gareth, his heart hammering in his chest. "What does he want?"

"Do what he says; remember we are supposed to be here, collecting wood for their fire."

"Come hither, bring that wood over here!" came the voice again.

"Yes sir, coming sir," answered Bran, in a subservient voice, before turning to Gareth and whispering, "Remember, do what he says, but let me do the talking."

Gareth followed him with his head still down, the hood shadowing his face. They dropped the wood down by the big blackened pile of ashes in the middle of the camp where the man was pointing.

"'Twill be a long cold night here, and that will not last the first hour. Set to and get more, lazy ne'r-do-all's." He reached out and swung a blow at Bran's head that almost sent him sprawling. Gareth's temper rose instantly at the mistreatment of his new friend and it was all he could do to keep from reaching for his sword.

"Yes sir, yes sir," answered Bran, with a series of grovelling bows as he backed away.

The man looked sharply at Gareth and he quickly followed Bran, doing the same. They scrambled off and rushed back to collect more branches under the watchful eye of the man. They collected several bundles quickly and deposited them in the same place. The surly man soon grew bored with watching them and turned away satisfied that they were working hard enough. They carried on bringing several armfuls until the pile was high, and now no-one was taking any notice of them at all as they came and went.

Finally as they headed back towards the trees, Bran tugged Gareth's sleeve. He looked back quickly, to make sure they were not being watched and dived into the bushes, dragging Gareth with him. They ducked down out of sight behind the thick foliage.

"What do we do now?" asked Gareth, hiding next to him.

"We wait for nightfall and then we can listen. The men will sit around the campfire and their tongues will loosen after a few jugs of ale. We can come and go now as we please, they will see us as the boys from the village sent to collect wood and do their bidding. We will not look out of place and no-one will pay heed to us. Later we can listen by the tents and find out where Medraut is, and with any luck we may hear his plans." Gareth nodded, still impressed by the boy's resourcefulness.

"The wood trick works every time, because the soldiers do not question it, they just think someone has told us to do it," Bran said, with a smug grin.

"How often have you done this?" asked Gareth with a smile.

"Only when there is something I want to find out! Well I suppose I do it quite often really!" he admitted with a laugh. "I go into Medraut's castle as well, I know secret ways in! They are so used to seeing me in there; they don't even give me a second glance!"

"Well I suppose that explains why you're so good at it then!" Gareth replied, laughing in open admiration. "We don't really know anything about each other do we? Is Bran your real name or is it short for something else?"

"Something else?" questioned Bran, looked at him strangely.

"I mean, like Pete is short for Peter, and Dave, short for David," Gareth continued, seeing Bran's puzzled look.

"No 'tis a real name," Bran answered, almost scornfully. "'Tis my name, a name I am proud of. 'Tis the name of the great chieftain long before Arthur, surely you know of him?"

"No I don't, but I'm not from here. Look I'm sorry; I didn't mean to offend you," Gareth replied, seeing the boy's proud stance and wishing he hadn't mentioned it.

They waited behind the bushes for what seemed an eternity. "Not too long now," said Bran. "The light is fading."

"You said Mordred killed your father and brother?" asked Gareth, remembering their earlier conversation. "Why did he do that?"

"Mordred?" asked the boy, looking puzzled.

"Sorry, you call him Medraut," Gareth explained. "We have a different name for him."

"I see," said Bran. "Medraut didn't kill my father and brother himself, they died doing his bidding. I was with them, but I ran off and hid or I would have been next," he finished sadly.

"What did they have to do?" asked Gareth, gently.

"Medraut came to our village and took two men; he said he had a task for them. They left and several days later he came back and said he had a task for three more men. He said they would be rewarded with great riches if they could do this task, and my father and brother stepped forward. I tried to stop them. I said 'Father, what of the others? We have not seen them since!' but they paid no heed, and they went with him. The promises of riches for their families were enough to make them go."

"But why would they trust him, what did he want them to do?"

"No-one trusts Medraut, but any man in the village would do anything to provide more for his family! As I told you before, we have to give most of our crops and livestock to the castle and by the time we have met their demands, often there is barely enough left for us to eat! My brother has a wife and two children, a third due soon, and my father wanted to provide for his own family, he sees it as his duty!"

Gareth nodded sympathetically, trying to understand how difficult it was for them, as Bran continued.

"They went off with Medraut, and I followed," continued Bran. "Medraut is an evil man, who cares naught for the lives of his servants! I had heard that his mother Morgause, the great sorceress, was with him, and I was frightened for them! It wasn't long before she knew they were being followed and she caught me and made me join them. We went through the passages until we came to the cave where Morgana was, with the bewitched woman with the golden hair!"

"Her name's Bronwyn, she's my mother and he still has her!" said Gareth quietly. "So what happened next?"

"I am sorry, I did not realise. I understand now why you follow him and would want him dead as much as me! She may be bewitched, but she is still alive and I will help you get her back!" announced Bran, as determined as ever.

"Thanks, and I'm sorry I interrupted, what happened to your father and brother?" asked Gareth.

"This is the strangest thing, all he wanted them to do was to pick up a casket, wrap it in sackcloth and put it in another box!" Bran answered, and Gareth nodded, guessing what was coming next.

"My father went first: he crossed the cave towards a strange glow. He started to behave strangely as though he was trying to walk, but could not because something was stopping him. He struggled forwards, putting his hands over his ears, as though he could hear something. As he went towards the casket he was thrown back, he landed on the floor and screamed! He writhed on the floor screaming, and then he was gone! In seconds there was naught but a pile of dust where he lay."

This was exactly what Gareth had been expecting to hear and his heart went out to the boy, for the story sounded worse than he could ever have imagined.

"My brother was next! He did not want to go, but Medraut said he would give him a hundred pieces of silver! A fortune! He could not resist that, but still I tried to stop him, but ..." he wiped away a tear with the back of his hand.

"I know what happened next, you don't have to say anymore," said Gareth, not wanting him to relive any more of his painful experience. "But you managed to escape at least."

"Yes, I could stand it no longer; I ran and ran, back into the tunnel," he sniffed, wiping his nose on his sleeve, trying hard not to cry.

"I'm so sorry about your brother and father! Mordred is the most evil person I have ever met! But we'll get the better of him and I'll tell Galahad and Merlin about your village and the way you're all treated. I'm sure when they know about it, they'll help you!" said Gareth, trying to comfort him in some way.

Bran nodded and wiped his eyes again. "You ride with Galahad; you have the honour of the knights. I trust this, and I believe you will do what you can for us. Because of that, I will in turn help you to get your mother away from him!"

Gareth nodded, and the two boys solemnly clasped hands in support of each other's cause.

"'Tis dark enough now, we will not be noticed," said Bran. "Stay here, I will look around the camp to see if 'tis safe, and then we will look for Medraut's tent!"

Before he could say anything, Bran disappeared through the bushes and Gareth was left on his own, still feeling saddened by Bran's dreadful story.

'Mordred!' Gareth could feel a powerful hatred welling up inside him, as he thought about Bran's father and brother, dead because of his obsession with the casket. He saw again in his mind, the pale unblinking face of Bronwyn, and felt guilty that he had been so reluctant to accept her as his mother, understanding now why she had gone to such lengths to protect them both from him. He thought about the figures in the cave he had left behind. Galahad, with wounds so bad, that he wondered if he had even survived them, their friend Johnny who was probably still under Morgause's dreadful spell, and his sister, who he had left to deal with them on her own. He felt sick at the thought of it all, and an intense hatred for the one person who had caused all of these dreadful things welled up inside him. Mordred! A man he decided he hated more than anyone or anything he had ever encountered, and he vowed to himself that he would do everything he could to put an end to this cruel, unjust man who ran roughshod over everyone to get what he wanted! His sombre thoughts were broken by Bran, emerging through the thicket.

"Medraut is here! He is in the black tent at the far end of the encampment. Come, 'tis quite safe!" said Bran.

Gareth followed him out of the bushes. They carried their last remaining bundles of wood and deposited them by the fire which the men were all seated around. There was a rowdy conversation between them as they swigged their jugs of ale. One of them passed two bowls with a chunk of bread and meat to the boys as they put the wood down. They nodded their thanks and carried the food to the far side of the camp, sitting down as close as they could, without arousing suspicion, to the black conical tent, listening carefully.

Mordred's voice was the first they heard, talking to his mother, Morgause.

"So when do they come, these old hags of yours?"

"They are two days away, and when they come, we will be a force to be reckoned with!" she cackled. "Rathyen and Gwynedd of Camarthynne are the two greatest sorceresses in the land, except for myself of course! Three druid sisters together, we can create a spell so strong, your men won't even need to fire an arrow! When you draw out the knights to fight, we will have the rest of the castle walking out like the dead and there will not be a knight among them able to defend themselves."

"I hope you are right, but what of the girl with the casket?"

"She does not want it, 'tis unlikely she even knows what it is! She will still bring the casket to you in exchange for the woman! We will send a rider to Tyntagyle, telling her to do so!"

"What of the woman Bronwyn?" asked Mordred.

"Oh, give them the woman, she is not important and 'tis unlikely she will even recognise them, or recover, she has been under this spell so long now."

"You dismiss the girls powers very lightly, Morgause, your daughter is dead because of her!"

They heard the old woman sniff dismissively and Mordred continued. "Do you not mourn your daughter, Morgause?" he asked sarcastically.

"Morgana was stupid, she deserved to die, she let her feelings get the better of her. The righteous Galahad no less! Stupid girl, any sorceress would know her powers would not work to seduce, when 'twas so blatant he was beguiled by another. He merely played her for a fool!"

"You may not be concerned by her death, but I will avenge it! I pledge that the Knight Galahad will be dead before the week is out, along with the Keepers and that old meddler, Merlin," shouted Mordred. "Tyntagyle will be mine and the whole of Cornwall will bow to its rightful heir! Tomorrow we will ride to my castle where you will install the woman Bronwyn, and we will await the casket, since you are so confident that the girl will bring it to us! When your druid sisters arrive, you will work your magic and we will take Tyntagyle!"

"Tyntagyle, is that all you are concerned about?" came the old, scornful, cracked voice. "With the power of the Chalice, you could be ruler of Briton, and the heads of Gaul, the Saxons, the Romans, and any other force would have to bow down to you! Do you not recognise the immense power you have here, and do you think I would have even considered helping you if I had not seen this?"

"Mother, despicable, black sorceress that you are, for a moment I actually thought that you would want your son to have what was rightfully his, since it was taken away by the righteous Arthur! Thanks to whom; I was forced to spend many a year listening to his pious plans for Cornwall and the liberation of every damned serf in the area, with the rest of his holy crusaders!"

"You were the one to kill him though, and these serfs need to be brought back in line, they need to know who their new master is!" she retorted scathingly.

"And that, mother, is exactly what I intend to do," they heard Mordred say. "It will be up to you and your druid sisters to prove yourselves, and after that, if the rest of the world wants to bow down to me, so be it!" he finished grandly.

The two boys exchanged a knowing glance and scuttled off back to the dark shrubbery before they were discovered. They dived back into the bushes at the edge of the wood, Gareth shocked to the core by what he had just heard.

"We have to stop them!" he said, as they settled deep inside a large leafy bush. "Although I have no idea how, and I dread to think who these druid sisters are that she has coming."

"More sorceresses by the sound of it," answered Bran. "'Tis less than a quarter of a days ride to Medraut's castle, we need to get there before them."

"How? We haven't even got any horses!" Gareth replied, worriedly.

"Oh, we shall have a horse, leave that to me! We must leave for my village before first light, but for now we must sleep, we have a long ride tomorrow," Bran answered. He pulled off some small branches covered in leaves and lay them under a large bush. He crawled underneath the bush and arranged the leaves into a makeshift bed, pulling its branches around him before curling up into a ball in his new den. Gareth copied him but unfortunately he was not quite as successful and had a very uncomfortable night with twigs and branches poking into him every time he moved. Finally he drifted off into a fitful sleep, only to be woken by Bran, as the dawn was breaking.

"Shh ..." the young boy said, with his finger at his lips. "Come, we ride!"

Gareth got up stiffly, amazed to see that Bran was accompanied by a large brown horse.

"How did you get him?" asked Gareth, rubbing his eyes, not quite awake yet.

"I took him; the guards are all sleeping off last night's ale."

"You'll get into a lot of trouble when they find out the horse is missing," said Gareth, concerned that Bran was going to make his own situation worse, as they both mounted the spirited horse.

"No, I have another trick," he laughed. "When we get to my village I will leave the horse outside the castle. They will think he has broken free and returned home."

"I take it you've done this before as well?" asked Gareth with a laugh, and the boy nodded with a satisfied grin.

The camp was quiet, and they rode through the wood, ducking low as the branches almost caught them. Once they reached the other side, a vast grassy plain stretched out before them, and their ride started as they quickly urged the great horse into a full gallop.

Gareth found the ride quite exhilarating, the horse was fast and they raced over hills and green pastures. They passed small villages, with rough stone houses clustered together in valleys, still quiet as the sun was just starting to rise. On and on the powerful horse went, never slowing its pace even though it carried two riders, its hooves thudding on the soft turf, still damp with the morning dew.

Eventually, when the sun was higher in the sky, they rode into a small village, alive with people, bustling about their daily duties. They slowed up and the horse walked sedately through the village, picking its way carefully past the children and a variety of animals all roaming freely around them. The village consisted of a small cluster of rough houses, simply thatched with straw roofs. The doorways were all open and their inhabitants seemed happy to be carrying out their chores outside in the morning sun.

No-one took any notice as they passed, the women carried on chatting as they scrubbed their washing in large wooden tubs and the men continued with what they were doing, although several waved a hand in greeting. When they reached the end of the houses, Bran pulled up the horse and jumped off. Gareth followed and Bran led him into a small dark cottage. An older woman, whom Gareth guessed was his mother, immediately chastised Bran as soon as she saw the horse outside.

"Never mind the horse, I'm going to take it back in a minute," he answered. "Mother, Imogene, I would introduce you to Gareth, he is a Knight of the Order. He rides with Galahad and he is going to help us, but you must keep him here, out of sight, until I return." The two women had no time to answer as Bran sped off to return the horse to the castle. Gareth found himself alone with Bran's mother and a girl whom he presumed must be one of his sisters. They were staring at him curiously.

"Ehmm, good day," Gareth said and bowed, thinking that it might be expected of him, not that he had any idea of how he was supposed to behave. In fact the whole thing was quite embarrassing.

"Good day," replied Bran's mother, followed quickly by his sister who curtsied, both looking extremely puzzled by him.

"Please excuse us sir, come and sit down. I will get you food and a drink, while you wait for my son to return," said his mother. "Imogene, where are your manners?" she directed crossly at her daughter.

"Have you travelled far?" she asked pleasantly as Imogene returned quickly with a bowl of steaming hot broth she had ladled out of a huge pot suspended over a fire in the corner.

Gareth murmured his thanks as he took the bowl from the girl, feeling guilty accepting it as he remembered Bran's words about the families not having enough to eat. Apart from the fact that he had no wish to offend them by refusing, his stomach rumbled at the thought of food, and hunger got the better of him. He quickly started to eat the broth with the large spoon that Imogene handed to him, almost burning his mouth in his haste. Their last meal had been the few scraps the night before, and the unappetising looking grey broth tasted wonderful to his hungry palate!

"I'm sorry, yes we have come a long way," he answered, after several mouthfuls, suddenly remembering he had been asked a question. "I'll let Bran tell you all about it though."

He returned to his meal, hoping that Bran wasn't going to be too long, as he had no idea what to say to them. He was guessing that they knew nothing about the death of his father or brother and felt very awkward indeed.

He finished his meal sitting on the rough wooden chair, his eyes watering with the smoky, dark atmosphere of the cottage. He handed back his empty bowl to Imogene and thanked them, after which came a difficult silence. The two women busied themselves, exchanging a brief uncertain glance at each other, as they all waited for Bran to come back.

Chapter Ten

The Elders' Decision

Gareth counted the minutes to Bran's return and smiled weakly at his sister and mother, having no idea what to say to either of them at all!

"Are you really a knight? You don't look like one!" asked Imogene, breaking the silence, curiosity finally got the better of her.

"I suppose I am, sort of," answered Gareth awkwardly, not sure what to say. He felt even worse when he detected a look between mother and daughter, indicating that they didn't really believe he was anyway.

Fortunately for him, Bran came bounding back in, having returned the horse to the castle, and Gareth breathed a big sigh of relief. A relief that was short lived, as Bran pulled him to one side and whispered sombrely that he would have to tell the two women about the fate of his father and brother. Gareth nodded sympathetically and quickly went outside so they could have some privacy. He sat down on a roughly hewn log, watching the children running around in the bright sunlight as though they hadn't a care in the world.

His heart was heavy and he felt a huge wave of compassion for these people for whom life was so hard. His world seemed far away, and he felt a pang of guilt remembering how he and his friends sought after the latest computer games or trainers, objects that now seemed completely unimportant, as he sat and tried not to imagine the tragic conversation that was now going inside the smoky cottage that was Bran's home.

A small girl in a ragged dress came up to him, breaking his thoughts. She looked at him curiously, and he forced a smile as she giggled and ran away again. She was followed by several young boys, who stared at him from a distance, whispering behind their grubby hands. Eventually Bran came out, and Gareth knew he'd been crying. His eyes were puffy and red, and he wiped his face with his sleeve as he left the cottage. The young boy put on a brave face as he joined Gareth, and Gareth felt an enormous pang of sympathy again.

"Are they all right?" Gareth asked, knowing it was a stupid question, but he couldn't think of anything else, and he felt he had to say something!

"'Tis a shock for them 'tis true," Bran answered, "but they will manage. Death is never a surprise here! My mother almost knew she would not see them again when they left with Medraut. She has been preparing herself for the worst since they left, though 'tis still hard for her to bare. My sister is very upset, but they will go together to break the news to my brother's wife. I have told them that you will help us, so they need not be afraid!"

Gareth nodded, hoping that he would be able to keep the promises he'd made.

"Come, we need to see the Elders, they need to know of Medraut's trickery. They must hear what he has done with our men, and what he intends to do next! Take off the tunic, you will need to look like a knight or they will not believe us."

"Who are the Elders?" asked Gareth, struggling to pull off the sack-like tunic as they walked back through the village.

"The Elders are the wise ones of our village, there are three of them. They decide what is best for our people, and make the decisions. In the past they have refused to stand against Medraut, as he once offered us protection against the Saxons, in return for our services. The Saxons never came here, but they still pledge their allegiance to Medraut. They think it easier to do his bidding whatever the cost to our people, in case we should ever need the protection of his army. Not that he would ever use it to help us anyway! But they still believe that he would. They won't take any notice of me, but they will listen to you, you are a knight!"

They had arrived at a large hut, much bigger than all the others, open at the front with several huge tree trunks holding up the rough thatched roof and forming a canopy over the steps. Bran pushed Gareth in front of him, "You have to tell them of Medraut's plans. They will believe you!" he finished as they mounted the steps.

"Me!" said Gareth, looking horrified. "Look, I don't know what you want me to say to them!" Too late, he found himself facing three old men, in long robes, with equally long beards, sitting at a huge wooden table.

"Ah, Bran, this is your friend that you bring to us. The Knight, Sir Gareth!" said an old man on the furthest side of the table. "Come forward. State your business, young knight."

"Well sir, I'm not really … Well I am sort of, I suppose … but I'm not really Sir Gareth!" Gareth mumbled guiltily, not making any sense at all. This was something that they seemed to miss entirely as they scrutinised him carefully.

"Aye, 'tis a Knight of the Order all right! He wears the tunic with the emblem!" stated the man in the middle. He seemed entirely happy that he recognised his attire, and completely ignored the fact that Gareth was shifting uncomfortably from foot to foot mumbling incoherently, embarrassed by his new title. They looked at him expectantly, and he glanced helplessly at Bran. He cleared his throat nervously, not sure where to start, but before he could say anything, Bran blurted out the whole story to the astounded men. He started with the deaths of the men that Mordred had taken to the cave, and concluded with Mordred's plans to take Tyntagyle.

"Is this the truth?" they asked Gareth. "Medraut fought under Arthur's banner, he was a Knight of the Order. He would not go against that honour; he made a pledge to their cause."

"I am afraid it is true, sir," he answered, thankful that he hadn't had to tell the story himself.

"I do not believe this!" stated the man in the middle. "Do you have proof of this dishonour?"

"My father and brother are dead because of him, is that not proof enough for you!" shouted Bran, the tears welling up in his eyes as he spoke.

"Your father and brother were good men, we understand your grief and your wish for revenge," said the old man with the longest beard. "But we have sworn our allegiance to Medraut for his help. We cannot go back on our word, 'twould be most dishonourable!"

"When has Medraut ever helped us? He takes our food and leaves us with nothing and our men and women must do his bidding whenever he pleases! It's him who is dishonourable!" returned Bran passionately. "He has his sorceresses with him and he will destroy everything that Arthur ever did! Is that what you want?" he asked them.

Bran's words immediately appeared to cause the elders some consternation, and they tugged at their beards and whispered to each other.

"I do not see that we can help, or even if we should. Medraut is powerful; his army would destroy our village in a second! This presents us with a great dilemma. I would be interested in your words as a knight, Sir Gareth," said the elder courteously.

"Everything Bran's told you is true! Medraut has no intention of protecting you or anyone else! He's using his mother and his sister, the sorceresses, in an attempt to destroy all of the knights that are left. He wants all of them dead. He will kill Merlin as well and anyone else that tries to stop him taking Tyntagyle. He isn't a real knight and never has been. Merlin and Galahad think he was the one that killed Arthur!" said Gareth feeling slightly braver now, as the Elders gasped in horror at this latest accusation. "He's holding my mother, and I have to rescue her! He wants us to give him something very powerful in exchange for her, something that Morgause, will use to kill all of the knights that are left!" Gareth continued, as the elders faces became whiter and whiter.

"We have a plan to stop him, but we will need some help!"

interrupted Bran.

"State your plan," returned the oldest man, looking at Gareth. Gareth had no idea that they even had a 'plan', much less what it was, and looked helplessly at Bran again.

"I know ways into Medraut's fortress," said Bran confidently. "We will hide ourselves there before they arrive back with Gareth's mother. We will smuggle her out, and hide her in the village. Without her, he will have nothing to exchange for the prize he wants and will be thwarted! All we will need is two horses and a diversion while we get her out!"

"No!" There was a resounding thud, as the man in the middle banged his fist against the table. "You will not bring her here! If Medraut found out, he would burn the village to the ground. You will not put our people at risk!"

"We can get her out, I know we can! We can hide her!" answered Bran stubbornly.

"Sir, if we could just have help to get her out, we won't come here. I will take her myself to Tyntagyle, to Merlin. He will rid her of the spell she is under and Medraut need never know that you were involved. I don't want to bring trouble to your village," Gareth interjected sensibly.

"What do we get in return?" asked the remaining man, who had so far been silent.

"We have to fight Medraut. He will attack the castle anyway, and we have to defeat him once and for all! He plans to use Morgause to create a spell to help them. We have the one thing they want, and we can use it against them. It will destroy her magic and defeat them! Once Medraut is gone, you'll all be free of the hold he has over you. You'll be able to trade fairly with your surplus food, keeping what you need to feed your own people, and if you help us, the knights will help you in return!" he answered, with much more confidence than he actually felt.

The men tugged their beards and muttered amongst themselves again, glancing at Bran and then Gareth, until finally the last man who had spoken stood up.

"The Council of Elders has reached a decision," he said with authority. "We trust the word of the Knight Sir Gareth, and we will give what help we can. You may have the horses, but the woman is not to come to the village, you must return her to Tyntagyle. We may be able to help with a diversion as long as our villagers are not implicated in the woman's rescue. State your plan for this!"

"We are due to take the hay to the castle," said Bran. "When we are about to bring the woman out, I will signal and the hay wagon shall be set on fire in the castle courtyard. This will keep the guards busy putting out the fire, and they will not notice us leaving."

After a great deal of muttering and beard pulling again, the man stood up.

"It shall be done!" he said.

"Thank you!" they said in relief. Gareth and Bran bowed and the Elders stood up and did the same. As they turned to leave, the man who had the final say came forward and spoke quietly to Gareth.

"In the days of Artorius, we were proud to fight his cause. 'Twas a sorry day he fell, and if it were at the hand of Medraut, in whom we have put our trust, this is a grave disappointment. We have kept up our allegiance to him, thinking him an honourable knight. This has been an allegiance we have kept to, despite the suffering it has caused us! 'Tis good to know that there are those who are still prepared to continue the fight, for the cause that Artorius began! May God go with you, young knight!"

"Thank you," said Gareth, bowing again as he left, extremely relieved that their audience was over.

As they walked back through the village Gareth was still recovering from their meeting with the Elders. He was unaware that the villagers all stopped what they were doing as they passed and nudged each other, whispering. It was only when he noticed a lady sitting on a stone bench scraping a large pile of vegetables into a wooden bowl, drop her knife and stare at him open mouthed, that he realised the attention they were attracting.

"Why are they all staring at us?" he asked Bran, as three men loading a cart with wood stopped what they were doing and whispered as they looked at them.

"'Tis not every day that I walk through the village with a knight," shrugged Bran. "And they will have heard my family's news by now!"

"Oh, yes I suppose so," answered Gareth, still feeling uncomfortable.

"When the sun is high, we will go straight to the back of the castle," said Bran undeterred. "You will have to cover yourself again, so that they do not recognise you as a knight."

"Look," said Gareth feeling he ought to come clean about his position. "I'm not really a knight. The Elders called me Sir Gareth, but I'm really not a 'Sir' at all. I come from somewhere very different."

"You ride with them, do you not?" answered the boy, looking puzzled. "I saw you with my own eyes. You were with the Knight Sir Galahad!"

"Well, yes, I was," said Gareth, "but I am not a Sir. Not like Galahad!"

"Have you not been knighted by the sword Excalibur, as all the others were, then?" asked Bran, looking confused.

"Well yes, I have," Gareth answered quite truthfully, remembering his first visit when he was knighted by Argante in the cave.

"Then you must be Sir Gareth, a Knight of the Order who rides with Sir Galahad."

Gareth sighed, there was no way he could explain all of the complications that surrounded his presence there. Bran's world was hard, but straightforward, and he wouldn't understand the story of them travelling through time from another century even if he tried to explain it! So he decided it was best not to even attempt it. Instead, he nodded resignedly and kept quiet, even though he still felt rather like an impostor.

They made their way back to the small dark cottage, where Bran went in to see his mother and sister again. He was not long and was followed out by Imogene, who handed Gareth a small bowl of water. He thanked her and drank it as she watched him curiously. Her pale, pretty face, now blotchy from crying, was framed by her dark tangled hair, and Gareth felt immensely sorry for her. Bran signalled that it was time to go and Gareth handed the bowl back to her. As he turned to go, Imogene caught his sleeve.

"I hope you get your mother back," she said quietly. "And when you kill Medraut, make sure he dies a slow, painful death: if not for your own cause, then for ours!"

"Um, well, yes, we will!" he answered, the guilty feelings of being a helpless imposter overwhelming him again, this time with a huge responsibility falling on his unprepared shoulders.

He followed Bran to a small wood, where there were two men waiting with the horses.

They took the reins from them, and the men bowed, wishing them well, before they led the horses away, deep into the wood. They journeyed on foot through the trees until they reached the other side, where Mordred's castle came into view standing on top of a small hill - grim, grey and imposing. His fortress was not an attractive sight, and in no way matched the splendour or size of Tyntagyle. It was a foreboding, square building with high walls around it. It didn't even look particularly impenetrable and Gareth noticed several gateways in its walls as they got closer. He mentioned them to Bran, who immediately informed him that they were always heavily guarded.

They left the horses out of sight in the wood and continued on foot again. A small stream ran at the back of the castle where a group of women, surrounded by large tubs, were washing piles of clothes in the water. One young girl in a dark grey dress stood up when she saw Bran and ran over to hug him, looking uncertainly at Gareth.

"He is a friend, you may trust him," said Bran reassuringly. "We need to get into the castle, can you help us?"

"You must come quickly then, in case the others get suspicious," she answered, coyly planting a kiss on Bran's cheek.

She handed them both two large pails, darting a look at the other women cautiously. "Fill these with water and follow me," she whispered.

Gareth and Bran did as instructed, filling the pails from the stream and following the girl up the incline to the castle wall and a large wooden gate. She knocked on it and it swung open to reveal a large, surly guard. They followed her in with their heads down, and the gate shut with a heavy bang behind them. The sentry pulled down a huge piece of wood on to a metal latch to secure it, and they made their way quickly across the open area towards the castle.

They entered through a small doorway and found themselves in a huge kitchen, bustling with young girls in the same grey, ragged long dresses. The air was thick with smoke from a huge fire in a recess, roaring and spitting as a large pig was roasting on a metal spit, with one of the girls slowly turning it. They scarcely looked at them as they left the pails of water in a corner and quickly left through another door on the other side.

"I must go back, before I am missed," said the girl, and was treated to another embrace from Bran. "Be careful, won't you?" she said over her shoulder as she rushed out into the courtyard, and back towards the gate.

"Come, we will hide!" said Bran and led Gareth quickly across the courtyard towards an archway in a nearby turret, not dissimilar to the one leading to Merlin's quarters in Tyntagyle.

They quickly ran up the stone steps, twisting round and round, until they were quite high. They stopped, out of breath, and leaned against an open arched window overlooking the approach to the castle.

"'Tis lucky for us that he has most of his men camped by Tyntagyle or 'twould not have been so easy," remarked Bran. "We are safe here; they use this as a look out, and for their archers to fire on an approaching enemy. They have no reason to use the tower as they are not expecting an attack."

Gareth leaned against the wall, surveying the countryside beyond, while he regained his breath.

"You can see for miles," he stated.

"Yes, we will see them coming from here," said Bran. "Yonder is the main approach to the castle," he said, pointing to a rough track leading to the main castle entrance further along.

"Who's the girl who let us in?" asked Gareth.

"Her name is Sarah; she is from our village, as are all the others at the stream. She and her sisters were taken when their father died in battle under Medraut's flag, and were left with no man to support them. They work from dawn till dusk as servants here," answered Bran, with a bitter note creeping into his voice as he was reminded of their treatment.

"I'm sorry, she seems very nice," said Gareth.

"She is more than nice. She is a truly lovely maid, and would that she were still in our village, I would take her as a wife."

"What? You're never old enough to get married, surely?" Gareth asked, with astonishment. "You can't even be as old as me!"

"I am old enough to fight, and to take a wife!" Bran answered defensively. "If she had not been brought here to the castle, we would have been betrothed by now!"

"Well can't you still do that, if that's what you really want?" asked Gareth.

"Of course not!" Bran answered scornfully. "She is Medraut's property now, and will marry who she is told to! One of his men I would expect!"

Gareth sighed again feeling rather useless, and said no more, not wishing to offend him again. They leant against the stone sill in silence as they watched the horizon for Mordred's party. 'This is most definitely another world,' thought Gareth, still amazed that someone younger than himself would even think about marrying anyone, however nice they were! His thoughts drifted back to his sister's giggly friends and he shuddered at the mere thought of being 'betrothed' to any of them!

Eventually, Bran nudged him and pointed to the riders on the horizon. As they drew closer they could see it was Mordred, Morgause and Bronwyn, with two men accompanying them. The solid gates were opened for them and they entered the castle compound. The two boys rushed to the window on the other side to see them dismount and drag a limp Bronwyn towards the castle.

"Stay here, I will find out where they are taking her!" Bran instructed solemnly, before he darted off down the steps, silently winding his way back down the stone staircase.

Gareth waited and waited impatiently, he could hear voices and a heavy door banging below him. He leant over the staircase as far as he could, but he still couldn't see what was going on. Eventually he saw Bran coming back up the stairs.

"What's happening?" Gareth asked, expectantly, as he met him on the top step.

"I know where they have taken her," Bran replied, smugly. "Two flights down, there is a door leading into the main castle, they are holding her in a room off there! Come; do not make a sound as they are still with her!"

Gareth followed him quietly back down the stairs until Bran motioned him to stop, as they heard Mordred's voice. They flattened themselves against the wall, out of sight, as they heard him say "Make sure you lock her in, the last thing I want is her escaping."

"Fool!" they heard the evil voice of Morgause scornfully answer him. "There are no locks that could bind the woman any firmer than my spell! She has no will of her own; she knows not who she is; or even where she is: and she has no desire to leave. If I did not tell her to eat or drink, she would die anyway!"

"As long as you are sure, Morgause ..." they heard him respond, doubtfully.

"Of course I am sure," she snapped. "Now show me the quarters my druid sisters will have. Only your finest rooms will do. I insist that they have the best and will be treated like Queens while they are here!"

"I am quite sure that anything other than a cave will be quite luxurious to them!" snarled Mordred, as the boys heard him disappearing down the stairs with Morgause, still arguing. Finally another door banged as they left.

The boys crept back down the stairs and through the door into a long passageway. Bran pushed open several doors gently, and peered inside at the empty rooms. They didn't find Bronwyn until they tried the very last door. Bran lifted the huge latch and motioned for Gareth to follow him in. The room was small and spartanly furnished. There were no rich trappings here, only a few pieces of heavy wooden furniture and a low pallet bed which Bronwyn lay on by the open window. The wind blew in through the open stone clad slit.

Gareth rushed over to her, but she made no move as he shook her gently. There was no recognition in the eyes that stared blankly at the ceiling.

"Bronwyn, it's me, Gareth!" he said in despair. "We're going to get you out of here!"

There was no response from the motionless figure.

"Bronwyn, Look at me!" he said pulling her up into a sitting position. She turned and looked at him, but there was still no recognition in her eyes. She was simply obeying a command. "Bronwyn, you have to come with us! Get up, we'll get you out of here!" She didn't appear to understand and stared blankly. "Oh this is useless!" he said to Bran in despair.

"Keep trying, we do not have much time! The hay wagon is coming into the courtyard below and we need to go before we are discovered!" Bran answered.

"Bronwyn stand up. You're coming with us!" tried Gareth again, and to his relief she slowly got to her feet. She didn't look at them and still stared silently into space, as though waiting for another instruction.

"Put this over her hair," said Bran, handing him a rough, dark shawl. "I stole it from the washing basket by the stream. If they see her hair they will recognise her straight away."

Gareth draped it over Bronwyn's hair and back over her shoulders, still marvelling at Bran's capacity to acquire whatever was needed. Bran opened the door and looked down the stairs, motioning that the coast was clear.

Gareth led Bronwyn firmly by the arm, and they followed him along the corridor and down the stone steps, with Bronwyn stumbling on every one of them as she continued to stare blankly ahead. When they got down to the next window, Bran halted. He leant out of the window with his fingers in his mouth and made a loud whistling noise that sounded remarkably like a screeching bird. He ducked back and looked out again carefully a few seconds later, when they heard shouts from below as people ran into the courtyard.

"Quickly, the hay is alight!" Bran said, as a plume of smoke drifted upwards. "We must escape now!"

They continued downwards as quickly as they could, with a reluctant Bronwyn stepping blindly as Gareth propelled her down the stairs. Suddenly a door opened at the bottom and they realised to their horror it was Morgause. She started up the stairs towards them, red faced and panting in rage.

"Stupid, stupid boys, did you think you could just walk in and take her without me knowing? I am the greatest sorceress in all of Cornwall," she screamed at them. "Of course I would know!"

The boys stopped in their tracks for a moment in panic, and then quickly tried to go back up the stairs. Morgause screamed in fury, then took a deep breath and blew. As the air left her mouth, it turned into a whirling, grey tornado that twisted its way up the stairway towards them. As it reached them and threatened to suck them into its grey twisting void, they clutched at each other as they were thrown back against the wall. The tornado raged for as long as Morgause's breath lasted and she cackled manically, with a laugh that was almost an assault in itself.

The tornado over they tried to go upwards again.

"Stay where you are!" Morgause screeched. Her command immediately halted Bronwyn, and Gareth found he could no longer move her, however hard he tried to push Bronwyn. "You will not escape me! Where is the girl?" the old witch asked, as she moved up a few more steps.

"She's not here, she's at Tyntagyle," answered Gareth, hoping that Rachel had actually made it back there with Galahad and Johnny.

"Well, maybe that is not so bad. The girl would have only been a nuisance, and she will certainly bring the casket now!" she grinned malevolently at them, as though in triumph. "With her mother and her brother, both in my captivity, how could she resist that?" She threw back her head and her evil cackle filled the stairway, ringing in their ears, making their heads spin.

Gareth shivered and remembering the pendant in his pocket, closed his hand firmly around it. 'Rachel, I don't know how this thing works, but I really need some of your magic now!' he thought to himself, as he tried again to push the unwilling Bronwyn back through the door that Bran was holding open for them.

"Bronwyn, come here," Morgause said sharply, beckoning with a long bony finger, and Bronwyn instinctively started to move forward towards her.

"No, No!" shouted Gareth jumping in front of his mother, grabbing her shoulders roughly and making her face him. "Don't listen to her, do you hear me? Don't listen to her!" Bronwyn still tried to step forward in her trance but then stopped, and for a moment Gareth thought he saw a flicker of recognition in her eyes.

Morgause must have noticed as well as she let out another loud yell. "Come here now!"

'The pendant!' thought Gareth, as he realised it was in his hand and he was pressing it against Bronwyn's shoulder. He quickly put it round her neck, fumbling with the catch. "Bronwyn, this is from Rachel, it'll help us. You mustn't listen to Morgause, you must listen to us!"

Another grey tornado spiralled towards them, flattening them against the wall. Its movement slowed, still whirling lazily, pinning them against the wall. Unable to move, Gareth looked down to see an enraged Morgause lifting her arms in a circle and the strange language they'd heard her using in the cave when she cast her spell before, was pouring from her lips again. Already the steady rhythmic force waves that Gareth had encountered before were starting to pulsate in their heads.

"Oh no, not again!" said Gareth, still holding the pendant at Bronwyn's neck with one hand. "Bran, try to get behind Bronwyn, cover your ears and don't look at Morgause, she's casting a spell!" he shouted.

Bran pushed himself behind Bronwyn as instructed, quickly covering his ears as the pulsing incantation got stronger and stronger with Morgause's chanting. Gareth tried hard to block it out and resist, but gradually it became more difficult for him to think and his hand slipped off the pendant that he had just fixed round Bronwyn's neck. His thoughts started to slip away altogether, to be replaced by a foggy greyness that was beginning to take over his mind completely.

Chapter Eleven
Mordred's Message

Back at the castle in Tyntagyle, Rachel breathed a big sigh of relief; as strong arms reached down to help them from their platform on the cliff face, up into the safety of the castle. Johnny scrambled up first and then Galahad lifted Rachel up into the men's arms and they heaved her up through the wooden trap-door. He passed the casket up to her, before climbing up himself.

"'Tis, Galahad, he is sorely hurt!" exclaimed the guards to each other, as they saw his blood stained clothes. Burly and tough as they were, their concern was genuine on all of their faces as they helped him up into the castle.

"'Tis, naught but a surface wound, I have suffered worse," Galahad declared unassumingly and they slapped him on the back and clasped his arm in turn showing their support.

Galahad turned to Rachel and Johnny, to make sure they were all right after their exhausting, treacherous climb. Even Rachel, still shaking from her ordeal, managed a relieved smile, only to see the young knight sway and slump to the floor in front of them.

"Oh no, what's wrong with him? Do something, get Merlin!" she shouted almost hysterically at the men, as she knelt down next to him. "This is my fault; I let him carry the casket! Galahad, wake up, please wake up!" she cried, shaking him. There was no response, his face was pale and his body was limp, making her even more frantic. "Get Merlin I said, didn't you hear me?" she screamed at them again.

One man dashed off and the rest of them stood back, not quite sure what to do with the hysterical girl as she loosened Galahad's clothing and pulled off his helmet. Merlin arrived out of breath a few moments later and gently pulled her aside.

"It's all right, leave him to me," he said reassuringly, as he knelt down next to her, inspecting Galahad's injuries. "He has passed out from loss of blood by the looks of it, but his heart beats strongly and he will soon recover."

Rachel stood up, relieved, the tears still running down her cheeks.

"Take him to my quarters, I will look after him," Merlin instructed the men, who immediately picked up the knight with ease and carried him away.

"Now then, I know young Johnny here, but where is Gareth? Is he not with you?" Merlin asked.

"No he's gone after Mordred. It's a long story," she added in a tired voice.

"Then we shall go to my rooms. I will attend to Galahad while you rest, and later you shall tell me all!" he answered.

Rachel and Johnny followed him through the castle towards his turret quarters. His long, elaborate blue gown swished and rustled as he walked in front of them.

Johnny was clearly in awe of his surroundings and tried to take in every detail as they passed through the great castle, almost walking into Rachel at one point as he caught a glimpse of the stone Round Table through an open door. Finally they climbed the stairs to Merlin's room, where Rachel flopped onto his large settle, exhausted, while Johnny, still beside himself with excitement, wandered around the room, looking at everything in wonder. He leant so far out of the window to look at the scene below, he almost fell out, reminding her of Gareth on their first visit, and she felt a pang of concern as she realised that they had no idea where he was, or what he was doing!

Johnny's exuberance was almost bubbling over, but Rachel was too upset and tired to even care. She left him to it and closed her eyes, pretending to sleep, only opening them when Isolde appeared carrying a tray with food and drink.

"Here Miss, Merlin said you are to drink this," she said, handing Rachel a goblet with a warm, sweet smelling liquid.

"What is it?" asked Rachel, sniffing the not unpleasant aroma of herbs and berries that emitted from the warmth of the goblet.

"It will calm you, miss!" Isolde answered, looking sympathetic.

Rachel took a sip of the ruby liquid, thinking that her hysterical behaviour must obviously be common knowledge in the castle and smiled weakly at the girl.

"Your knight will recover, you need not worry," Isolde said knowingly. "Merlin will make sure of that!"

"My knight?" said Rachel, almost choking on the drink as the girl's words registered. "He's not my knight!" she answered indignantly, but her words were lost, as Isolde had already closed the door behind her. 'Oh no, was that what they were all thinking? How embarrassing!' she thought to herself, as she sipped the warm liquid, which strangely enough, did calm her and she began to feel quite drowsy.

Eventually Johnny managed to contain his enthusiasm and calmed down enough to join her on the large settle, sitting down gently as Rachel appeared to be asleep again. He tucked into a plate of food silently, still marvelling at his surroundings.

When Rachel awoke she found Merlin sitting talking quietly with Johnny on the far side of the room.

"How's Galahad?" she asked immediately.

"He's fine," answered the old wizard. "He will sleep till morning and with rest his strength will return. I must say though, I am at a loss to see how he has lost so much blood, or indeed what injury caused it. There were no fresh wounds that I could find, only some strange scar tissue on his neck and arm. However I am sure there is an explanation for this," he added wisely.

Between them, they told Merlin the story of what had happened after she had left the castle with Gareth and met up with Johnny.

He listened carefully until they had finished.

"Splendid, splendid, do you have the casket with you?" Merlin asked, unperturbed by the horrific tale of how they got it.

"Yes, I put it upstairs in the little bedroom for safety," answered Rachel. "I don't understand - how was I able to touch the casket, when those poor men died trying to do the same thing? That's why I was so worried about Galahad, I thought it had killed him because I'd let him carry it up the cliff. And Johnny, I made him touch it as well, but he's all right, so why did it let us do it?" asked Rachel.

"Well firstly, the casket had nothing to do with Galahad's collapse; in fact it was the Chalice that saved his life. No-one ever recovers from the bite of a shape shifter, while they are in animal form! The wound, however small, never heals; it festers until it poisons the whole body. I also believe that if Galahad had not carried the Chalice he would have collapsed on the cliff face and fallen to his death. No-one could make that climb, with half of their life's blood gone!"

"But why did the casket allow me to pick it up and let Johnny and Galahad touch it as well?" she asked again.

"You were able to pick it up, because you wanted nothing for yourself from it," Merlin answered. "I do not know about the men that died, as we do not know their motives, but you wanted it to save Bronwyn. Johnny was in a trance, and did not touch it of his own free will and Galahad was aware of the risk, but took it from you anyway, as he knew that you could not have managed the climb if you were carrying it. These were all selfless acts, for which it would not harm any of you."

"But originally I was going to give it to Mordred in exchange for Bronwyn, so surely I did want something from it?" asked Rachel.

"Something else must have happened when you went to get it," stated Merlin.

"I heard voices and I said I was sorry, and that we would make sure to take it back to safety. Then I saw someone ghostly, they spoke to me and said it was all right and they would protect us, but that I mustn't give it to Mordred. That's why I didn't give it to him, but it backfired because he ran off with Bronwyn and now Gareth's following them all on his own. We might have the Chalice but it's all still a dreadful mess!"

"It may seem like that, but you are forgetting that you have accomplished the most important thing. You have removed the casket from Mordred, and it is safe here with us!"

"Well, I'm glad you think so," answered Rachel angrily, "but Mordred's still got Bronwyn and Gareth's missing as well now, and I find that much more important!"

"Yes, my dear of course you do, but I don't think you realise how much power you have on your side now. In living history there are but a few who have ever heard, much less seen, the Guardians of the Chalice, and to be allowed to hold it and use it to heal Galahad and Johnny is even more remarkable!"

"I suppose so," answered Rachel begrudgingly.

"The Guardians have entrusted you completely with the Chalice, and will help you, but afterwards you must fulfil your mission and take it back to where it belongs."

"But what about Gareth and Bronwyn? They haven't got anything to help them!"

"But they have my dear, don't forget that Gareth is a Keeper of the Power, and Bronwyn before him. They have their own protection."

"That's all very well, but Gareth has no idea how to use it, and Bronwyn is under Morgause's spell!" she said miserably.

"Then ask the Chalice, ask it to protect them and keep them safe! You are holding the power here, use it!" the old wizard replied.

"He's right, if it can help me and cure Galahad, it'll help the others as well, I'm sure!" said Johnny, whom she had almost forgotten was there.

"Spoken like a true friend!" said Merlin. "A young man who has risked much to be here with you and has more faith in your capabilities than you appear to have yourself!" he admonished. "And now we shall sleep, for tomorrow will bring us the opportunity to defeat Mordred and return your mother and brother to safety!

Now Johnny, you shall sleep here, you will be comfortable enough on the settle. I will bring you a blanket and Rachel you shall sleep in the turret room. Tomorrow you will contact your brother and we shall make plans to help them!"

"Contact him, how are we going to do that? I can hardly phone him and ask him where he is!" asked Rachel, her temper and frustration rising again.

"You will see, there are other ways of contacting someone when you need to!" Merlin said resolutely, as he handed a blanket to Johnny and went to the door. "I will see you both tomorrow."

Johnny and Rachel looked at each other as he left, and Rachel shrugged her shoulders. "He always does this! He always leaves with the promise of a plan, which I'm sure he hasn't got, and then we'll find out tomorrow that we're going to do something that doesn't even bear thinking about!" she said crossly.

"I'm sure it'll be all right," said Johnny, trying to reassure her. "I'm just sorry that I haven't been much help. I don't even remember half of what went on today, and I really wish that I could have gone with Gareth to help him!"

"That wasn't your fault; anyway, I am glad you're here to help me! Otherwise I'd be on my own!"

Johnny's face lit up. "I'll do anything to help, you know that!"

"I know and I am really grateful that you're here!"

"I suppose we'd better go to bed like he said," answered Johnny, "and don't worry, we'll sort it all out tomorrow, we'll get them back!"

"I hope you're right!" she answered as she went to the small staircase.

"By the way, I've still got your book here," he added, handing it to her before she left.

Rachel took a candle up to her bedroom and got into bed. She was far too worried to go to sleep and opened the yellowed pages of the book they had gone to such lengths to keep with them. She studied it carefully, something they had not had time to do, and was amazed to find strange pages at the back of the book containing passages that sounded almost like spells. *"To summon the Power against thine enemies,"* and *"To evoke the Power to vanquish sorcery,"* caught her attention and she read them nervously. Eventually she closed the book, frightened that if she read any more of the spells, she wouldn't sleep at all. She turned her attention instead to the casket, which was sitting on the small table next to the bed. She inspected it gingerly in the candlelight, noticing the intricate designs on the lid, depicting a picture of an oblong table with men seated behind it wearing long robes. There were more pictures on the sides, each showing another scene, which were difficult to see in the dim light. For a moment the enormity of what she was holding suddenly hit her. She knew that inside the beautifully decorated box lay an old, indistinctive looking earthenware goblet that could possibly be the Holy Grail, which they had heard about only in stories, and she hastily put it back on the table.

Before she blew the candle out, she looked at the casket and said quietly, "You promised to help me, please protect my brother and Bronwyn as well, and help me get them back."

She pulled the bed-covers over her ears, worried again that if she thought about it too much, she would never get to sleep!

Not realising how exhausted she was, not only did she go straight to sleep but was surprised to find that the morning light was soon streaming through the window. She quickly remembered the previous day's events and was soon wide awake. She splashed her face with cold water from the pitcher and dressed quickly in one of the other dresses that she had discarded the day before. She didn't pay much attention to what it looked like, as she was eager to get downstairs.

The room was empty, but there was evidence that Johnny had eaten his breakfast, by the amount of crumbs left on the table, along with the platters that Isolde had obviously brought earlier. Rachel smiled; Johnny's appetite was like her brother's and she sat down with a drink and a plate of food, wondering if Gareth had managed to eat breakfast somewhere. Before she was allowed to get too despondent, Merlin appeared in the doorway.

"Ah Rachel, I am glad you are up. I have sent Johnny to have a look around. Dear boy, he was up at first light and could not wait," he said.

Rachel smiled again, as she remembered how excited Gareth had been on their first morning at the castle, when everything had been new to them.

"Ah good, I see you have eaten, you can take this broth in to Galahad for me, it will do him no end of good."

"Oh, I don't know … I don't think I ought to … " she stuttered, nervously.

"Nonsense, I am sure he will be glad to see you!" he said, thrusting the hot bowl into her hands. "Second door down the stairs, off you go my child, while I find out where Johnny has got to." He held the door open for her and closed it behind her firmly, leaving her with no choice but to take the soup downstairs to Galahad.

She knocked timidly at the door and there was no answer, so she let herself in quietly and was relieved to see that Galahad was still sleeping. She put the bowl down on the small table next to the bed and was pleased to see that his face had lost its pallor of the day before. She looked closer, seeing the red, livid scar left by the wolf's attack, which was now looking quite healthy. She couldn't help but notice the many old, deep scars that covered his chest and a jagged puckered line that reached right across from his shoulder. She was also surprised at how young he looked without his armour and chain mail. She had automatically assumed that since he was a knight he must be much older than her, but looking at him now, she realised that he could not be much more than about nineteen. It was then that she realised that the dark brown eyes were open and his usual arrogant grin was back.

She stepped back so quickly with embarrassment, that she nearly knocked the bowl off the table.

"I am touched that you watch over me, fair Rachel. For a moment I thought 'twas an angel, come to take me away," he said, with a laugh.

"I wasn't watching over you. Merlin asked me to bring you some broth!" she answered defensively. "Anyway, I'm glad you're feeling better, and I'll leave you to eat," she said over her shoulder, as she made for the door.

"Do not leave, I was only jesting. I would enjoy some company," he answered, sitting up and wincing slightly. Rachel hesitated with her hand still on the door. "It would make me feel better, besides I cannot reach the bowl from here."

Rachel laughed and handed him the bowl. There was no spoon, so he took it in both hands to drink from it. She sat down gingerly on a wooden chair, not quite knowing what to say.

"How did you get all those dreadful scars?" she asked eventually, curiosity getting the better of her.

"Battle trophies," smiled Galahad.

"You don't look old enough to have been in so many battles."

"Age has not much to do with it, if you have the strength and the skills you are old enough to do battle. I mastered the sword at an early age." He wiped his mouth with the back of his hand and handed the bowl back to her. "But if the truth be told, I got some of the scars mastering the art of the sword!"

"That's even worse then!" she said, as she put the bowl back on the table.

"Not really, if you took the shirt off every man in the castle, you would find them covered in scars from their efforts in the battles they have fought!"

"I still think it's dreadful!" she replied.

"Dreadful they probably were at the time, but wounds heal and after any battle, we are grateful when we wake up to find another morning!"

She nodded in answer, not knowing quite what to say, coming from a world where, thankfully, she did not have to experience such things.

"Rachel, I fear I have an apology to make," he said seriously. "I may have appeared disrespectful in the cave. My might is with the sword. I have no defence against the kind of weapons that Morgana and Morgause use, nor do I even understand them. I thought at best, I could at least keep Morgana away from you. I am familiar with the way she uses her magic, and I sought to distract her by playing to her vanity. I knew she would protect me from

Morgause's spells, if she thought I was under her enchantment. It was the only way I could help you."

"So you were playing along with her? You seemed to know her very well."

"Our paths have crossed many times," he said wryly.

"She was very beautiful," said Rachel, slightly enviously.

"Beautiful indeed: no man would ever dispute Morgana's beauty on the outside, but on the inside, she had a heart as black as the night, and as cold as the snow in winter."

They lapsed into silence as they both reflected on Morgana's final attack on Galahad, causing the injuries that had nearly killed him.

"Merlin said you're Lancelot's son," she said, valiantly trying to change the subject.

"I am indeed," he replied.

"You must miss him."

"Not really, I hold no great affection for my father," Galahad said seriously. "Although there was a time when I did."

"I'm sorry, I didn't realise," she replied, feeling as though it was her turn to apologise. "I assumed that since you were both Knights of the Round Table, you must have followed in his footsteps I suppose."

"And follow in them I did. I followed a father who I held in utmost respect, 'tis no secret," he shrugged, "until he betrayed our King and our cause. My father's downfall was always women, but to betray Arthur with his own wife Guinevere, the woman he had made his Queen, was unforgivable."

"I'm sorry, I assumed that Guinevere was your mother," apologised Rachel, feeling awkward again.

"Indeed she was not! My mother was Elaine of Corbeck, another woman my father apparently loved, with an even more complicated story! In fact, it could indeed be said that my father excelled himself with difficult relationships!" he answered scornfully.

"What went wrong with your mother and father?" she asked.

"It has been said that my mother used sorcery, to trick him into thinking she was Guinevere, and when he found out she wasn't, he tried to kill her!"

"That's awful!" said Rachel.

"If it were true it would be, but I do not believe it. I think that my father amused himself with her for a while, and when he grew bored with her he left," he answered bitterly. "Many women were enamoured by my father, and my mother was one of them, but the only woman he ever really loved was Guinevere, despite the fact that she was the wife of our King!"

"So you grew up with your mother?" she asked.

"I do not remember her, I lived with her for a short while I believe, and then I was sent to Malmesbury, to be brought up by the women of the church. When I was old enough, I went in search of my father, the great Lancelot, as I too was enamoured by the stories of him. He taught me the sword, and I joined the knights to fight alongside him. I was proud to do so, I admired him greatly."

"Did you know about Guinevere then?" asked Rachel quietly.

"Not initially, it was a well kept secret and I was very young. I joined my father, and became a Knight of the Order, to serve under Arthur. He was a great man and was probably more of a father to me in the short while that I knew him, than my own had ever been. He did more for the people of Cornwall than any other and he died for his cause, betrayed by two of the people he loved and trusted most!"

"I shouldn't have asked, I'm really sorry," said Rachel, feeling guilty for prying into his past.

"'Tis of no consequence," Galahad shrugged with a smile. "'Tis up to our parents to make their own mistakes and up to ourselves not to repeat them. My feelings towards my father are no secret. I make my own destiny and I fight for what I know to be right."

"Well, I'm sorry anyway, and I'm really pleased that you're feeling better, you helped us so much yesterday. Mordred would have killed Gareth if you hadn't stopped him."

"And I in turn owe you my life! Were it not for you I would surely be dead."

"It wasn't me, it was the Chalice!" she said her cheeks colouring up with embarrassment, as he took her hand and kissed it solemnly.

"I do not know what magic you used, but I know that I should not have survived Morgana's attack. I shall not forget this and I will be at your service, for as long as you need it."

Embarrassment finally getting the better of her, she snatched her hand away, red faced, and mumbled that she had to find Johnny. She left so quickly that she realised halfway up the stairs that she had left the bowl behind. When she entered Merlin's room, she found them waiting for her. Johnny had been chatting comfortably with the old man, and jumped up when she came in.

"There you are," Johnny exclaimed. "You've been ages!"

"I'm sorry," she said, still flustered. "Galahad was telling me about his past, about his mother and Lancelot."

"That's very unusual. He does not generally speak of such matters," replied Merlin.

"I asked him about them, and then I felt dreadful. I had no idea he grew up without either of them!" she answered truthfully.

"Galahad judges his father harshly, with good reason. He was let down by him as a child and then again as an adult. The truth is that Lancelot was guilty of falling in love with someone he could not have, the wife of the King! He did immense good when he fought side by side with Arthur; he was a fearless supporter of his cause. In the end their love was something they both paid a heavy price for!"

"I had a dream, when I was here before, and you told me that I'd seen Galahad watching his village burn. Was his mother killed there too?"

"No, Galahad's mother left him when he was very young. You saw the burning of the village at Malmesbury where he grew up. The women of the church were his mothers and Galahad had a huge respect for them. He was away fighting with knights when the Saxons took the village. They burnt the church first with all the nuns in it and the women who had looked after him all perished in the fire. He rode back with help when he heard of the attack but they were too late to save them."

"That must have been so dreadful," she answered, remembering the anguish she had felt in the dream: feelings that were Galahad's.

"For him it was," replied Merlin. "Galahad fights with a passion that most do not understand. He is bound by loyalty and honour, a code he took from his father, and one that he saw him fail in completely. Arthur treated him like a son, and he valued that above anything."

Rachel nodded understandingly, and said no more, feeling guilty that she had previously judged Galahad rather harshly, seeing him as an arrogant young man who took pleasure in ridiculing her. She realised now that his flippant exterior was a cover, behind which were feelings of betrayal, and heartache from his childhood. Instead she now felt a great sympathy towards him and admired the way he seemed so intent on being different to his parents. Her thoughts were interrupted by a knock at the door, and the arrival of Bors, the knight they had met on their last visit.

"Merlin," he said with a bow. "There is a rider outside the main entrance; he rides with Medraut's flag and seeks an audience with you."

"Thank you Bors, we will be down immediately," replied Merlin. "Let him no further than the perimeter wall."

"He is being guarded very carefully at the gate. No-one under Medraut's banner would get any closer than that!" Bors replied with a laugh, as he disappeared out of the door.

They all made their way down the stone steps, out into the courtyard and across to the main gateway in the perimeter wall, where a large unruly looking man with a scar across his cheek was still seated on his horse. He was scowling and quite obviously annoyed by the castle guards surrounding him with their swords pointed towards him.

Merlin waved the guards aside and they stepped back to allow the wizard through.

"At last!" the stranger said disrespectfully. "I have a message from Medraut."

"Deliver your message," answered Merlin curtly.

"I am to tell you that Medraut is still prepared to exchange the woman for a trophy the girl has. He says that they must deliver it to the castle alone. No harm will come to them, provided they do as Medraut asks."

"Ridiculous," answered Merlin sharply. "Medraut is not master here, and I would not send my charges alone on such a journey: they would not even know how to find Medraut's castle."

"They would not be alone if they travelled with me," said the man, with a sneer.

"Indeed, they will not be travelling anywhere with you!" answered Merlin firmly.

"That is for you to decide, but I have been told that I am not to return without your answer," returned the man sourly. "So what is it to be then?"

"My answer is, that we will think about his offer," replied Merlin.

"Medraut will not be pleased, he wanted the girl to come back with me," answered the man, glowering again at Merlin.

"Well your master will have to be displeased then! You have my answer! Now be on your way, and be thankful that you are riding out of here!" Merlin turned his back on him and walked away. "Show him out!" he said majestically to the men at the gate.

"You 'eard, be on your way!" said a burly man pointing his sword higher, quite obviously delighted at this task.

The messenger turned his horse around and shouted over his shoulder angrily, "You have until the sun is high tomorrow, if Medraut does not get what he wants, the woman will be killed."

He galloped away over the causeway, taking no notice, in his fury, of the sheer drop on either side.

"Insolent dog!" exclaimed an angry Merlin, as he turned back.

He walked quickly, unused to being threatened, and clearly angry at the man's lack of respect. They found themselves almost trotting to keep up with him. They passed back through the second gateway and he strode towards the courtyard, with Rachel barely having time to notice the difference in the activities there. The perimeter was a bustle of activity, and the atmosphere was tense.

There were sentries everywhere along the battlements, and everyone was busy. There were no children in the courtyard and the animals were tethered. The archers were making ready their arrows, swords were being sharpened and many were making piles of huge round boulders at points next to the castle walls. Several men pushed a huge piece of wooden apparatus towards the battlements next to the piles of boulders.

"They really are expecting an attack on the castle, aren't they?" Rachel asked worriedly. "What on earth is that?" she said, pointing towards the wooden scaffolding being pushed towards the exterior wall.

"They are preparing for battle, but let's hope that it will not come to that!" Merlin answered, noticing her concern. "That is a sling shot, a marvellous invention! If the enemy try to scale the walls, it will fling boiling oil, or boulders on top of them. Better to be prepared!" he finished, and continued towards the castle.

"Do you really think Mordred will attack the castle?" asked Johnny.

"He would be stupid to try!" answered Merlin.

Rachel and Johnny looked at each other apprehensively.

"Do not fear, Tyntagyle is virtually impregnable, by its very position. It has held off much larger armies than his, and remained intact," Merlin said, as they reached the entrance to the stairway. "But now we must play our own part, we must find out what your brother has been up to."

"But how are we going to …?" started Rachel, interrupted by a dismissive wave of Merlin's hand.

"All in good time, all in good time," he answered vaguely, as he marched up the stairs.

Glancing at each other again, Rachel and Johnny followed him apprehensively to his turret quarters. As they reached the top of the stairs a dreadful feeling passed through Rachel, she shuddered violently as a cold, black ripple went through her. She was left with a sense of evil and impending doom and she knew with certainty that Gareth was in danger.

Chapter Twelve

The Journey through the Orb

Galahad was waiting for them in Merlin's room, and as soon as Rachel entered its cosy warmth the feeling of danger left her.

"I trust you are feeling better my friend?" inquired Merlin.

"I am indeed; maybe there was magic in the broth that I was so kindly served," Galahad answered, good-humouredly, with a sideways glance at Rachel.

"Well if there was, it was nothing to do with me," answered Rachel immediately. "It must have been Merlin!"

They all laughed at her indignant reply, and she felt her cheeks growing hotter and hotter.

"Well you must be feeling better, since you're making fun of me again!" she answered, put out by their amusement.

"I came to tell you, my riders have informed me that Mordred's camps are making ready for battle," said Galahad seriously to Merlin. "I have summoned the knights that are here to the Great Hall, as we will need to plan an attack from behind. You are welcome to join us Merlin. We are so few now; we would welcome your wisdom."

"We will join you. I would be most interested to hear your plans," Merlin answered.

They followed Galahad back down the stairs and through the castle. They pushed open the solid doors to reveal five men already seated around the great stone table. They all stood up and bowed. Galahad and Merlin returned the gesture and sat down.

"Come, take a place. The days are gone when we would fill all the seats!" instructed Percivale, noticing that Rachel and Johnny were hovering, unsure of whether they should take a place at the famous Round Table, or whether it might be considered irreverent to do so.

Rachel smiled in acknowledgement, remembering him from her last visit, and sat on one of the vacant heavy seats. Johnny was still gazing around in awe at the high domed room, with its shields and stone plaques that decorated the solid walls, and she had to tug his sleeve and motion for him to sit down.

"We have news that Medraut's men are to attack the castle upon his return," stated Percivale, intent on getting down to business.

"There is no sense to this at all," replied a large man with a thick beard. "Medraut has left his men to prepare for battle, yet he has returned to his castle. Surely, if an attack was his intent, he would be there with them?"

"I agree, they have been camped here for many a night, waiting for what?" said Kay.

"There is something strange afoot. They have no surprise attack on their side, and there are not enough of them to take Tyntagyle!" said a knight in an orange tunic.

"Aye, 'tis is a bad omen, and no mistake. I would give anything to know what they wait for!" joined in Bors.

"We all have men coming, I have a hundred, Percivale has fifty or more. What of you, Kay and Bedevere? How many men do you expect?" asked Galahad.

"I have forty a day's ride away and Kay has eighty or more, half a day away," answered Bedevere. "Owain will bring another hundred."

"But there is still no sense to this, Medraut may be many things, but he is not stupid!" joined in Percivale. "Why would he camp his men for days, so that we may know their intent, and prepare for it? He knows this castle, and how difficult it is to attack, and he surely knows that we will bring reinforcements and attack from behind. He knows that we can far outweigh him and that his men will have nowhere to go but the sea! I still cannot believe that these are his intentions! Medraut is too experienced to risk this!"

Rachel felt a chill go through her, and she knew with certainty that this was exactly what Mordred wanted! The last of the knights and all of their supporters gathered in one place!

"I think Mordred was expecting help of a very different kind, which at present he does not have," Merlin answered gravely.

"So why continue?" asked Galahad, knowing he was referring to the casket.

"If I could answer that question with certainty, I would! For now, you must make your plans to attack them from behind and if I learn anything else, I will let you know!" said Merlin.

"I do not like this. Sword against sword is our business, but if he is looking to use sorcery with his old witch of a mother …" Bors started.

"We have our own sorcery, leave her to us!" interrupted Merlin. "Continue your plans."

Galahad, wincing slightly from his wounds stood up and led the talks. They sat quietly as the men made their battle plans. Johnny listened in awe. To sit at the Round Table with the knights was something he could not have envisaged even in his wildest dreams. The Great Hall seemed to resound with ancient voices of the past, in a time that they could only imagine, where Arthur had sat planning for bygone battles with his knights. The scenes the great stained glass windows had witnessed, and the battle plans that had echoed against the thick stone walls were easy to imagine as they sat listening to the last remaining knights around the enormous stone table.

Rachel looked across the table and, for a moment, she saw Arthur again. He looked worried and shook his head in consternation. She felt another cold chill spread through her as she looked back at the men discussing their tactics and she knew that this was a warning. If the battle they were planning were to continue, she knew that they would all be destroyed!

Eventually they all stood up, clasping each other's arms in turn as they wished each other luck. Merlin wished them well, before they returned rather sombrely to his quarters. Rachel's recent knowledge worried her and although she was aware of Johnny's excited chatter about the Hall and the knights she couldn't join in.

"Why is he planning to try and take the castle without the casket? Surely that was his original plan, to use the Chalice to help him?" questioned Rachel, as soon as they were back in the privacy of Merlin's room.

"It was indeed. He is either still expecting to get it back or he has something else to help him. He would not attempt it otherwise," answered Merlin.

"What are we going to do? If he doesn't get the Chalice, he'll kill Bronwyn. You heard what the rider said: we've only got until tomorrow! I had the most dreadful feeling in the Hall, that this is exactly what he wants; all the knights together, with all of their men so that he can get rid of them all in one go!"

"You seem very certain of this," answered Merlin.

"I saw Arthur again, and I'm sure he was trying to warn me!" she said.

"Maybe he was, we need to heed that, and we also need to start using some of our own magic! Fight fire with fire, I would say!" nodded Merlin emphatically. "Starting by finding out what your brother has been up to."

"How?" asked Johnny, bemused.

"As I said before, it is not always necessary to use a telephone!" answered Merlin with a chuckle, as he went over to his ornate cabinets. "Could you get the casket please, Rachel?"

By the time Rachel returned, Merlin had put the ancient Orb of Resolution on his desk, and she put the casket down next to it.

"Good, good," said Merlin rubbing his hands together. "Now we must turn the tide in our favour again!" he said, as Johnny's eyebrows disappeared into his long shaggy fringe in wonder, and he sat down on the settle to watch.

"Now then, Rachel, first of all, I want you to ask the casket to restore my powers. We must get rid of this wretched binding spell that Morgause has left me with."

Not quite sure how she was to do this, Rachel put her hand on the casket and asked silently for Merlin's powers to be restored. Nothing happened, and Merlin looked disappointed. But as she looked at the casket longer, it appeared to be silently telling her what to do.

"I think it wants you to hold it," she said, picking it up gently, holding it out to Merlin. "It's all right, it wants me to give it to you!"

Merlin took it gingerly in both hands as he looked down at it reverently. At that moment the room filled with whispering voices and a strong gust of air blew the parchment papers off Merlin's desk, all over the floor. Merlin's hair lifted as though an electric current passed through him, and the voices got louder. Suddenly the room was silent and the breeze stopped. Merlin looked flushed and elated, and slowly his hair fell back down around his shoulders again.

"Oh, I have felt the power within!" he breathed. "It is indeed the greatest honour, and such a privilege!"

"Have your powers returned though?" asked Rachel.

"I do believe they have," said the old wizard. He excitedly raised his hands until every candle and torch threatened to ignite the room, and then plunged them into near darkness as he lowered them again quickly. "Oh glory, I do believe they are stronger than ever!" he said laughing. He pointed towards Johnny and they were plunged into darkness again, as Merlin played with his new found powers. When the light returned back to normal again, they found that Johnny was hovering several feet in mid air above the settle, still in a sitting position.

"Whoa ... steady on there!" Johnny shouted in shock, as he looked at the space around him and moved his legs frantically in the air. "Merlin! Put me down!"

"Oh I'm so sorry, my dear chap, I got quite carried away there," said Merlin, and with a wave of his hand, Johnny landed back on the seat with an unceremonious thud.

The old wizard seemed oblivious to Johnny's distress, despite his loud groan as he landed, and returned with a feverish enthusiasm to the Orb and the Chalice on his desk.

"Now, my dear, I want you to use the Orb as you did before," Merlin said, bringing the ancient frame to the front of the table for her. "Just concentrate and ask to see!"

Rachel did as he asked and looked into the round translucent ball again, watching it float inside the metal frame, its sheer movement becoming quite absorbing.

"Ask and then clear your mind. Let it lead you!" said Merlin, his voice almost a whisper.

Rachel looked deeper into the Orb's shifting matter, transfixed by its merging colours of soft translucent shades. It was really quite beautiful, she thought to herself. She was vaguely aware that Galahad had entered the room and had sat down quietly beside Johnny. She felt the same chill pass over her, as she had in the Great Hall, but was unable to take her eyes away from the Orb. Gradually through the shifting threads of colour a picture started to emerge. Soon it became quite clear and it was almost as though she were watching a scene on a television.

"I can see him, I can see Gareth!" she said excitedly.

"Go on, my dear, what else do you see?" asked Merlin.

"He's going up a stairway, it's a bit like yours here and he's with someone else, a boy!"

Merlin nodded encouragingly. "Wonderful! Wonderful! Do go on."

"I get the impression they're friends, I'm sure the boy's helping him! They've arrived at a doorway, and they're going in. Oh, Bronwyn's in the room! I can see her, she's lying down: it looks as though she's sleeping and Gareth's trying to wake her, but she isn't taking any notice. Oh no, she must still be under Morgause's spell! No, wait, Gareth's talking to her and she's getting up! She's going with them and Gareth's leading her out by the arm. They're rescuing her and I know where they are, they're in Mordred's castle!"

All the time she was talking eagerly, she never took her eyes off the smoky globe, and her hand went repeatedly from her neck to her left wrist. Merlin noticed the strange involuntary action and went quietly over to his cabinet, returning with a small box. He opened it and lifted out a heavy silver bracelet, which he snapped on to the wrist she kept holding.

"Is this what you were reaching for?" he asked softly.

Rachel ignored the question and the bracelet that he had just put on her arm. She appeared to be completely unaware of Merlin's actions. She continued as though nothing had happened, except that she immediately placed her other hand over the bracelet on her wrist, clasping it firmly.

"Bronwyn's going with them and they're all going back down the stairs. Oh no, no! Morgause is there, she's stopped them and they are trying to go back. She's started chanting, just like she did in the cave. She's casting the same dreadful spell again!" she continued narrating, her voice rising with the horror of her brother's predicament. "Gareth's put the pendant I gave him round Bronwyn's neck. Why's he doing that? Doesn't he realise that the spell will affect him again, the same as it did last time? Oh no, it is already, I can see him drifting away again, his face is going blank. Oh for goodness sake, Gareth, fight it!" she shouted in frustration. "Bronwyn, wake up will you! Do something! Wake up and help him!" she cried again, as though they would hear her. The pulsating waves from Morgause's spell were extending through the Orb and Rachel could almost feel them herself as she watched in fear, narrating the events out loud. Galahad and Johnny exchanged a worried glance, her distress evident, as she saw her brother falling motionless under the same dreadful spell as before. "Oh, no this is awful!" she said, as she watched the blank look creep over his face, the same as it had done with Johnny, before in the cave.

"Channel your thoughts, send the power from the Chalice to them," said Merlin, looking as worried the others.

Rachel looked on helplessly, still gripping the bracelet on her wrist as she watched the picture in the Orb. It depicted Gareth and the boy gradually becoming motionless and expressionless. Morgause was grinning manically at them as she stepped towards them, still chanting wildly. Then Rachel noticed Bronwyn's hand moving stiffly up towards the pendant at her neck, her fingers closed round it, and her lips began to move, slowly at first, until she regained her voice. She spoke quietly but firmly until her voice grew stronger. Bronwyn faced Morgause determinedly, reciting something back at the old sorceress and Rachel listened carefully, as the words were sounding somehow familiar.

"Bronwyn's awake, she's taken a stand against Morgause, and she's saying something back at her! I know the words, but I can't remember where from!" Rachel told the audience behind her. "Where have I heard them before?" she asked herself out loud. "I know, I haven't heard them, I've read them! It's a spell from the Keeper's book, I know it is! Get me the book, I can help them," she said, excitedly. "Johnny, get me the book, quickly!"

Rather taken aback, Johnny rushed off in the direction of her room as instructed, and reappeared after a few minutes clutching the black book. He put it on the desk next to the Orb, and Rachel pushed him away in her haste to open it.

"I remember this, I read it last night, oh where is it?" she muttered, flicking through the ancient pages to the back, where she found the words that Bronwyn was reciting. She waited until she found the exact line that Bronwyn was quoting and confidently joined in.

"Thou shalt not oppose the power of the righteous.
May the Power of the great ones defeat the spells and sorcery of the darkness.
Let the light of the true, shine through to extinguish the fires of Hades.
We evoke the Power against our enemies of darkness.
We evoke the Power against the darkness itself, and those who follow it.
We evoke the Power against those who oppose the great ones."

Maugause stopped chanting and looked up and down the stairs in bewilderment. She could hear Rachel's voice quite loudly, it echoed eerily all around the stairwell, as though it came from the air around them, but the girl was nowhere to be seen.

"Be silent, those who oppose us,
Be still, those who oppose us,"

Bronwyn ignored Maugause and carried on.

"What sorcery is this? Where is the girl? I can hear her, where is she?" Morgause asked with a scream, as all of the doors below them flew open with a crash and a blast of air rushed up the stairwell. She looked upwards in bewilderment as she saw Rachel's face appear on the wall in front of her in a cloud of smoky colours. It filled the wall like a huge television and she stared at it stunned, as the two voices said in unison:

"By all that remain sacred
We evoke the Power.
And in the name of the Power we bind you!"

A white ball of light shot from Bronwyn's hand and exploded in front of Morgause, who fell back, as though she had been forcibly struck, screeching loudly like an animal. She hit the wall and shrank into a huddle of tattered gowns, muttering obscenities at Bronwyn, who faced her firmly, still holding the pendant at her neck with her other hand.

Bronwyn's voice started to drift into Gareth's otherwise blank mind and the pulsing sensation that had stopped his mind from functioning began to diminish. For a moment he thought he heard his sister's voice joining in with Bronwyn. He was sure he heard two female voices chanted together, echoing eerily, and then he heard a sound rather like an explosion and heard Morgause howling like a banshee. As he came back to his senses he was convinced that Rachel was there with them, until he looked around for her and met only Bran's frightened look.

"Bronwyn, you're all right!" Gareth said almost stupidly, as he tried to understand what had just happened. "I thought I heard Rachel! She was joining you, I did hear her, didn't I?" he asked, confused. "Where is she?"

"I heard a girl's voice as well, 'twas coming from the very air around us!" joined in Bran, still looking fearfully around him.

"Rachel was with us, for a while anyway. She must have found a way to help us," answered Bronwyn. "But never mind that now, we must get Morgause into the tower room and lock her in. Don't worry, she can't hurt you, we've taken away her powers for the moment."

The two boys looked at each other apprehensively, before taking hold of the old woman who was still spitting ineffective spells at them. They pushed her back up the steps into the room, barring the door with the heavy wooden latch as she cursed and hammered on it with her fists.

"We must go quickly, before anyone hears her!" said Bran,

tugging at Gareth's sleeve. "If she keeps yelling like that, she will have the entire castle up here!"

They all began to run down the winding steps. The hammering stopped and they could hear Morgause screaming out of the open window above.

"She will have every guard in the place on their way here by now; we cannot go across the courtyard," said Bran, as they reached the heavy wooden door. "We must carry on downwards. There are passageways under the castle; one of them leads to a gate in the wall."

They carried on down and the steps twisted round and round until they reached a dark stone corridor hewn out of the rocks that the castle stood on. Bran grabbed a torch off the wall and struggled to light it.

"Here, give it to me," said Bronwyn, taking the conical torch. She passed her hand over it until it gradually began to glow. They ran on and on down the domed, airless passageways until they reached a door. Gareth pushed it, but it was solid and wouldn't budge.

"It's barred from the outside," said Bran. "This is the door that leads outside, by the wall."

"What do we do now?" asked Gareth.

"We will have to wait until the commotion dies down and hope that we are not found. Then I will have to go back and open it from the outside. If I could have got word to Sarah, she would have opened it for us," said Bran.

"Well, we're here now, so we'll have to just wait and hope that they don't look here. We might be able to escape when it's dark," said Bronwyn. "We came through a door further back in the tunnel. Run back and lock it, at least we'll be safe for a while, until we can think of something else!"

Gareth and Johnny ran back through the passage and secured the door with a heavy latch.

"What are our chances?" he asked Bran, and the boy shrugged his shoulders.

"They are not good, it will only be a matter of time before they realise we are here," he said.

Rachel still watched them in the translucent Orb back at the castle.

"They're trapped, they can't get out," she told Merlin. "I have to help them. There's a girl called Sarah, she can let them out. I have to find her!"

"No," said Merlin. "You cannot do any more, you have done enough! Come away now, this could be very dangerous!"

"No, I have to tell the girl. I know where she is, and I know how to do it!" replied Rachel, looking deeper and deeper into the Orb.

She was vaguely aware of Merlin's voice somewhere in the distance behind her, warning her, as she became part of the floating substance that was the Orb itself. Her body felt light, almost fluid. It wasn't an unpleasant sensation at all, and it was quiet and peaceful in the Orb. She floated just like the matter itself, surrounded by the beautiful colours, until eventually they cleared and she felt sunlight and a breeze blowing against her face. The sound of water and birds filled her ears, followed by the chatter of young girls. She knew that she was in the right place when she felt firm ground underneath her feet again.

She could see the group of young women with their large wooden baskets by the edge of the stream and she tried to walk towards them. The effect of exiting the Orb was as strange as entering it and she found walking extremely difficult. Her body felt as light as air, and she had to concentrate hard to make herself go forward, putting one foot in front of the other. She walked, or maybe even floated, she wasn't quite sure which, towards the group by the stream. She picked up a pail, to blend in, and joined them at the water's edge. She knew instantly who the girl with the rosy cheeks and the big smile was, and she knelt down next to her.

"Sarah?" she asked.

"Who are you?" asked the girl in alarm.

"I'm Gareth's sister. He's with your friend. You helped them into the castle."

The girl looked even more nervous, and she glanced quickly around at the other women in case they were listening.

"You must help them. They can't get out," continued Rachel. "They're in a tunnel under the fortress, by a door. It's set in an archway, and it's close to the wall, but it is barred on the outside.

Do you know where it is?"

Sarah nodded dumbly as she looked Rachel up and down. "You don't look real," she answered finally, looking frightened.

"Never mind that, I'm real enough. Do you know where the door is? They came down the steps from a turret and came through some underground passages towards the wall. Do you know where it is?" she repeated, and the girl nodded, still dumbstruck.

"How do you know of this? How did you get here?" she asked, still unsure of Rachel.

"I am a seer, that's how I know where they are," Rachel answered, slightly irritated at the effort of having to explain herself. "Will you help them?"

"Yes, yes, of course I will. I will go now." Sarah scrambled up and picked up her heavy basket. "Will you be coming with me?" she asked, almost fearfully.

"No, I can't, I'm sorry, you'll have to go on your own, but I have a message for my brother. Could you tell him to ride to Tyntagyle, but to only go as far as the woods, for Mordred has camps on either side of the causeway and they won't be able to get through. Tell him to hide there and we'll come to find them."

"I will tell him," answered Sarah, and she started up the slope towards the castle wall.

"Thank you," answered Rachel, finding it an effort to even speak now.

She just had time to see the girl disappear through the gate, before the swirling sensation of falling backwards consumed her completely. A sudden rush of colours surrounded her, and she guessed that she was back in the Orb again, but this time it was not so gentle. The force pulling her back was so great that she was whirled into a spiralling cloud of flashing colours.

Meanwhile, Galahad and Johnny had watched her ignore Merlin's warnings and place her hands on the metal frame, staring fixedly at the Orb, her appearance becoming almost translucent as she fell silent.

"What's she doing?" asked Johnny eventually. "Why has she gone so quiet?"

"It is all right, she will be back with us soon," answered Merlin, unconvincingly.

"What do you mean, back with us? What is she doing?" asked Galahad, rising, looking as worried as Johnny.

"She has entered the Orb, to go to them!" Merlin answered gravely. "I did try to stop her, but she would not listen! I do hope she can cope with it, she is very new to all of this!"

They turned as they heard Rachel gasp and let out a long sigh, her eyes fixed on the Orb. She stepped back, still holding on to the frame until her arms were outstretched and she could go no further without letting go of it.

"What do you mean cope with it, could this harm her?" asked Galahad insistently.

"I'm sure she is all right," Merlin answered. "Do not be alarmed."

Rachel moaned again and Galahad stepped forward. "I do not understand magic, but I do know that this is not right. You must put a stop to it at once!" he demanded.

Merlin put a hand on Galahad's arm in an attempt to calm him. "You must not interfere, it could be very dangerous to try and stop her now," he said.

Rachel gave out a long moan and her arms began to shake. The movement travelled into the rest of her body, until she was trembling from head to foot.

"No, this has to stop!" Galahad said, alarmed. Ignoring Merlin, he went towards her.

"Don't touch her Galahad!" warned Merlin, but it was too late as the knight had already taken her by the shoulders.

"Rachel, please stop this now, 'tis not safe!" Galahad said in concern.

Rachel heard his voice, and felt his hands on her shoulders, and the whirling motion in the Orb stopped abruptly. It felt as though she had slammed into a wall. It knocked the breath out of her and plunged her into blackness. She felt someone holding her up, and gradually his face came into focus. For a moment she was back in Merlin's room, and she realised it was Galahad. She gasped for breath, and the room stopped spinning for a second, before she was plunged into another vision.

This time, she was outside the castle, where three old women dressed in black stood on a hill, performing a ceremony over a large flat stone in the moonlight. She recognised Morgause, but not the others. The picture changed, it was daylight, and the three old women now stood on a hill, chanting, with their arms outstretched. Below them was a battle scene, which Rachel quickly realised was taking place outside the castle. She could see the knights on their horses in combat, their swords slashing as they were met with silver blades and heavy axes. The scene was violent and full of frenzied fighting. Suddenly the fighting stopped and the knights froze. The castle gates opened and the people walked out, unarmed and somehow oblivious to the battle that had been taking place in front of them. Men, women and children walked over the causeway towards the frozen scene. The knights remained motionless, unable to move as their enemy turned on them, slashing with axes and swords, while the others launched themselves towards the defenceless people on the causeway.

Unaware that she was screaming, Rachel realised she was being shaken firmly by the shoulders, and the vision stopped. She found herself back in the turret room looking straight into Galahad's white face, and she heard Johnny and Merlin's voices somewhere in the background, but she couldn't shake off the vision and the horror of the scene she had just witnessed. Her head spun and she felt sick with fear.

"You've got to stop your men coming. All of them!" she shouted at Galahad, grabbing his arms forcibly. "If you don't, they'll all be killed! You'll all be killed along with everyone in this castle. Do you hear me? You have to stop them!"

She didn't hear his answer, as the dizziness consumed her completely and she felt the room slip away again, as she fainted.

Chapter Thirteen

The Stalker in the Wood

Galahad scooped Rachel up and carried her to the settle, where he put her down gently, stepping back as Merlin rushed to her side, followed closely by Johnny.

"What's happened to her? She will be all right won't she?" asked Johnny.

"Yes, she's fainted that's all. Nothing serious and I did say not to disturb her!" answered Merlin, with a brief, cross look at Galahad. "She has been brought back too quickly; the shock to her system has caused her to faint."

Eventually, Rachel's eyes fluttered open, and the two worried faces in front of her gradually became clear. She struggled to sit up as she remembered her vision. Merlin motioned for her to stay calm and handed her a goblet containing the warm, sweet smelling liquid that Isolde had given her before. She sipped it slowly and recounted her experience. Merlin listened carefully, nodding, and Johnny's eyes grew wider and wider, as she repeated her last encounters in the Orb. Galahad remained silent throughout, and sat on the other side of the room.

"The two women with Morgause, what did they look like?" asked Merlin, tugging his long beard thoughtfully, as she described them.

"I feared so; they sound very much like two powerful druid high priestesses from Wales. Though why she would invite them here to help her, and why they would consider joining forces with her is a mystery. They will have travelled a long way for this, and they must be expecting some great prize in return for their trouble!"

"A prize like the Chalice?" stated Galahad dryly, breaking his silence.

"I fear so!" answered Merlin. "The scene you described, my dear, sounds as though they will cast a spell to immobilise the knights and make the castle inhabitants turn themselves over to Mordred! This is not something Morgause could do alone, but with the help of the two druid priestesses, maybe it could indeed be possible."

"I saw it clearly! It will happen, and I know this was what Arthur wanted to warn me about!" said Rachel, getting upset again. "I wish I hadn't seen it, because it was awful!" she said and covered her face with her hands.

"Do not upset yourself," answered Merlin wisely. "You have seen the picture of what will happen if their intent is allowed to be carried out, but forewarned we can stop it."

"How?" asked Johnny with an excited look on his face. "I'll help! Give me a sword, and I'll help you fight them!" he said, turning to Galahad.

"'Tis not a sword you will be needing against sorcery like that," answered the knight, almost curtly.

"No, it's magic," answered Merlin. "A magic that can surpass anything that even their druid powers can conjure up!"

"You mean the Chalice, don't you!" said Johnny. "We can use it against them!"

"No. I don't!" said Merlin firmly. "At all costs we have to protect the Chalice and see that it does not fall into their hands!"

"What do you mean? Are you saying we can't use it to help us?" he asked, looking deflated.

"No. We have to protect it. No one person has a right to use the Chalice, and we certainly cannot ask it to help destroy others in order to keep it ourselves."

“I don’t understand,” joined in Rachel. “You said the Chalice would help us.”

“Not in a battle over the Chalice itself, it is not something to be owned,” replied the old wizard. “The Chalice was left for all mankind. Sadly, mankind makes its own choices, and some of them are not always for the good of others! No, it is up to us to make sure that it never falls into the wrong hands. That is why it has been safe for hundreds of years hidden in Avalon, where it could never be found. Think back over your history lessons. How many leaders would have used it for their own ends, and what would have happened if they had! No we have to protect it at all costs! Galahad, what say you?”

“Aye, we have a responsibility to return the Chalice to a place it can never be found again! Too many have lost their lives over it already! But I also have a responsibility to the men who will fight at my command. So if you have a plan to stop this with your sorcery, I would be pleased to hear it!” Galahad answered brusquely.

“Our plan, yes of course, now let me think …” Merlin replied tugging his beard again, deep in thought. Rachel caught Johnny’s eye as they both had the same thought, that so far Merlin’s plans hadn’t been particularly good.

“First light tomorrow you will meet up with Gareth and Bronwyn. Galahad’s men will be advancing towards Mordred’s camps, to position themselves ready to attack if he makes an attempt on the castle. It is unlikely that he will do this until he has had an opportunity to try and gain the Chalice. If he does, get your men to delay them for as long as they can. The Chalice must remain here; I will lock it away, and stay with it. I will put a spell on the room, so that none may enter and we will dupe Mordred into thinking you have it with you. The three sorceresses will be quite visible when they cast this spell, and the four of you will have the chance to position yourselves in between them and the knights to ward it off.”

“The four of us, who do you mean? And how are we going to ward it off?” asked Rachel in horror.

“The four people who have the connection with the Power:

yourself and Gareth as the Keepers of course, and Bronwyn and Johnny, who by rights should have been a former Keeper," Merlin answered, undeterred.

"Hang on a minute," questioned Rachel. "Are you telling me that we are going to go out there and take on three druid high priestesses, casting spells even worse than the ones that Morgause managed all on her own?"

"Have faith, my dear, never before have four Keepers ever called upon the Power. Your strength will be immeasurable!"

"But I don't know how to do all this magic stuff, not like Rachel and Gareth," butted in Johnny nervously.

"You don't need to," answered Merlin. "Your strength is an added bonus, as you were cheated of your heritage by an accident caused by Mordred, the same as Bronwyn by the death of her brother. To alter the natural course of the Keepers will have made Mordred its enemy, and this partnership of Keepers could be the strongest force so far to ever call upon the Power for its help. It will not deny you."

Johnny looked as though Christmas had just come. He had desperately wanted to do more to help his friends, without whom he would never have been a part of all this. Ever since his accident, everyone including his family had treated him like a child, and for the first time in a very long while he felt accepted, useful and strong. This meant more to him than he would admit to anyone. Merlin smiled as though he knew, and patted his shoulder.

"You have a very important part to play, both you and Bronwyn!"

"I still don't see how we're going to do this. How are we going to use the Power against them?" interrupted Rachel.

"The Power will guide you," answered Merlin, with a dismissive wave of his hand. "Open your mind and ask. You will know exactly what to do when the time comes!"

Rachel sighed, instantly recognising another of Merlin's plans where they were about to wade into the unknown again. She looked at Merlin rather crossly, at his now apparent satisfaction that the problem was solved, and then more sympathetically at

Johnny who was looking so proud to be included in this important task, and obviously had no real idea of what he was letting himself in for! She felt as though a huge weight had just been put on her shoulders, and she wished that her brother was there to share it with her.

She glanced hopefully at Galahad, who had so far said nothing. The brooding expression on his face told her instantly that he was not entirely comfortable with Merlin's plan either. She caught his eye for a second, but he looked away immediately, leaving her feeling as though she had somehow lost a strong ally.

"Good, that's settled then," continued Merlin, "you will meet up with Gareth at first light."

"How? The causeway is surrounded by Mordred's men!" asked Rachel in a tired voice.

"We have the horses by the rock face on the south wall, we will go out the way we came in, and use them," answered Galahad, before Merlin could speak. "I will take you to your brother."

"But you can't, you're not well enough and I can't go down there again," finished Rachel feebly at the thought of having to repeat the climb.

"I have said that I will get you to your brother!" answered Galahad, rising. "I will ride with you to the woods and we will find them. I will then carry on and join my men. Now if you will excuse me, I have preparations to make." He bowed and made towards the door and after a brief exchange of words with Merlin, he left.

Rachel knew he would do his duty, he had pledged his support, but his sudden change in attitude concerned her. He had left sharply, leaving her feeling as though she had done something wrong. She felt deflated and tired.

Isolde came and went, leaving a steaming stew, which Merlin and Johnny tucked into straight away, and insisting that she had some. She humoured them by eating as much as she could, and then made the excuse that she was tired and was going to her room. This was partly true, as her experience using the Orb had left her feeling drained. She picked up the black book and asked Merlin if he had paper and a pen. He handed her a piece of parchment, some ink and a quill and she left, determined to write down and memorise as many of the spells as she possibly could, in case she needed them the next day.

She put her candle on the table next to the bed and climbed in. She began to read from the old book, picking out the passages that seemed most appropriate. She copied them onto the thick paper in the dim candlelight, until eventually the flickering light began to fade and she gave up. Tired and worried, she pulled the blankets around her in the slightly lumpy bed and tried to sleep, while the words and passages went round and round in her head.

Meanwhile back in Mordred's castle, Gareth, Bran and Bronwyn were sitting leaning against the wall, in the stifling, airless tunnel, next to the locked door. They were waiting until it was dark, in the hope of sneaking out somehow. The floor was rough and uneven and none of them were very comfortable. For what seemed like an eternity Bran had been listening intently by the door for any sounds outside. There had been a commotion initially, but miraculously, no-one had followed them down there.

Suddenly the heavy latch moved and there was a grating sound as the huge wooden door began to creak open. They all jumped up and moved back, expecting the worst. The door stopped and there was a silence. There was no movement from outside and Bran and Gareth quietly moved forward in anticipation, expecting the guards to seize them at any moment. The door creaked again and they heard Sarah's voice whispering Bran's name. They all breathed a sigh of relief as she ducked inside the door quickly, looking as frightened as them.

"You must leave quickly, they are still searching the castle for you!" she said looking over her shoulder fearfully towards the main building. "I must go, if they find out I have helped you, they will surely kill me!"

"How did you know where to find us?" asked Bran, as he hugged her briefly.

"A girl came to me at the stream; she said she was his sister. She told me where you were and asked me to let you out. I have a message from her," she said, turning to Gareth and relaying Rachel's warning about Mordred's camps by the causeway at Tyntagyle.

"Rachel was here? You saw her? Where is she now?" Gareth asked incredulously.

"I don't know, when I looked back she was gone. Your sister, she … she is alive, isn't she?" she asked haltingly.

"Yes of course she is, why would you ask that?"

"Well, she did not look real; she looked ... well almost like a spirit! I wondered if …"

"Thank you so much for helping us, Sarah," interrupted Bronwyn deliberately. "You must be very careful that you are not caught. You need to go straight away; we can't risk endangering you any more, after you have been so good. If you go first, we won't leave until you are back in the castle, and then we'll make a run for it!"

"Thank you, and yes I must go, before I am found out!" Sarah said, looking frightened again as she hugged Bran.

"Do not go back to them, come with us," Bran said.

"I cannot, I wish I could, but if they found me gone, they would know it was me, and my family would suffer! I cannot risk that. I know what they are like if disobeyed. I have to go!" She hugged him again tearfully and rushed away in the direction of the castle.

They waited until Sarah had entered the main castle building, and once she was out of sight they prepared to go.

"Come, quickly now, we'll run to the horses!" said Bran determinedly. He crept out and made sure the coast was clear before he motioned for them to follow him. They filed out silently behind him, through the gate that Sarah had left unlatched in the castle wall, and out towards the stream. Its banks were now deserted, as everyone was within the castle compound, leaving them free to run unnoticed towards the safety of the wood.

The horses were where they had been left and they quickly untied them, leading them quietly into the sheltering cover of the trees. Once they were deep enough inside not to be noticed, they were able to stop for a moment to catch their breath.

"Look," said Gareth, pointing through a gap in the trees. "There's a group of people riding towards the castle."

They all stopped and looked through the bushes, across to the castle entrance, where a small party was riding up slowly towards the main gates. The solid gates opened as they approached and closed firmly behind them as they disappeared into the castle compound.

"There were two women riders dressed in black, surrounded by eight men. I did not recognise their armour or banners. They are not from anywhere I know of," reported Bran, who had crept forward as far as he could to get a better look.

"I bet it's those women with the strange names that Morgause is waiting for. They called them her druid sisters when they were talking about them in the camp, if you remember," answered Gareth.

"Aye, I do remember," agreed Bran. "It could well be them!"

"We'd better get a move on then, if Morgause has more druids arriving," said Bronwyn, sounding concerned. "She won't be very pleased if her guests have to release her from my binding spell. I think we have just made a very bad enemy there!"

"Oh, I would so love to see that!" answered Gareth laughing.

Bronwyn frowned, indicating that it was not something that was in the least bit funny. As they all began to mount their horses, Bran stopped them again.

"Wait," he said cautiously, "I hear someone coming."

"Quick! It'll be the guards, they're after us," answered Gareth, about to mount his horse in panic. "Quick everyone!"

"No this is only one person. I can tell!" said Bran listening hard.

Gareth listened, but he couldn't hear anything, and gestured silently at Bran to indicate this. The boy raised his finger to his lips, motioning them to be silent. They all listened hard, not moving, scarcely daring to breath, until eventually they could all hear the rustling of branches, and snapping of twigs as someone walked over them. The approaching person was breathing hard as they drew nearer, and they gasped for breath as though they'd been running.

"Stand back, hide yourself," Bran instructed Bronwyn. "Gareth, take the other side of the track, we will jump them as they come through."

Gareth nodded, concealing himself in the same way, while Bronwyn disappeared behind a large bush, away from the pathway. Gareth's heart began to hammer in his chest in anticipation as he heard the person panting as they drew nearer, but before he could do anything Bran had already leapt out, and there was a stifled shriek as he threw his full weight on their follower, knocking them to the ground.

"Sarah!" they heard him exclaim with relief.

"Oh Bran, you scared me something dreadful! I thought you was the guards!" she said, sobbing as he helped her up. Her face was already streaked with tears, and she was completely out of breath. "They know it was me that helped you, they locked me in the cupboard in the kitchen, but Martha from the village let me out, and told me to run for it. Please say you'll take me with you!"

"Of course we will," said Bronwyn, appearing from behind the bushes. "It's our fault that you are in this position, and we'll make sure that you're safe!"

"Thank you, miss," she answered, bobbing a curtsy automatically before turning back to Bran. "They are questioning all the others from the village, it won't be long before they realise that it was one of our own that I was helping. They will soon guess it was you! Oh Bran, there is talk that they will torch the village, if they don't catch the ones who have helped her escape! Medraut is in a complete fury! He has ordered two people to be flogged already because they would not answer him!"

"Don't worry, it will be a long time before anyone from the village talks, they all hate Medraut, and they will buy us time!" said Bran, consoling the distraught girl. "They will look after their own, and they will not let anything happen to the village."

"We'll make sure you're both safe. Merlin will let you stay at Tyntagyle," said Gareth, concerned that they were going to suffer for helping him.

"Thank you," answered Bran. "I will lead you back to the woods that will take you to Tyntagyle, but there I must leave you. I have to return, I am concerned for the safety of my mother and sister. I must go back to protect them, in case Medraut's men attack the village," said Bran. "I would ask that you take Sarah with you, and look after her."

"Of course we will, she can come to the castle with us!" answered Gareth.

"With any luck, Medraut will be occupied with entertaining his visitors for a while and there may be enough time for me to get back before he sends his men into our village," replied Bran sombrely. "We need to make haste, we must leave now before the sun goes down and there is enough light to ride fast!"

They all agreed upon the urgency of his request and mounted their horses: Sarah riding with Bran, and Bronwyn and Gareth on the other horse. They started back on the ride to Tyntagyle, pushing the horses as fast as they could go once they had left the confines of the wood. The strong animals made light work of carrying two riders, their hooves thudding on the grassy plains in a full gallop.

The ride was hard and fast, the miles eaten up by the two pounding horses, never slowing for a second. Even as the light began to fade, Bran drove them faster and faster over the open grassland, past the villages, towards the sunset. Eventually darkness prevailed and they were forced to slow their pace, but Bran still urged them forward relentlessly, and as though by instinct, the horses picked their way deftly through the blackness.

Gareth felt guilty, realising that the fast, dangerous pace that Bran was so intent on keeping up was because he was worried about the rest of his family, left in the village.

He wished he could take the women back himself, so that Bran could return straight away. He knew he couldn't though as the landscape looked so different in the dark, and he had no idea where they were! He wished desperately that he could do more to help his new friend, whose loyalty was proving to be more than he would ever have expected from anyone. All he could do was follow him blindly with Bronwyn seated behind him, hoping that the journey would soon be over. He had no idea how far they still had to go, or even what time it was, as they urged the horses on.

Eventually they came to a thick dense wood and, once inside it, Bran dismounted. They were all glad to follow suit and climbed down wearily, tired and saddle sore.

"We will rest here for a while, the horses are tired and we can go no further in the dark. On the other side of this wood is Tyntagyle. If you follow the path you will be able to continue from here without me."

Gareth nodded, recognising the terrain, and was extremely glad to get off his horse. They helped Bronwyn and Sarah dismount, both looking exhausted.

"I will stay with you while the horses recover and then before daybreak I will ride back," said Bran to Gareth, taking him aside. "Will you be able to carry on with the women?"

"Of course, you've done more than enough taking us this far, and I know you've got to get back to your family," answered Gareth. "You've helped us so much! I couldn't have got Bronwyn back without you! I'm just so sorry that we may have made things worse for you!"

"We both fight the same enemy, my friend, and I have been glad to help you!" answered Bran, clasping his hand and arm in the same way that Gareth had seen the knights do.

They joined Sarah and Bronwyn who had already sat down against a tree trunk. Bran sat down next to Sarah who immediately put her head comfortably against the boy's shoulder. He wrapped his cloak around her protectively and they both closed their eyes, feeling safe with each other.

"You've made a good friend there!" remarked Bronwyn, as Gareth sat down next to her.

"I know," agreed Gareth. "I just hope we can do something for them, they've risked so much for us."

"You will! Those who do good things are always rewarded for them, in some way or another," answered Bronwyn profoundly.

Gareth smiled weakly in answer, as tiredness overwhelmed him and he closed his eyes, hoping that she was right.

Chapter Fourteen

The Sorceresses and the stone

Despite her fears on reading the spells in the book, Rachel finally fell asleep, only to find herself being woken roughly by Johnny shaking her.

"Rachel, wake up, we've to go now!" he said, in a half whisper.

"What?" she questioned, sitting up abruptly, realising he was holding a candle and that it was still dark. "I can't go down that cliff in the dark. It was bad enough in daylight!" she said, panicking immediately at the mere thought of it.

"No, you don't have to. We're going out through the main entrance, while it's still dark. Merlin has cast a spell over the men in the nearest camp, to keep them asleep! Galahad has brought the horses round into the castle, but we have to go quickly as Merlin says it will only last for about an hour!"

"Ok, ok, just let me get dressed!" said Rachel, still half asleep, waving the excited Johnny away with her hand.

He took the hint and dashed back towards the small staircase, the light from his candle going with him.

"Wait! Light a candle here for me, I can't see anything!" Rachel cried, as the room went dark when he disappeared through the door.

"Oh, sorry, I forgot!" he said, rushing back. "Here, I'll light this one for you," he said, picking up a candle from the dresser. He lit it from his own and dashed back out of the door again.

Rachel wished she felt the same excitement as Johnny, as she dressed quickly and went down apprehensively, to join them in the room below. They were waiting for her rather impatiently.

"Ah, good you're here, Rachel!" Merlin mumbled, without looking at her. He pushed aside a small mountain of parchments on his overloaded desk, revealing the Casket, sitting in the middle of the clutter. "We must be quick; we need to work some magic before you go! The Chalice will remain here, I will lock it away safely, and guard it myself, but I want you to take the casket with you. Mordred must think that you have the Chalice. They will not dare to challenge you, whilst they think you have it in your possession."

Rachel nodded, still slightly dazed. That made sense, she thought, to take the casket but not the Chalice itself, and she went to open the casket to remove it. She tried to open the clasp, but it wouldn't budge and however hard she tried the casket remained firmly shut.

"I don't understand this, it opened so easily last time," Rachel said, as she attempted to lever the clasp open again. The room started to fill with the same whispering voices she had heard before, and she paused to listen to them.

"They don't want me to take it out! The Chalice has to stay here in the casket. They want them both to stay here. They say they understand our reasons to protect it, but they want me to do something else."

"Listen to them, and we will do as they say," instructed Merlin.

Rachel listened hard and then put her hands on either side of the casket as the voices instructed. She didn't touch it, instead she gradually moved her hands upwards. Once she had cleared the box, she found she was holding a perfect shining replica. The casket still sat on the table, but to the undiscerning eye, she still held it in her hands! She placed the replica casket on top of a pile of Merlin's parchments, the only space she could find amongst the clutter, and they all looked in amazement at the two identical boxes.

"Ingenious, Ingenious!" said Merlin, picking up the real casket. He took it to his cabinet and locked it safely away. "That's even better; no-one will be able to tell the difference!"

They realised that Galahad had joined them, and stood impatiently in the doorway.

"We are almost ready, a few final preparations and they will be with you," Merlin informed the impatient knight. "The minute you have gone, I will put a spell on this room to protect the Chalice: and no-one will be able to enter until I remove it," he said triumphantly. "Now then, be off with you and good luck!" With that he shooed them out of the room, anxious to be rid of them to work his spell.

They followed Galahad down the turret stairs and through the castle courtyard towards the entrance. If he had seen the last bit of magic he didn't mention it, in fact he strode ahead saying nothing at all. Johnny was so eager to be going, he chattered constantly to Galahad all the way, and the knight answered him courteously when necessary. Galahad however ignored Rachel completely as she followed behind the two young men.

When they reached the huge gates, they saw their horses, saddled and waiting for them. Rachel was delighted to see Rufus again and the big horse whinnied, in recognition, as soon as he saw her. She climbed into the saddle with the aid of a large, bald man, who lifted her up so easily that she almost disappeared over the other side. She regained her balance by clutching onto a handful of Rufus's mane and was comforted by the familiar, solid, black horse, who didn't seem to mind at all!

She tucked the replica casket carefully into a large drawstring pouch that Merlin had given her and wedged it in front of her. She patted the pocket at her side and felt the silver dagger and the parchment paper with the spells on, safely concealed in their depths. She knew that she was as ready as she would ever be for this. Galahad handed Johnny a sword as he was about to mount his horse.

"Do you fight? Can you handle a sword?" he questioned, as the boy hesitated.

"I would rather have an axe sir, if I may?"

"An axe?" said Galahad, looking slightly startled.

"Yes sir. I am good with an axe," replied Johnny.

"An axe it shall be then!" said Galahad, smiling for the first time. "Get the boy an axe!" he instructed and the large man who had helped Rachel onto Rufus quickly disappeared, returning a few moments later with a heavy axe. He handed it to Johnny, who took it solemnly before he mounted his horse.

"Are you sure about the axe? It looks really heavy!" asked Rachel, as they all moved off through the castle gate.

"Oh yes," he replied. "I use an axe all the time at the farm. I cut all the logs for the fire."

Rachel laughed, partly with nerves and partly at the whole incredulousness of their situation.

"No, I am really good with it!" said Johnny, looking offended.

"'Tis better the boy has a weapon he is familiar with," cut in Galahad flatly.

Rachel felt the reprimand, and said no more as they followed him silently now across the causeway. What was left of the moon lit up the way, casting eerie shadows all around them. They crossed the open grassland and Mordred's camp came into sight. They carried on slowly and cautiously towards the perimeter of the camp, where all was quiet and still. They could see the embers of the fire glowing faintly in the middle of the camp, surrounded by conical black tents. As they drew nearer, they could hear loud snores coming from their inhabitants.

"Looks like Merlin's spell worked," whispered Johnny. "Look, even the sentry's asleep," he said, pointing at a man leaning back against the tent, half slumped and still holding his bow, although the arrows were scattered all around him on the floor.

Once they had passed the camp, they galloped towards the wood and rode in as far as they could until it became too dense, and the branches too low to continue riding. They continued on foot with Galahad taking the lead. Soon the thick trees obscured the moon, and apart from the odd sliver of light in places as its rays penetrated their branches, they were mostly in darkness. They followed a rough track, but stumbled often over the roots and fallen branches. Rough brambles caught their legs and made it even more difficult for Rachel as they pulled at her long skirts. She tripped again for the umpteenth time, landing on all fours and grazing her hands.

"If you were not a sorceress, I would say that this is no place for a woman," remarked Galahad as he took her arm and helped her up.

"I'm not a sorceress!" replied Rachel indignantly.

"Well you are certainly more than just a seer. I have known women before with powers such as yours, and no good has ever come from it!"

Rachel was stunned and really hurt by this remark. She knew that he was comparing her to Morgana and Morgause.

"I'm not like them," she said quietly, in her defence.

"If you say not," he answered, curtly. "Come, we have no time for idle banter, we need to make haste if we are to find your brother."

Johnny took her arm as Galahad took up the lead again. "Take no notice of him. I don't think he's very comfortable with magic!" Johnny whispered.

"Well he's not the only one; I'm not 'comfortable' with it myself!"

"To be honest, I think you scared him to death with that Orb!" said Johnny. "His face went that white I thought he was going to pass out next to you! In fact you scared all of us!"

"I didn't mean to," she replied, with tears prickling her eyes.

"I know that! We all know that you and Gareth are good people. You'd never use magic in a bad way!" he said sincerely. "In fact, you're probably the best friends that I've ever had."

"Oh, thanks, Johnny, that's really nice," answered Rachel, with a sniff, as a tear escaped and ran down her cheek. She hung on to his arm to stop herself from tripping. Eventually, they reached the other side of the wood but there was no sign of Gareth, so they followed its perimeter slowly, peering into the trees. Rachel was just beginning to worry that they wouldn't be able to find them, when Galahad held up his hand for them to stop.

"'Tis them, 'tis Galahad!" came a voice from the bushes. A young boy jumped out, and Rachel recognised him from her vision in the Orb as Gareth's friend. He was quickly followed by Gareth, Bronwyn and Sarah who looked at her nervously.

"Bronwyn! Oh thank goodness you're all right!" Rachel exclaimed, hugging her.

There were a few moments of delighted chatter, in the relief that they were reunited. Bran and Sarah were introduced, and Bran bowed low in respect for Galahad.

"'Tis a great honour to meet you, Sire," he said.

"The honour is mine," Galahad replied, warmly. "You have shown great courage in the way that you have helped Gareth."

"We both have our grievances against Medraut," answered Bran sombrely. "I do not wish to be discourteous, but I was preparing to leave, I have to return to my village." He looked up anxiously at the sky, where silver threads of light were beginning to penetrate the blackness.

"Bran, don't let us keep you any longer," said Gareth, briefly explaining to Galahad about Mordred's threat to his village.

"How many men do you think Medraut has left at the castle?" asked Galahad.

"Most of the men are gone, there can be no more than twenty, Sire," answered Sarah shyly, with a small curtsy.

"This is unlike him, he is spreading his men very thinly," said Galahad thoughtfully. "If he travels back here with Morgause, he will not travel alone: he will take men with him. There will not be much of a defence left at the castle. Your villagers, would they ride with us?"

"If Medraut's men torch the village they might," answered Bran cautiously.

"I ride to meet my men, and we will pass not far from your village. It may be possible for us to take the fortress, but the villagers would have to stay there to defend it. Would they be prepared to do that?"

"No, the Elders would be too frightened of what Medraut would do if he came back," replied Bran.

"I understand, but if there is trouble in your village when you return, send word to me and we will help you," said Galahad, moving towards his own horse.

"Try and get the villagers to join us," said Gareth. "The women could go somewhere safe, and they can go back to them afterwards. If anything goes wrong, they can come to Tyntagyle, they'll be safe there."

"Aye, Gareth is right! Tell your Elders that if they ride with you, they will be riding with the Knights of the Order. Ask them to join us and show them this," Galahad said, in agreement. He unclipped a metal brooch and handed it to Bran. "Your Elders will recognise this, as they rode with us once before in Arthur's time. Tell them that Galahad's message is that if they ride with us again, we will make sure they are protected."

"I will, Sire, and thank you," said Bran, scrambling on to his horse.

"And if you are to ride with the knights, get yourself a sword!" Galahad shouted after him as he began to ride away.

Shortly afterwards Galahad left them to join his men and the five of them all moved back into the wood, under cover again. Sarah was in tears after Bran's departure and Bronwyn put an arm round the girl's shoulder to console her.

"He'll be all right, don't worry," she said, as Sarah sniffed and wiped her nose with the back of her hand. They decided it would be safer to move into the middle of the wood where they would be less likely to be seen. The small remaining party set off down the winding rough track through the dense wood, a journey that seemed much easier now it was starting to get light.

"We're going to have to stay here; we can't get back to the castle, as Mordred's camps are there. His men are supposed to be attacking the castle as soon as he joins them!" said Rachel.

"Mordred will be on his way there by now. That ceremony that you told me you saw in the Orb would have taken place last night," answered Bronwyn. "There's an old sacred druid stone not far from Mordred's castle. They would have been using that!"

"Do you know what they were doing?" asked Rachel.

"I can only guess that they were using a pagan ritual of some sort, to combine their powers. I shouldn't worry too much about that though," she added, seeing Sarah's frightened look. Rachel could tell that Bronwyn was uneasy, and was deliberately not saying too much.

They stayed deep in the wood until it was daylight and eventually they could hear noises coming from the other side. They looked apprehensively at each other, each thinking the same, that this was probably the start of Mordred's attack on the castle.

"I'm going to go and see if I can find a safe place just inside the trees, so we can see what's going on," said Gareth. "Stay here, I'll come back for you when I've found one."

Johnny wanted to go with him, but Gareth insisted that he stayed to look after Bronwyn and Rachel. He looked crestfallen, until Gareth reminded him that if he was caught, it would be Johnny's job to protect the women and finish the mission for him. His disappointment disappeared quickly and as Gareth left, he stood like a sentry with his axe in his hand.

It was a while before Gareth returned, announcing that he had found some large, fallen tree trunks they could hide behind, near enough to see, but camouflaged enough to stop them from being spotted. So again they led the horses forward, treading carefully as the noise grew louder. They tethered them behind some large trees, and crept down on the floor, following Gareth through the thick bushes. They ducked down behind the huge trunks, and Gareth dragged over some large leafy branches. He put them up against the logs so that they could look through them without being seen. No-one was looking towards the wood anyway; all of their attentions were on the castle, as Mordred's archers, hidden on the slopes either side of the causeway, rained their arrows upwards over its solid walls.

"They haven't got a chance, they can't get near enough!" said Johnny, in admiration, as they watched a battery of stones hurl down from the battlements onto the unfortunate perpetrators who got too close to the castle.

"They'd have to get on to the causeway by the gates, to be close enough to do anything," agreed Gareth, "but if they do that, they'll be in full view of the archers on the battlements. They haven't got a hope!"

A few men had started to scale the cliff on the right of the castle and their screams were heard as something was tipped on them from above. They lost their hold, and were seen falling down towards the rocks.

"This is horrible," said Rachel, with a shudder.

They continued to watch, horrified and still hidden by the leaves, as Mordred's men continued their futile assault. Then they heard a thundering noise in the distance, and the ground began to vibrate as it got louder. They peered anxiously through the leaves and soon the cause of the vibrations became evident as they watched hundreds of horses pounding over the hill towards Mordred's men.

They knew that these were the reinforcements that Galahad had talked about in the Great Hall. The men sent by the knights to attack from behind and defend the castle. The knight's men ploughed into Mordred's small army of men, and there was a clash of steel as they met their swords. This was closely followed by the thundering hooves of another wave of horses riding in from the left, from Mordred's camp, as though they were waiting for their arrival. More of the knight's horses streamed down the hill, meeting them from behind, and a vicious battle commenced. The noise was dreadful as the combat began. The clashing of steel against swords and axes combined with the screams of the injured and those who met their fate was quite sickening.

"This is dreadful, I cannot watch," said Sarah, putting her hands over her ears and turning away. Having only just recovered from Bran's departure, the battle proved too much for her and she hid behind their leafy barrier, shaking in terror.

"I know what happens next!" said Rachel in alarm. "This is exactly what I saw in the Orb, and the next thing will be Mordred arriving with those women. They'll appear on that hill and walk down towards the battle. They'll spread out, then cast their spell. That's when the battle will freeze and his men will start to kill them all. We've got to get out there now, before they come. We're going to have to be in between them and the battle if we're going to stop them!"

"Ok, as soon as we see them on the hill, we'll go out," answered Gareth.

"No, we've got to do it now, before they get here, or they'll see us," said Rachel adamantly.

"Rachel's right, we need to go now, before they get here! Two of us need to get to the other side, so that when they start to cast their spells, we can move across, two from each side, and position ourselves at intervals in front of the battle!" said Bronwyn. "If we ride across now, we won't be noticed."

"Ok, Rachel and I will go," said Gareth.

"No, let me go with Rachel," said Johnny. "I'm better with an axe than you are with that sword and you are more important in this than I am."

"No!" stepped in Bronwyn again. "I will go with Johnny, because we are both the least important."

"No, you can't I …" started Gareth.

"This isn't negotiable, Gareth," said Bronwyn, firmly. "We haven't got much time and we need to be organised. We must have complete protection against their spells before they cast them. If we can find something that connects us all, it will increase our unity against them. Rachel's got the casket, and I've got Guinevere's pendant, that just leaves Gareth and Johnny," she continued.

"Gareth can have Guinevere's bracelet, it's part of a set," Rachel said, taking it off her wrist and handing it to Gareth.

"That's brilliant, and if you give Johnny the pouch that the casket was in, there should be enough of its power left on it to help him," Bronwyn said, satisfied that they all had something that would protect them. Rachel went to retrieve the replica casket, still strapped on to her saddle on Rufus's back.

"I'm not happy about this," Johnny said quietly, as she lifted the casket out of the pouch and handed it to him.

"I know, and I'm really sorry that I haven't got anything better to give you," she whispered back.

"I'm not bothered about that, I've got my axe," he replied, brandishing it firmly. "Anyway, this pouch held the real casket with the Chalice before, but you haven't got the Chalice; you've got an empty box. It's not even the real casket!"

"It doesn't matter; I've probably got more strength against Morgause than anyone here. Don't forget I've challenged her before, and I think I can do it again," Rachel answered quietly.

"We must be completely united when we turn to oppose their spell," continued Bronwyn, before Johnny could say any more. "We are all going to summon the Power together, by using a spell made especially for its Keepers, to use in times like this! You all need to learn it before we leave. I need you all to hold hands and repeat what I say."

They all solemnly joined hands listening carefully to her.

"We invoke the Power as its keepers.
We invoke the Power to protect us.
We invoke the Power against our enemies.
We invoke the Power against the magic that threatens us.
We ask for the Power's protection as its keepers.
We ask the Power for protection against the dark ones that threaten us.
We ask the Power for protection against the powers of evil.
We ask the Power to protect us, only in its cause, that we may do its bidding.
We invoke the Power against our enemies!"

They repeated the words, over and over again, until Bronwyn was satisfied that they knew them and Rachel had begun to feel quite light-headed. Her hands, held by Johnny on one side and Gareth on the other, were beginning to burn uncomfortably. She was relieved when they all broke hands and wished each other luck as Bronwyn and Johnny mounted their horses to go.

"Now remember what I say, when you walk out to meet us, the sorceresses will already be in place. Repeat these verses over and over and think of nothing else, don't look at them, don't listen to anything you might hear, and do not be distracted by anything that might be going on around you," said Bronwyn. "Walk forward, and concentrate hard on the words. If we say them together, we will all be summoning the Power, and it will give us the protection we need against them!"

Gareth and Rachel watched as Bronwyn and Johnny edged forward until they were level with the perimeter of the wood and then rode hard in a headlong gallop behind the battleground and across the grass. They held their breath, peering through the leaves once again, as they saw a man ride out towards them, his lance pointed towards Johnny who had taken up the rear. He urged his horse towards them, and they saw Johnny skilfully turn his horse to avoid the lance and take a swipe firmly with his axe, catching his opponent heavily and almost decapitating him. Bronwyn rode on and Johnny followed, swiping at several others that came near to them, until they disappeared from view.

"Wow, that was spectacular!" enthused Gareth, impressed. "I couldn't believe it when I saw Johnny with that enormous axe, but he's really good with it! Did you see that? I'm sure that man's head came off!"

"Don't! I don't even want to hear about it!" said Rachel, covering her eyes. "I can't stand this, have they got across?"

"Yeah, they're okay, and we've got visitors! Looks like the witches have arrived as well!" he said, looking towards the hills.

"Where?" she asked, uncovering her eyes immediately, and sure enough fourteen black horses stood in a line on the rise, overlooking the battle. Three figures dressed in long, flowing black garments dismounted and began to walk downwards, spreading out as they went, until they were quite a long way apart. They stopped and raised their arms to the sky. Black clouds rolled across and the sky went dark as if by command, and a strong wind began to blow, rustling through the trees.

They watched silently, almost frightened to breathe, as suddenly everything went quiet and still.

"We need to go now!" said Gareth. "It's starting!"

"Will you be needing me to come with you?" asked a pale-looking Sarah, as they both started forwards.

"Sarah, I'm so sorry, we'd forgotten all about you!" exclaimed Rachel. "No don't get involved with this! Stay here; hide yourself in the thickest bush you can find! No-one knows you're here with us, so they won't look for you. If it all goes wrong, go to the castle or back to your village."

The girl nodded and Rachel could see tears forming in her eyes. Realising Sarah was frightened out of her wits; Rachel reached into her pocket and brought out the silver dagger.

"Here take this, and protect yourself if you have to. We will come back for you, once this is all over. I'm really sorry but we've got to go!"

The girl took the dagger, relieved that she wasn't going to have to take part in whatever magical thing they were doing, yet on the other hand, she was equally terrified at the prospect of being left on her own.

"Good luck, miss!" she said sincerely, as she put the dagger in her pocket.

Rachel smiled at her briefly before Sarah scuttled away quickly, in search of better camouflage. She joined Gareth again and they made their way on foot towards the edge of the wood.

They reached the edge of the trees, already rustling ominously in the wind that was whipping through the branches in frenzy.

"Ok, we'll hold on to each other until we get a quarter of the way across, and then I'll carry on towards Bronwyn in the middle," said Rachel. "Do you know the words?"

"I'm saying them already!" replied Gareth. "But I think I ought to be the one that carries on."

"No, I've got the casket. I need to face them with it in the middle. Bronwyn will be next to me I know!"

"All right, if you're sure," he answered. "Come on then, it's now or never!"

They stepped out from the trees and were hit by a blast of wind that took their breath away and made it difficult to walk. It caught Rachel's skirts and almost blew her back again. They tried to ignore it and walked on as purposely as they could towards the figures of Bronwyn and Johnny who they could see in the distance making their way forward. The battle on the left of them had dissolved into slow motion, where armour creaked eerily and clashes of swords slowed. The movements beside them took on an unnatural and peculiar pace until they stopped completely. Rachel and Gareth walked quickly past with their heads down, trying hard not to look at it as they struggled against the wind, muttering over and over the words that Bronwyn had given them.

From the safety of a large bush, Sarah watched them in awe as they strode out past the battle, the wind whipping furiously at them, the clouds above growing dark and threatening.

"May God go with you!" Sarah said quietly, "and may he keep you safe!" she whispered, shaking with fear, as she ducked down as far as she could into the bush, frantically pulling at the branches and leaves, until she was completely covered and totally concealed.

Chapter Fifteen

The Spectres of Light

The further away from the wood the twins got, the stronger the wind became. It became a battle in itself just staying upright, and walking against it was almost impossible. They struggled forward, clutching on to each other, murmuring Bronwyn's passages over and over again, the wind whipping their words away as soon as they had uttered them. The battle to the left of them had become eerily silent, and Rachel tried hard to concentrate on the words and not be distracted by it. The sky was dark; it was almost as though night were approaching, as the thundery clouds threatened to shut out the smallest glimmer of sunlight. As they drew nearer the middle they could see Bronwyn and Johnny struggling towards them in the distance. Suddenly they felt another force joining the strength of the gale. Or was it all one and the same? It was difficult to tell.

It was almost like walking against a current, rather like an electrical force, and as they battled against it, they started to feel tingly and numb. Their limbs felt strange and each footstep took more effort than the last. They repeated the passage from the Keepers book, and it appeared to be working, as the sorceress's spell they were walking into didn't seem to be affecting them. However the effort of going forwards in the force field and wind, and trying to remember their words, became increasingly difficult and took every vestige of concentration they could muster.

Once they were about a quarter of the way across, Rachel left Gareth and carried on alone towards Bronwyn, who was almost nearing her position. Out of the corner of her eye she could see that the old women had spread out in a line, chanting with their arms outstretched, palms forward towards the battle. She immediately tried to block any thoughts of their incantations out of her mind by saying her own words as loud as she could against the howling wind.

As Rachel approached the middle, she saw Bronwyn indicating for her to stop. Bronwyn waved her arms at Rachel, pointing towards the castle and Rachel instantly realised that she meant for them to turn towards the battle and she motioned to Gareth to do the same. They all faced the strange motionless scene with their backs to the sorceress's stretching out their arms in the same way, apart from Rachel who held the fake casket in front of her.

The tableaux in front of them remained eerily still, with the knights frozen in strange positions. Some had been in the middle of a strike, their swords still in the air, poised to come down on their enemy's weapons. Others were still leaning forward from their horses ready to attack. They remained in their rigid positions like wax models as though someone had pressed a pause button on a DVD player! Even the horses were not flinching or moving. The only movement in the strange tableaux was that of their flags and banners fluttering in the wind.

Slowly Mordred's men began to move; as though emerging from a sleep, they looked around bemused by their new situation as they gazed in amazement at the knights around them, so still and unseeing. In the distance Rachel noticed with even more horror that the huge castle gate was opening. She knew exactly what would follow as she had seen the people walk out to their deaths in her vision. This was the moment she had been dreading, as she knew that the appalling scene she had witnessed in the Orb was about to become reality.

Fortunately, the witches' spell had affected Mordred's men as well and although they had obviously been released from it, they were still completely dazed. They gazed stupidly at the strange scene, looking fearfully at the unmoving knights. Realising that there would only be a temporary delay before they took advantage of the situation, Rachel shouted to Gareth and Bronwyn.

"This isn't working, we need to do something else!" she screamed against the wind and beckoned frantically to them. Reluctantly they left their positions and joined her in the middle, still chanting their protective words.

"We have to do something else!" Rachel insisted. "This isn't stopping the spell!"

"There are other spells in the Keeper's book, but I can't remember them," said Bronwyn, struggling to make herself heard above the blustering wind, while Johnny and Gareth carried on delivering their words of protection.

"I copied some out last night, I've got them here," shouted Rachel, pulling the parchment out of her pocket. She had to get Johnny to help her hold it, as it threatened to blow away whilst they tried to read it.

"I'm sure this one will work," said Rachel, pointing to the one that she had copied out last. "I wasn't going to write it down as I was so tired, but something made me carry on! This time we need to face them and hold on to each other. I'll hold the casket out in front of me."

"Well whatever we're going to do, we need to do it quickly," shouted Gareth. "Look, they've started coming out of the castle!"

They all gasped in horror as they saw the slow trickle of people in the distance, walking slowly out of the gateway towards the causeway, their trance-like state making them oblivious to the danger they were in.

Mordred's men seemed to suddenly come to their senses, gleefully realising their enemy would be the easiest captors they had ever taken. They let out a great cheer and half of them ran towards the causeway brandishing their swords, whilst the rest turned on the knights, their screams of delight filling the air as they swooped down on their frozen mesmerised opponents.

"Oh no!" said Johnny. "Look, over by the wood, that's Sarah, I'm sure it is! The spell must have affected her as well!"

They all looked in despair as the pale figure of Sarah walked slowly, as though hypnotized, towards the battle scene.

"Oh no, not her as well!" said Gareth, distressed that the poor girl had unwittingly been dragged into this. "I said I'd look after her, we should have brought her with us!"

"Never mind that!" snapped Bronwyn. "If we are going to help any of them, we need to do it now! Concentrate on what you're doing, hold hands and start reading that spell!"

The sudden urgency of what they had to do returned, and they all grabbed each other's hands with a new determination and turned to face the sorceresses. Rachel held the casket in front of her with Bronwyn and Johnny holding her arms so that they formed a circle. Johnny was the only one with his back to the old witches, as Bronwyn read out the words on the parchment and they all repeated them after her, their words almost lost in the wind.

"In the name of the Power and all it holds sacred.
We ask the ancient ones, in their wisdom, to come forth and vanquish our enemies.
Vanquish the powers of darkness.
Vanquish the dark forces of Hades and the underworld.
Vanquish the forces from beyond the grave itself.
Vanquish our enemies that use their dark arts against us.
Vanquish those who seek to destroy us with their vile intentions and protect us from their darkness.
Vanquish the powers of their sorcery.
Bind their spells and curb the tongue of the darkest being himself, he that talks through his servants.
Vanquish them all!
May the forces of the heavens, vanquish them!
May the forces of the earth, vanquish them!
May the souls of the great ones gone before us, vanquish them!
And may the power of the creator and all that is good be upon them!"

The force of the wind blew so strongly that their circle was broken as a great blast of air hit them and they struggled to stand up. The dark clouds above them rolled furiously; there was an enormous crack of thunder, closely followed by another, and two jagged bolts of lightning streaked towards the ground. They hit the grass with a sound like an explosion, loud enough to stop everyone in their tracks. Mordred's men looked up fearfully, and the spellbound castle inhabitants on the causeway stopped walking and looked around at the scene below them in total confusion.

The dark, foreboding clouds parted and a shaft of light shone through, like a veil of brightness, from the clouds to the ground. It separated them all from the witches on the hill, dropping down like a curtain of soft white radiance that illuminated them all, almost blinding in its brightness. For a few seconds everything went silent again and the carnage stopped. The druid witches' spell was broken, and for a moment they thought that the sorceresses on the hill may even have been struck by the lightening, until they got used to the light and saw the old women struggling to get up and regain whatever momentum that they could.

The dark clouds above them swirled in a strange way, moving quickly in a circular motion as though about to turn into a whirlwind. The gale returned and as the beam of light faded, the darkness returned again.

"Its worked! Look its worked!" shouted Johnny. "The people from the castle are all running back, look!"

They all turned to see that he was right, the stream of bewitched people were now dashing back to the safety of the castle, and the gate closed firmly behind the last person. The battle began to rage again behind them, as the knights, now freed from the spell, fought back against their enemies with a new ferocity, and once again the air was filled with the frenzy of clashes of steel and the screams and shouts of the battlefield behind them.

On the hill, the three old witches had managed to get to their feet but struggled to keep their balance as the force of the wind turned against them. It caught their long flowing robes and threatened to drag them backwards again as they huddled together, their positions on the hill abandoned.

"What sorcery is this?" demanded a toothless old hag. "You said they had no sorcery equal to ours. Who is their priestess?"

"Which one is it?" demanded the other.

"'Tis that damned girl, with the casket," answered Morgause

venomously.

"Is she their priestess? You said they had none," asked Rathyen.

"She is no priestess; she is naught but an inexperienced seer!" Morgause replied, vexed at being thwarted again by this annoying girl.

"She cannot be so lowly; I think you must have underestimated her powers, sister!" said Rathyen haughtily.

"I have not underestimated anything: she holds the Chalice, without that she would be little more than useless!" Morgause answered furiously.

"Then we shall take the girl out, and the Chalice shall be ours!" Rathyen replied, her accomplice nodding in agreement, and they both moved forward again.

"Not while she holds the casket," said Morgause fearfully.

"You shrink back, Morgause," the druid priestess said as they both turned on her. "Do you doubt your great powers? Are you frightened of a young seer, who you say has no powers of her own? Or maybe you have lied to us, and she is indeed a sorceress of worth!"

"She is not a sorceress, and she has no worth!" screamed Morgause.

"Then we are not afeared, we have powers passed down to us from those far greater than you or her, and we can do well enough without you!"

This was more than Morgause could stand. Not only had she been completely humiliated by having to ask her two guests to free her of that wretched woman's binding spell when they arrived, but now even worse, they mocked her status as sorceress and dared to imply that she was frightened of a mere peasant girl. A girl who, at worst, was a seer and had been nothing but a nuisance ever since she had first appeared in the cave, daring to flout herself against her own great magic!

"My sorcery is famous throughout the whole of the land. People walk in fear of me!" Maugause said indignantly, drawing herself up. "I am with you, kill the girl and we shall have the casket!"

Unnoticed, the old evil sorceresses' walked back to their vantage point and huddled together, chanting an incantation. Suddenly they straightened up and pointed three bony fingers, from which came three bolts of green lightening that hurtled down towards the unsuspecting party below. Their magic was directed solely at Rachel, and as the three crackling green bolts joined together there was a ferocious, crashing discharge almost equal to that of the lightning earlier. They all turned quickly, too late to do anything as the magical spell knocked Bronwyn, Gareth and Johnny to the ground and enveloped Rachel in a green light as it hit her.

"Rachel!" Gareth shouted, struggling to get up, as he watched his sister rooted to the spot, surrounded by a green effervescent cloud that was crackling viciously like electricity.

"Don't touch her; you can't do anything," said Bronwyn, holding him back.

Rachel looked as though she was being electrocuted inside the green crackling force. Her body shook and her face was masked with pain, but she still hung on grimly to the casket, holding it firmly in both hands.

Suddenly the casket lid flew open and out of the box flooded transparent wisps of smoke-like substances, which quickly changed into white unearthly beings that flew up into the air. They circled around Rachel, as more and more flooded out of the box until they surrounded her completely. For a moment the others couldn't even see her as she was completely swathed in a vortex of translucent smoke-like beings. The apparitions penetrated and absorbed the green light that had been holding her in its magical grip. It became a white, unnatural, moving cloud that swirled around her, with ghostly faces appearing from time to time.

Bronwyn, Gareth and Johnny were still unable to get up. The forces in play were so powerful that they were reduced to watching helplessly in awe, as Rachel disappeared completely behind her whirling protectors. The green light sent by the druid sorceresses had gone and one by one, the spectres broke free of their cloud surrounding Rachel and darted off. To the left, to the right, hovering for a moment as terrible faces appeared from their translucent, wispy forms before they shot off towards the battlefield and towards the three druid sisters on the hill.

Rachel was left still holding the open casket, from which the spectres still flooded in a seemingly never-ending stream. The air around them was completely full of the delicate white beings of iridescent light that transformed hideously in the air into unearthly white ghouls that descended towards their victims.

On the hill, the three sorceresses watched in astonishment as their second spell backfired, and they saw a steady stream of spectres sweeping towards them. Morgause was the first to turn tail. She lifted up her tatty, black skirts and ran as fast as she could towards Mordred and the other men on top of the hill, who were still on horseback. She didn't even stop to see if her two druid sisters were following.

"Ride, you fools, ride! They have unleashed the whole of the underworld upon us!" she panted hysterically, grabbing the reins of her horse.

Mordred needed no second invitation; he didn't even bother to help his mother as she struggled to mount the large horse, aware of the ghastly spectres heading up the hill towards them. Instead he turned his great black horse and galloped off, with his men following close behind him.

Morgause was still trying to mount her frightened horse when the ghoulish apparitions caught up with her, swirling up and around. If she had turned back before, she would have seen the fate that her druid friends had met as the spectres had consumed them. Her screams could be heard across the valley as the spectres whirled around her, disintegrating her body until there was nothing left but a pile of black rags left on the grassy hill.

Gareth, Johnny and Bronwyn were still forced to the ground, watching, speechless and incapable of movement. Rachel stood stiffly with the open casket still in her hands, until the last ghostly whisp emerged and the lid snapped shut. She reeled backwards from the impact and gasped for breath. She looked down gratefully at the tightly shut replica casket and noticed that it was now fading in front of her. It became fainter and fainter until eventually her hands were completely empty and the replica casket was gone!

Released from the spell, Bronwyn, Johnny and Gareth scrambled quickly back to their feet and rushed over to Rachel. They hugged each other in shock and relief as they watched the spectres swooping down, descending onto the battlefield. For a second there was a silence again as the fighting stopped and the men watched in fear as the ghostly army headed towards them. Then screams of panic and horror filled the air as complete mayhem began.

The spectres darted in and out of the figures on the battlefield, singling out Mordred's men, who screamed as they met their terrible fate. The rest of his men ran, fleeing in all directions, tripping over the bodies and wounded, in their haste to get away. Others fell to their knees and prayed, covering their faces in terror. Most grabbed the nearest horse, dropping their weapons and fleeing towards the woods. The knights ducked as the ghoulish wisps of light flew straight past them, not even stopping or giving them a second glance as they swooped down on the enemy. The knights dropped to the ground and most covered their eyes in dread. The rest of the horses reared up in fear and bolted, adding even more to the confusion as the main body of men tried to reach the safety of cover in the woods, closely followed by a swirling cloud of spectres.

All Gareth, Rachel, Bronwyn and Johnny could do was huddle together in fright and watch the battlefield thrown into chaos as Mordreds men scrambled over each other to escape.

"Where's Sarah?" asked Rachel suddenly. "What happened to her?"

"She was coming across from the wood when we saw her last," said Johnny.

"I hope she's all right," said Gareth, as they all looked over to the wood, hoping to see her amongst the chaos of fleeing men. "She must be in the middle of all that!"

"There she is, look!" shouted Johnny, pointing, and sure enough right in the pathway of the men and horses was a terrified Sarah. Still dazed and confused, she was obviously so frightened she didn't know what to do and was almost knocked to the ground as the horses pushed roughly past her.

"She's right in their path, she's going to be killed if she doesn't move away!" gasped Johnny.

Two spectres swooped down next to her and enveloped two men fleeing past. She turned and ran in terror, back towards the woods with the others. Not many appeared to reach the safety of the trees as the apparitions darted amongst them, consuming most, after which they disappeared up into the sky, leaving all but a few of the enemy escaping. Seeing this, one of the last of Mordred's men grabbed Sarah as he rode past, dragging her along with his horse, half on, half off it, struggling wildly with her feet still trailing on the floor.

"Oh no, that man's got her, he's one of Mordred's men!" shouted Johnny.

They all looked on helplessly, too far away to do anything apart from watch as he pulled Sarah upwards, trying to drag her across the saddle in front of him.

Suddenly Sarah's assailant halted, drawing up his horse quickly, as a fierce, scruffy-looking band of men armed with clubs, axes and all manner of crude weapons emerged from the wood, blocking their escape. They waved their weapons menacingly at the last of Mordred's men, most of whom were now unarmed. A band of riders came swiftly round the side of the wood, hemming them in. There were no banners flying and none of them appeared to have any armour.

A slight figure on the leading horse sped straight towards Sarah, but before he could reach her they saw her captor clutch his side and fall sideways off his horse, dragging Sarah down with him. They both landed hard and the horse's hooves appeared to go over them. The man didn't get up, but Sarah did and she ran to the new rider's horse, holding out her arms to be swept up onto his saddle, where she clung to him.

"I don't believe it, that's Bran!" shouted Gareth. "Look, all the villagers have come with him!"

The knights were slowly getting up, as the last spectre flew upwards towards the clouds, finally disappearing like the others. Still dazed and not entirely sure of what they had just seen, they regained their composure and headed towards the last of Mordred's men who had been rounded up by the newcomers. All that was left on the battlefield were the bodies of the dead and the injured. Some of the knight's men were helping each other, and were limping towards the castle supporting each other.

By the wood, Bran's party and some of the knights were leading their prisoners back towards the causeway, with the rest of them going back to help the injured.

Bronwyn, Johnny and the twins started to make their way back towards the castle knowing that, to reach the causeway, they would have to cross the remains of the battlefield. Four horses headed towards them. Bran and Sarah arrived first, riding together, closely followed by Galahad leading two more horses for them.

"Come, you shall ride back to the castle, we will go around the battlefield by the wood and approach the causeway from the other side," said Galahad, not wanting the women to have to step through the corpses left strewn across the field.

"That's very thoughtful of you, thank you!" said Bronwyn with relief, as she had not relished the idea of having to walk past the dead, and she knew that Rachel would have been completely traumatised by it. Johnny and Gareth climbed up onto a large brown horse, and Rachel was about to mount the smaller dark grey horse that Bronwyn was already seated on when Galahad leant forward and offered her his hand.

"Come, you may ride with me," he said.

Normally she would have protested, but she was too tired to be bothered and allowed him to pull her up, seating her in front of him.

"I wish we had been able to get here quicker," said Bran, drawing alongside Gareth's horse, as their party started off. "We came as fast as we could."

"No matter, the very fact that you all came is enough," returned Galahad. "If a normal battle this had been, we would have been glad of your men."

"The Elders' have come with us; they want to talk with you," said Bran.

"I'm sure there is much we can discuss, they may stay at the castle and join in the feast tonight, along with your men. 'Tis no less than they deserve, and tomorrow we will talk."

"They will not say no to that!" laughed Bran.

"May I join in the feast too?" asked Sarah shyly.

"Most certainly," laughed Galahad. "For you, we will set a place of honour, one befitting your bravery in helping Gareth and Bran rescue Bronwyn."

"Thank you, Sire!" she breathed, her eyes shining. She had delivered the food and filled many a jug of ale at Mordred's banquets, but she had never been a guest at one before!

"Oh miss," she said, remembering Rachel's dagger. "I am so sorry, your knife, I have it no more. 'Tis still with the man that I used it on!"

"What knife?" Gareth asked his sister, intrigued. "I didn't know you were carrying a knife!"

"Merlin gave it to me when we went to the cave in case I needed it. I gave it to Sarah when we left to protect herself," she answered dismissively.

"Good job you did, by the sound of it," answered Gareth. "So that's why the man that was dragging you fell off his horse. You stabbed him! We didn't realise that! Good for you!" he directed at Sarah who blushed at the praise. "Here, you'd better have this bracelet back now, it looks a bit silly on me!" he said to Rachel, handing it back to her. "I didn't think it would work when you gave it to me, but it must have done because their spell didn't affect me at all this time! By the way, where's the casket? Have you still got it?"

"No, it disappeared afterwards," she said, uncomfortable talking about it.

"Disappeared, what do you mean disappeared? Aren't we supposed to be taking it back somewhere?"

"It wasn't the real one!" she answered flatly. "It was a copy, a fake. The real one's back at the castle with Merlin."

"Wow, if it wasn't the real one how did you ...?"

"I don't want to talk about it," she interrupted in a tired voice. "I'll tell you all about it later."

Fortunately for her, they had to break into single file to cross the causeway. This prevented Gareth from launching a battery of questions, which she really didn't want to answer in front of Galahad, who had been so disapproving of her before. As they passed through the gate they could see Merlin rushing through the crowds towards them. The castle was a hive of activity in the aftermath of the battle. The courtyards were full with the extra men that had travelled with the knights and from the village with Bran. Large jugs of ale were being passed round as they celebrated their victory, albeit a strange one.

The inner courtyard had become a temporary hospital and the wounded leant against the walls where the women attended to them. Rachel just wanted to get away from all of it, and retreat to Merlin's rooms. Galahad jumped down and reached up to help her off the horse.

"Everything that Merlin gave you to protect yourself, you gave away to the others," he said seriously, as he lifted her down.

"I had the casket," she answered defensively.

"Merlin had the casket; I was there when he locked it away," he replied. "You had an empty box, and not even a real one at that!"

"Well, whatever it was that I was holding worked anyway!" she answered, turning to follow the others.

"Rachel," Galahad said, stopping her at the bottom of the stairway. "I fear I have done you a great disservice. I compared you with the other sorceresses that I have known, and I wronged you by saying that you were like them. I should not have done this, as I know that you are not!"

"That's all right," she said, surprised and, as usual, embarrassed by his frank way of talking. "Look, I just want to join the others, I'm really tired," she answered.

"Of course, I will not delay you," he answered, stepping back quickly.

She ran up the steps, not looking back, anxious to get to the quiet safety of Merlin's room. By the time she reached the top step, her cheeks were still red with embarrassment, but a warm glow spread through her due to his apology and the knowledge that he didn't think badly of her any more.

Chapter Sixteen

The Amber Potions

"Woah! What on earth's happened to your room, Merlin?" exclaimed Gareth as they entered. "It looks as though a hurricane's gone through it!"

"Something very like one, my dear boy!" answered Merlin distractedly, as they all stared at the state of his room. It may have been an untidy muddle before, but now it was in complete chaos. Cushions, papers, parchments, lay strewn around the floor, even the curtains were in a tangle. One was actually ripped in half, and for the first time, his desk was completely empty, as its usual clutter now adorned the floor. Oddly enough he didn't seem too concerned by the mess, and it was clear that something else was causing his great agitation.

"Ah Rachel, there you are!" Merlin said in relief, as she walked in behind them. "Do you have the casket?"

"No, you had it," she answered, puzzled by his question. "You locked it in your cabinet. I had the fake, don't you remember?"

"Yes, yes, of course I remember, but do you have it?"

"No, it disappeared in my hands after those … those things came out of it."

"Oh no, this is even worse than I feared," he said, putting his hands to his head. "I fear 'tis lost!"

"What do you mean lost?" asked Gareth. "How can it be lost?"

Merlin sat down heavily on the settle, his lined face pale. "'Tis lost, lost!" he said miserably, putting his head in his hands.

"It can't be, you locked it in your cabinet, and put a spell on the room!" said Rachel.

"I did! Oh, I did indeed! I put a spell so strong around this room, that no earthly being could penetrate it. I was so sure it was safe! I was watching the battle from the window when all of a sudden an enormous blast of wind blew the door open. It circled round the room like a small tornado and everything rose into the air and flew around. The force was so strong that I had to hold on to the window frame to stop myself from being dashed against the walls! The cabinet doors all burst open and everything was sucked out. I could do nothing, my powers left me completely. Then suddenly it went quiet and everything dropped to the floor. I went straight to the cabinet to check on the casket, but it was gone! The doors were wide open and the locks were broken. The casket with the Chalice in it was gone!"

"Are you sure?" said Johnny rushing to the cabinet and turning the handle, expecting it to open. "It's locked!" he said, turning to Merlin.

"No, it can't be. The lock was broken in the force, when the doors burst open," he answered. "I saw it all with my own eyes!"

"Well, it's locked now," Johnny answered insistently. "Look, the key's here on the floor!"

"It can't be, I haven't locked it! The doors were all still wide open when I came down to meet you," said Merlin jumping up. He took the key from Johnny and opened the heavy doors with shaking hands, and there inside was the casket, exactly as he had left it.

Rachel gently picked it up, and opened the clasp. The Chalice still laid nestling in its silken covers. She closed it up and put it back in the cabinet, and Merlin, still shaking his head in disbelief, locked it up firmly away from sight again.

"I don't understand: it definitely wasn't there before. Oh, what a relief! What a relief!" he said, still trembling.

"When you were looking out of the window, what was happening as the wind blew the door open?" asked Bronwyn.

"I saw you hold off the sorceresses. You broke their spell, the people ran back to the castle and the battle started again. Morgause came back down the hill with the sorceresses and they sent a destroyer spell to Rachel. I saw the green bolts and I saw it hit her. It was a few seconds after that when it happened," he answered, stroking his long beard thoughtfully.

"That's exactly when those ghostly looking things came out of the casket," said Johnny.

"I did not see this, tell me about it!" Merlin demanded excitedly, and Gareth and Johnny recounted the events for him.

"Maybe the tornado came from inside the room, after all," Merlin said. "The real casket holding the Chalice must somehow have transferred itself to you, Rachel. You must have been holding the real one for the apparitions to appear. The spectres you have described sound remarkably like the protectors of the Chalice itself! There can be no other explanation; they came to your aid when you needed them. It was the Chalice that finished the battle and destroyed Mordred's men!"

"Well, thank goodness we've sorted that one out!" said Bronwyn wryly, as she picked up the papers and put them back on Merlin's desk. The others began to help her and soon the room was back to some semblance of order again. In fact by the time they'd finished it almost looked tidier than it usually did!

"Tonight there will be a great feast to celebrate the safety of our castle. We will join in the merriment and make our own private toast to the Chalice, for tomorrow we must keep our side of the bargain and return it to safety!"

"We?" inquired Gareth dubiously. "Who exactly is 'we'?"

"Well, you know what I mean, Rachel and yourself of course!" answered the old wizard, quite unconcerned by the look of horror on both of their faces. "Now I must go and prepare myself for the feast. I will be back later," he said, ignoring their concern.

"I don't know why you even bothered to ask that question,"

said Rachel with a heavy sigh, as she sat down. "It was always going to be us! Is there ever going to be an end to all this?"

"Doesn't look like it!" her brother answered, laughing at her pained expression. "Well, not yet anyway!"

As it grew dark the noise of the festivities drifted upwards and they assembled in Merlin's room ready to go and join in. Bronwyn and Rachel appeared in long embroidered dresses, their hair half braided in the fashion of the period. The boys were waiting in equally fine attire with Merlin, who smiled his appreciation and offered his arm to Bronwyn as he led them down through the castle towards the smell of food and the sounds of music and laughter.

The doors of the Great Hall were open wide and the room was ablaze with a bright orange glow from the flaming torches. The long wooden tables were filled with food and a hungry throng of people sat round them. The noise of their banter almost drowned out the players strumming their instruments around the tables, singing words that were lost in the raucous atmosphere. They followed Merlin as he swept past the tables in his long emerald gown, his white hair flowing down his back, framed by a pointed, matching hat, the perfect vision of a wizard of his standing. As he passed, men bowed in respect and he nodded courteously in return.

They made their way towards the top table, where the knights sat. Bran and Sarah were seated at the next table and stood up excitedly as they arrived.

"Oh, miss, look at the dress they have given me to wear!" said Sarah excitedly. "Is it not the most beautiful dress that you have ever seen?" she cried, as she twirled round holding out the cream skirts.

"It certainly is," agreed Bronwyn. "You look quite beautiful, Sarah!"

"Oh, do I? Oh thank you, miss," she replied, still stroking the folds of the cream, embroidered dress that replaced her usual course servants attire.

"Bless her, she's so excited," said Bronwyn quietly to Rachel, as they moved towards the next table. "I'm sure she has only ever thought that she would wear a dress like that in her dreams!"

"She deserves it, I'm so glad that she's happy!" answered Rachel.

The knights automatically bowed to Bronwyn and offered her a seat, moving up to make room for her. Gareth sat down next to Bran, and Johnny joined them, leaving Rachel to sit opposite, in between Galahad and Bronwyn, as Merlin sat at the head of the table. The men exchanged uneasy glances as Rachel passed them and the table grew quiet. They were met with a stern look from Galahad and they quickly fixed their attention on their plates, resuming their eating and drinking, albeit in a much quieter fashion, leaving Rachel feeling uncomfortable as she joined them.

Galahad stood up and banged his tankard on the table.

"My friends," he said loudly as the room fell silent. "We drink to a victory. Our great castle remains safe and our enemy Medraut is defeated!"

Normally he would have received a raucous reply, but instead the room stayed quiet, a few nodded, but most shifted uneasily and stared at Rachel.

"Aye, this was not a usual battle, we know that for certain! But we met our enemy, blade for blade!" he continued. "Though 'tis a sad day when one of our own, that used to fight side by side with us, is so consumed by greed and jealousy that he would leave his sword in its scabbard and resort to sorcery in an attempt to kill those who were once his friends!"

This was met with agreement from the crowd and they nodded, muttering to each other in quiet support of his words.

"You all know me as a plain speaker, and I speak from the heart," Galahad ploughed on determinedly. "I know there will not be a man present in this room that is comfortable with sorcery on a battlefield, but 'twas not us that brought it there. 'Twas our enemy, Medraut! It took four people to hold his sorceresses' magic, and one risked her life to stand out against them. She defeated them with a magic that was not of the same nature as the dark powers that Medraut has brought here. I do not pretend to understand this magic, but I do know that we would have been doomed without it. You may look upon this girl and see a sorceress, but today she was every bit as much of a soldier as any man on the battlefield! So I would say that we drink a toast to our victory and to our own sorceress!" He held his goblet high and waited for the response.

There was a few seconds of silence, during which all eyes fell on her and Rachel wished a hole in the ground would appear and swallow her up. Suddenly there was a loud scraping of heavy chairs as they all stood and shouted resoundingly, "Aye, aye, to our victory! To our sorceress!" The noise was quite deafening as they all banged their vessels on the table and resumed their noisy banter.

"Thanks for that!" said Rachel rather sarcastically, having hated the attention that had been directed towards her.

"You do not need thank me, I spoke only the truth!" Galahad answered simply, her sarcasm entirely wasted on him. She smiled, realising that he had missed her point entirely, but was also relieved to see that the men had all sat down and resumed their festivities, thankfully ignoring her now as though she were one of them again.

"Well, thank you anyway," she answered, slightly more affably.

"My pleasure!" he replied, spearing a large chunk of meat on his knife. "Now eat, drink, today is over, enjoy the feast!"

The rest of the evening passed in a much more relaxed atmosphere. Gareth, Johnny, and Bran on the next table seemed to have struck up a great friendship; evident by the way they laughed and joked together. There was a bond created between them, even though they all came from different times and circumstances. Rachel was almost envious as she watched them. Bran turned to include Sarah, making sure she was not left out, and she held his hand and hung on their every word. Only Johnny remembered to include Rachel, by beaming a smile at her whenever he caught her attention across the table. Even this didn't stop her from feeling slightly left out.

"I would say that the young knave is sweet on you!" remarked Galahad, observing Johnny's frequent glances at Rachel.

"Johnny? No, he's just a friend!" answered Rachel, embarrassed.

"Nevertheless he is sweet on you!" he replied seriously.

"No, you're wrong, he's definitely just a friend," she insisted.

"If you say so," Galahad laughed, annoying her again, as it was obvious he didn't agree with her.

Merlin stood up. "Alas, I am too old to stay into the night with the rest of you and tomorrow we have much to do, so we will take our leave."

Gareth and Johnny groaned, but were ignored as Merlin signalled that they were leaving. The rest of the table stood up, acknowledging this. The men bowed to Bronwyn and Rachel as they stood, moving back courteously for them to pass.

"Thank you, Sire," said Bran, clasping Galahad's arm. "Our men have never had a night such as this; they will remember your hospitality for a long time to come!"

"'Tis no less than they deserve," answered Galahad. "I have not had a chance to talk to you Bran, but you showed great courage today. You have the heart of a knight. There is a place here for you and your lady if you want it."

"To ride with you and stay here at the castle?" breathed Bran, clearly overcome by this offer. "Do you know what that would mean to me? Oh, thank you, Sire, thank you! You will not regret it!"

"I take it that you accept my offer," replied Galahad, laughing at the boy's enthusiasm. "You will have much to learn if you are to ride with us, but we will teach you if you are willing."

"Willing?" Bran answered, "I will work harder and learn faster than anyone you have ever taught. Thank you, sire, thank you!" he finished, with a low bow.

"I have no doubt that you will, and tomorrow I will talk with your Elders!" Galahad answered with a smile as Bran bowed again. He left excitedly with Sarah, to join their friends on the table further down the room and tell them of his good fortune.

Bronwyn and the twins followed Merlin out of the Hall with Gareth and Johnny still protesting. The revelling was still in full swing behind them as they made their way back through the castle to his quarters. The lamps were flickering in Merlins room when they arrived back, and the sounds of merriment drifted upwards in the night air.

"A good night's sleep, that's what we all need now. We have much to do tomorrow. We shall meet here early, and make our arrangements to complete our mission," Merlin said as he swept out, leaving them to sort out their sleeping arrangements.

Rachel and Bronwyn went off to the small room upstairs and the two boys went down to the room Galahad had recovered in. Sleep came quite easily to all of them, especially Gareth and Johnny who had managed to sneak a small goblet of ale each at the feast when no-one was looking.

They all assembled in the morning in Merlin's room. As usual there were trays of food and drink and they helped themselves.

"I wonder what he meant by 'arrangements' last night," said Gareth, in between mouthfuls. "I would have thought for once that this one would be easy! We can all go together to Valonia and put the casket back in Arthur's grave."

"Oh that it were that simple," came Merlin's voice as he entered the room, catching the last bit of the conversation.

"Well, we're going back to Valonia anyway, so why can't we take the Chalice back with us?" asked Rachel. "Don't tell me we can't go home!"

"Well not immediately, my dear, you must take the Chalice to Avalon first."

"Hold on, Avalon, Valonia, aren't they the same place?" asked Gareth.

"They are, but they are both in different times. Avalon is the place where Arthur was put to rest, in a time slightly ahead of this one. Over the years the name changed to Valonia, just as our place names differ from yours - for instance Landinium has become your London."

"I still don't understand. If it's the same place why can't we just take it back with us?" asked Gareth.

"You must remember one of the very reasons that you came here was because time had altered in Valonia, thanks to Morgause's spells. It is very important that things are done correctly to restore it again. One slip up and we could have even more problems to deal with!" answered Merlin.

"So how are we going to get it back there?" asked Rachel, looking worried.

"The Chalice must be returned to the time that Mordred took it from, in order to restore the balance of time, which is a very delicate thing. In your world back in Chesterton, the events of the past have happened. They are long gone and leave you all where you are today, in your time. If the events of the past were somehow altered, it would alter the future, which is where you come from. This is what Mordred wanted when he started to meddle with the time in Valonia. He wanted it to slip back until you two wouldn't exist, and therefore, you could not be the Keepers of the Power. Now as far as we know, the time in Valonia has still continued going back while you have been here. This is very serious, very serious indeed! We have to restore time back to where it was before Mordred altered things before you can go back. Do you understand?" he finally asked.

They all nodded, silently, still grappling with the enormity of it.

"To return the Chalice and set the balance of time straight, you must take it back to the exact time that Mordred stole it from. Then you will have to come back here to this time and return back through the tunnel as usual into Valonia, which by then, should be back to normal," he continued. "It is imperative that these steps are done correctly."

"Will you be coming with us?" asked Rachel dubiously, almost knowing that he wouldn't be.

"Alas I cannot, I was here when the chalice was stolen, and that is where I must be when it is returned," he replied.

"I'll come with you," said Bronwyn immediately.

"And me, I'll come as well!" joined in Johnny.

"No, no, my dears, you can't go!" said Merlin, patting Bronwyn's hand. "They must do this alone. If you were to go it would upset the balance of things. You were here before them Bronwyn, and you must remain here until they come back. We cannot return you straight to Valonia as we have no idea how far time has gone back there, so you must wait until it is restored and you can all go back together."

"Well I came after them," said Johnny firmly. "So I don't see why I can't go!"

"Ah Johnny, we have a different problem with you," said Merlin shaking his head sadly. "You have been a good and true friend, but it would be very dangerous for you to go, as the time changes have already affected you."

"No they haven't, I'm fine, it affected everyone else in Valonia but not me," he replied adamantly. "I was the only one that knew what was going on!"

"You may not realise it, but it has affected you," said Merlin gravely. "It has taken you back to the time before your accident, when your mind was still strong. I have no idea why it had no effect on your memory as it did with the others, but the plain truth is that I don't know what effect this venture would have on you! It would be even more dangerous if you went with them to yet another time!"

"Are you saying that if the Chalice manages to put time right, I will go back to how I was after the accident?" asked Johnny quietly, the mere suggestion of returning to his former confused state, striking dread into his heart.

"You may have to prepare yourself for that possibility," answered Merlin. "I am so sorry to give you this news, my dear boy."

The room was silent as they all took in the dreadful thought that Johnny, who had been with them all the way through, so anxious to do anything to help, would be reduced back to his former childlike state.

At first he looked devastated by this news and then a defiant look came over his face..

"Then I am going with them!" he announced firmly.

"No, Johnny, you can't," said Rachel immediately. "You really can't! You heard what Merlin said! It could harm you! You can't go: you've got to stay here!"

"She's right mate, you can't risk it," agreed Gareth.

"I don't care, I'm coming with you!" Johnny answered, even

more defiantly. "What have I got to lose? By the sound of it as soon as time goes back to normal, I'm going to become a half-wit again anyway. So I might as well feel useful and do something exciting while I can."

"Johnny you can't risk …" started Rachel.

"'Tis the boy's decision," Merlin interrupted. "A brave one too, I might add, and if it is what he wants to do, you must allow him that."

They nodded silently and Rachel could feel the tears welling up in her eyes, at the thought of what could happen to their friend. She got up and poured some water into a goblet on the other side of the room so that Johnny wouldn't see her tears.

"You don't have to do this for us," Gareth said quietly, putting his arm around Johnny's shoulder in admiration and sympathy. "You've done enough already!"

"I'm not, I'm doing this for me, while I am still able," he answered.

Hearing this, the tears poured silently down Rachel's cheeks and she brushed them away with the back of her hand.

"Now, make your preparations, I am waiting for Galahad to come with news of Mordred before you leave," said Merlin.

With heavy hearts they went to collect their things. Rachel came back with a thick cloak and the black book, which she gave to Bronwyn to keep for her, and she placed the casket back in the pouch, ready to travel. Gareth and Johnny returned, all ready to go, just as Galahad joined them.

"I do not bring good news," he said. "My men have scoured the area all night, but not one of them has news of Mordred. His remaining men have fled, they are not a threat as they will be in hiding, but no-one knows where Mordred is."

"I'm sure he has retreated back to his castle to lick his wounds," answered Merlin, unconcerned.

"No, that would not be possible, my men took his castle yesterday, and some of the people from the village remained to defend it. The others rode back to join them with some of Bors' men early this morning."

"This bodes ill, my friend," said Merlin gravely. "This means he is still at large and will stop at nothing to avenge this."

"I will escort Gareth and Rachel on their mission with my men to make sure they come to no harm," answered the knight.

"Oh that it were that simple," answered Merlin stroking his long beard absent-mindedly. "You can only escort them so far and after that, they must travel alone."

Galahad looked about to insist, and was firmly silenced by Merlin. "You must understand that this is a quest of a very different nature!"

"I understand that, and I understand that the Chalice must be returned, we are at your service to help in any way we can. We will escort them as far as we can and then await their return," said Galahad.

"That will be service enough, my friend, and I thank you," said Merlin gratefully.

"I will take my leave then," said Galahad, bowing to Merlin. "The horses will be ready for you by the gatehouse," he told Gareth as he left.

Bronwyn hugged them both tearfully. "Be careful, please be careful," she said as they were about to leave. "Oh I wish I was going with you!"

"Now then, I have something I want you to take with you," said Merlin, handing each of them a small bottle. "Use it only if you have to."

"What is it?" asked Gareth, looking at the amber-coloured liquid in the small oval bottle suspiciously.

"It is a potion!" said Merlin. "We will call it plan B, just in case anything goes wrong and you inadvertently end up in the wrong time or find you can't get back for any reason."

"Oh great!" said Rachel, horrified at the prospect that something might go wrong.

"Don't worry, my dear, the tunnel is the key to travelling through time, and it is unlikely that it will fail you, but just in case, the potion will transport you to wherever you need to go. All you have to do is drink it and imagine where you need to be and it will take you there. Use it only as a last resort as I believe it works very quickly and you can only use it once."

"Does it work?" asked Gareth, looking doubtfully at the bottle.

"The recipe is an ancient one and has been used by many in the past," said Merlin proudly.

"How many?" asked Rachel, suspiciously. "And did it work?"

"Well, I don't really know exactly how many," answered Merlin vaguely. "But I am confident that it will be quite effective!"

They put the bottles away, still not entirely convinced.

"Now before you go, there is something else," continued Merlin. "When time is restored to its proper balance, things might seem different when you come back."

"What do you mean different?" asked Rachel, now looking really worried.

"The events that have happened over the last few days were due to Mordred's actions. These were all things that weren't supposed to happen. So once time is restored, it could be that they simply won't have happened, and no-one's save us, will remember anything about them or the parts that you have all played in them."

"I don't understand," said Rachel.

"I do!" said Gareth. "He means that when we come back no one's going to know anything about it! But what about Bran and Sarah, will they remember us?"

"They may not," answered Merlin.

"But what about Bran? He's so thrilled about joining the Knights and living at the castle with Sarah. And what about the villagers that helped, do you mean they'll all have to go back to being Mordred's slaves? Surely not, not after all of this!"

"I don't know," answered the wizard, seeing his distress. "I am just warning you, in case this is what you come back to. As I said before, time is held by a very delicate balance and things may be different, once you have put it right."

"What about Galahad, surely he'll remember?" asked Rachel feeling her heart sink. "He was part of it all!"

"These are questions that I do not have the answers for, my dear," answered Merlin. "I wish I did, but whatever the consequences are, they are certain to be for the good of mankind! It is imperative that time is put back on its correct course!"

They said their goodbyes and made their way down, slightly despondently, to the courtyard, where Galahad and eight of his men were waiting with their horses. They mounted and followed them out of the castle gateway onto the causeway, with the safety of the castle getting further away with every step as they embarked on their final mission.

Chapter Seventeen

Shifting Sands and a Stone Effigy

They rode across the open plain towards the tunnel entrance. There was hardly any conversation between them, as each of them was secretly dreading what was in store. Gareth was wondering silently about his new friends Bran and Sarah and whether they would have a life at the castle after all. Rachel was just terrified at the thought of yet another adventure that she would prefer not to be taking part in, and Johnny, despite his bravado and determination to go with them, couldn't help but wonder what might happen to him, even though he would never admit it to the others. Even Galahad was quiet, although he glanced at Rachel several times, noticing her white knuckles gripping the reins.

"I will gladly go with you, if it would help," he said eventually, drawing his horse up beside hers. "You are frightened."

"Frightened isn't the word," she said, with a nervous laugh. "Thanks for the offer, but you can't help us with this one."

"I have chosen eight of my toughest men to ride with us, the others all search for Mordred. Once we get to the tunnel I will await your return, however long that takes. We will wait for you and escort you back."

She smiled weakly in return, but as the tunnel entrance came into view, two riders galloped up behind them, pulling up their horses beside Galahad.

"Percivale, what brings you here?" he asked, puzzled.

"I have news of Medraut!" Percivale answered. "We have heard that he entered the caves last night under the cover of darkness and he has several men with him. We believe they may be taking shelter there. 'Twould not be safe for you to travel through them."

"Thank you for letting us know, this is bad news indeed," replied Galahad.

"I will return to gather extra men and we will search the caves until we find him, but as you know well, these caves cover a great distance. They run under the length of these hills and go so deep that some have never been explored. It may take time to find him!" said Percivale, before he rode off.

"We're going to have to go through the tunnel," said Gareth firmly. "It is the only way we can get to Avalon."

"Mordred would know this, he may even be expecting you!" insisted Galahad.

"There isn't any other way of getting there," said Rachel. "We have to take the Chalice back, what are we going to do?"

"There may be another way," said Johnny, unexpectedly. "If the tide's out, we could go round the headland past the caves where Mordred was before."

"Can we get all the way round to the village? It's an awfully long way!" asked Gareth.

"It would depend on the tide, if it's far enough out we could make it on the horses," replied Johnny confidently.

"Hang on a minute, that last bay, that's the one with the quicksand," put in Rachel. "I've already had one bad experience there, and I'm not going to risk having another one!" she finished, shuddering at the memory of the quicksand that had slowly sucked her under until Gareth had rescued her. "No, it's far too dangerous!"

"Do you have any better suggestions?" asked Gareth.

"No I don't! But I am still not doing it!" she answered adamantly.

"Rachel, if we ride hard and fast on the last two bays, it is possible for a horse to cross the quicksand as long as it doesn't stop," said Johnny. "Galahad, you must have heard of people doing it?"

"I have heard tell that there are those who have crossed it on horseback," said Galahad reluctantly. "But this is not a route that I would recommend. The quicksand can be deceiving unless you have someone with you who knows exactly where it begins and ends!"

"Exactly," said Johnny triumphantly. "And I know where it is! It covers most of the big bay past the rocks where the caves are, right along the middle to the point. I've ridden across it with my sister several times, although we only ever got half way and had to turn back quickly because the tide was coming in."

"Have you really done it before?" asked Rachel.

"Yes several times, before my accident," stated Johnny. "All right, it was a stupid thing to do and we got an almighty telling of for it, but we came to no harm."

"That's settled then, we'll go that way, it's the only option," said Gareth, urging his horse on again.

They all followed him as he headed down towards the beach, with Rachel silently hoping that the tide would be in and they wouldn't be able to go. She was disappointed to find that it wasn't, in fact it couldn't have been further out! It was merely a thin shimmering line in the distance.

"That's so lucky, it's still on the way out, we should have plenty of time," said Johnny.

They rode to the left, avoiding the rocks towards the cave where they had left Morgana for dead, and when they drew level Rachel shivered, remembering their last encounter with her. Galahad signalled for his men to ride ahead into the cave to search for Mordred. They returned a few minutes later to report that it was empty and there was no sign of him. Rachel looked towards the cave entrance where they had left Morgana, but her body was gone, much to her relief. The horses pawed at the ground expectantly while they all looked down the long sweep of beach past the rocks, where their escorts would leave them.

"I'm still not happy about this," said Rachel, looking nervously at the long stretch of sand ahead. The thin line of water in the distance shimmered innocently in the morning light.

"It'll be all right, honestly!" said Johnny. "I wouldn't even suggest it if I didn't think we could do it!"

"We will wait for you at the tunnel entrance. My men will find Mordred!" added Galahad, looking at her with concern.

"Rachel, ask the Chalice for help, you're holding the damn thing! Ask it to help us!" said Gareth, irritated by her reluctance, and apparently having more faith in the vessel than his sister. She looked dismally at the sand ahead of them.

"Ok, just give me a minute," she answered, having quite forgotten the Chalice in her fear. She held it tightly, willing it to get them there safely, her heart racing with the thought of what they were about to do.

"All right, now, before I change my mind!" she said taking a deep breath, and they lined their horses up just past the end of the rocks.

"Ok, one, two, three, now!" shouted Johnny, as he took off, urging his horse into a gallop as they cleared the rocks. Rachel followed behind him on Rufus who went straight into a fast pace, sensing her urgency. With Gareth close behind, they drove their horses faster and faster. Rachel's hair and cloak streamed out behind her as she leant forward in the saddle, clinging on to the pounding horse.

"Oh get us there, please, please get us there!" she said out loud, to the box bumping around in front of her.

"Once we get out past the next headland, the quicksand starts, we need to come back in close to the rocks. Follow directly behind me, in single file," Johnny shouted across to them. "When we've cleared that bay, we need to go out towards the sea, just follow me, and don't slow down for anything!"

They followed his instructions, galloping behind him under the shelter of the huge cliffs. Jumping several small sets of rocks, they cleared most of the sweeping bay and could see the point looming up in front of them where Rachel had got stuck in the quicksand before. The rocks on the beach were getting bigger and Johnny started to head out diagonally towards the furthest tip of the point, facing the sea. The horses rode through the shallow waves, their hooves sending up a spray of salty water, soaking their legs as they still pounded on. Terrified, Rachel fixed her eyes on the rocky point and just rode.

"Oh, please, please get us there! Please, just get us to Valonia safely!" she murmured in fear to the Chalice.

Johnny headed out further into the sea to reach the tip of the point and for a moment she thought she couldn't hear Rufus's hooves pounding or splashing any more, even though the big black horse had turned deeper into the waves.

"We're ok, we're almost there!" shouted Johnny over his shoulder. "We're going to have to jump the last bit of the point though, as the tides turning and will come in fast here. Don't worry though, there's a thin stretch of rocks there, just follow me."

As they approached a lower section of the rocky point, Johnny's horse leapt upwards, clearing the rocks easily. Once on the safety of the next beach, he slowed up and stopped to look back at Rachel and Gareth as their horses jumped over the rocks.

Breathless and relieved they rode up the sand towards the cliffs.

"We've done it! Yeah, Woo-hoo!" shouted Gareth, slapping Johnny on the back. "See, I told you it would be all right!" he said to Rachel who was still shaking from the ordeal, as the two boys whooped with delight. "Right come on, let's get this over with, we'll have to go along the beach and take the horses up the jetty, then double back to the church. Won't take long!" said Gareth, once they had caught their breath.

They rode slowly up the beach, now there was no danger of the sand swallowing them up, and they all felt temporarily relaxed as the jetty got nearer.

"Hang on a minute. Stop!" said Johnny suddenly, pulling up his horse. "This is my village! This is Valonia!"

"Are you sure?" asked Gareth.

"Of course I'm sure, I live here! That's old Mr Gill there tidying up his fishing nets, and there's Luke and Edward repairing their boat!"

"We're in the wrong time then! How's that happened?" said Gareth. "Do you think it's because we didn't use the tunnel?"

"It can't be, we've gone through time anyway, just too far forward! We'd better stop in case they see us!" Johnny answered, drawing his horse up towards the cliffs, where they pulled up next to him.

"I have a horrible feeling that this is my fault," said Rachel. "I was asking the Chalice over and over to get us here, and I think I may have said Valonia instead of Avalon. In fact I'm fairly sure I did! Oh no, what have I done?"

"Oh great, well done!" said Gareth angrily.

"It's not her fault, she was frightened! Anyway, if it wasn't for her, we might not be here at all," said Johnny, defending her.

"Well we are here, and we're in the right place, but the wrong time!" Gareth snapped.

"Look, I was worried when we had to go out into the water by the point because that stretch further out is where the quicksand is at its worst, and I've only ridden on it when it was dry," said Johnny, pulling him to one side. "When we had to go in deeper I was holding my breath, and yet suddenly, the horse wasn't even splashing! I looked back at Rachel's horse and there was no spray at all! Do you remember your horse's hooves splashing there? Because I don't!"

"I can't remember," Gareth said rather sullenly. "So, what are you trying to say?"

"I am saying that I don't think our horse's hooves were even touching the quicksand by the point. I think the Chalice saved us there!" insisted Johnny.

"Do you? Maybe it did, I can't say that it seemed very deep at all, and yet looking at it now, those waves are really big! Maybe you're right," Gareth admitted begrudgingly. "But we've still got to get back to the right time. We need to be in Avalon not Valonia!"

"I suppose we could try Merlin's potions," said Rachel, reluctantly. "He did say to use them if we ended up in the wrong time!"

"I'm not sure I like the idea of that!" answered Gareth, as they all pulled out the bottles and looked at the amber liquid in trepidation.

Johnny pulled the stopper off his bottle and gingerly sniffed at it. "Oh please tell me it doesn't taste like it smells!" he said, with a cough, and replaced the stopper quickly.

"Probably does!" said Gareth, doing the same. "Yuk, that's awful! The only way we will ever be able to drink this is to hold our noses and down it in one!"

"All right, we'll tell it where we want to go and do it on the count of three," agreed Johnny, still wrinkling his nose. "Merlin said it works quickly!"

"Ok, everyone ready? Take us to Avalon, to the time just after Mordred stole the Chalice. One, two, three, go!" said Gareth as they all held their noses and swallowed the potion, choking as the foul-tasting liquid burnt its way down their throats.

Instantly the ground began to shake and everything started to move around them. The waves came in and went out at a frightening speed, the sky turned dark then light again in an instant, and figures appeared and went. It was as though someone had pressed a rewind button on a video, with them in the middle of it! They clung to their horses as they began to feel quite dizzy. Suddenly it stopped, the beach was empty and the waves were back on the horizon.

"Wow, that was really weird, I feel quite sick!" said Gareth. "Do you think it has worked?"

"Well there's no-one on the beach, the boats and the fishermen have gone," answered Johnny. "There's only one way to find out, let's go up towards the village."

They rode up to the beach entrance, where they found that the jetty was replaced by a rough track and the wall and buildings had gone. As they ventured up the track, they could see a settlement to their right in the distance, and a small group of stone buildings with conical roofs, rather like the ones in Bran's village. There appeared to be a larger building at the back, circular with a large, wooden coned roof. There was a small stockade fence around the small village that looked as though it was only to keep the animals from straying, as it would not be any use as a defence.

"I've seen drawings of this in the old books at the shop in Valonia showing the history of our village," said Johnny. "This is definitely how it would have looked when it was Avalon."

"Looks as though we're in luck then!" said Gareth, remembering the dusty old book shop.

"Even so, we'd better get a move on, in case we're seen," Johnny replied, looking nervously towards the village.

They sped up until they reached the safety of the track leading towards the church, where they were hidden by the trees and high hedges. When they got there, they were surprised at the difference. There was no fence or tall gateway and the pretty stone church they were used to was replaced by a small, ugly, square stone building, with no steeple and only a short square tower at one end. The small slits that were windows made it look more like a small fortress than a church. They dismounted, leaving the horses by the hedge at the entrance.

They walked quietly through the graveyard, looking at the mounds of earth with small stones or wooden crosses that replaced the neat stone graves they were used to seeing in Valonia.

"So which one do you think is Arthur's?" asked Gareth, as they inspected the graves.

"It can't be these, they don't look important enough," answered Rachel as they had exhausted their inspection. "What are we going to do if we can't find it? We can't take the Chalice back!"

They retraced their steps and started the search again, inspecting every grave and every small headstone, their efforts proving futile.

"It's got to be here, one last look and if we can't find it we'll have to go back," said Gareth. "I'll start at the back again, you two do the front."

He walked to the very back of the churchyard and started again, finding he was getting a pain in his neck from leaning over to read the inscriptions. He was so absorbed he didn't notice the boy until he was almost beside him. Gareth jumped with surprise but he recognised him straight away. It was the young boy who had led him back to Merlin's room on their last visit, when he had been captured by Gwelliant and Alfrick in the tunnels beneath the castle.

"What on earth are you doing here?" asked Gareth incredulously, since he knew the boy came from the castle in the time they had just left.

"You search for Arthur's tomb!" stated the boy, ignoring his question.

"Yes, but how did you know that?" Gareth asked in surprise.

"The tomb is inside the church, you must look there," he answered. "I cannot stay long, but I have come to warn you to be careful, Medraut is looking for you!"

"Thanks for the warning," replied Gareth, "but what are you doing here? You were at the castle when I saw you last. This place is in a different time!"

"I live here," said the boy. "I must go now, return the Chalice as quickly as you can and go back to Merlin. You are not safe here!"

"We will, and thanks again!" said Gareth, still puzzled, as the boy disappeared round the church.

"Who was that?" asked Rachel, as she walked towards him.

"You're not going to believe this, but that was the boy that helped me, when we were here last time. Do you remember I told you that he led me back to the rooms after Gwelliant and ...?"

"Yes, I remember your story," she interrupted. "But I've seen him before as well! It wasn't at the castle though; it was when Argante made her prophesy. I recognised him straight away."

"I don't understand," Gareth said, looking puzzled. "He wasn't in her cave, how could you see him there?"

"No, he wasn't in the cave, it was when she put her hand on me, I saw lots of things. Mostly things from my own life, as though she was looking into it, but right at the very end, I saw a boy. I had no idea who he was, but I saw him quite clearly. I will never forget what I saw that day, and I know that he is definitely the boy I saw in the vision."

"That's really odd, I wonder who he is?" pondered Gareth.

"I know, there must be some reason why I saw him then, it's really strange!" she answered. "What did he want anyway?"

"He came to warn us that Mordred's looking for us and to tell us that the tomb is in the church. He said to return the Chalice and get back as quickly as we can."

"How does he know we've got the Chalice?" asked Rachel.

"What's going on?" asked Johnny, joining them before Gareth could answer.

"I think the tomb must be in the church," said Gareth quickly.

"Could be, good idea, let's have a look," agreed Johnny leading the way.

They turned back towards the church entrance and pushed open the heavy door. It was dark inside, the air was cool and there was a strong musty smell. There were some rough wooden pews either side of the aisle that led up to a bare-looking altar, raised on a stone platform, above which was a large carved cross. The walls held banners and flags similar to those in the Great Hall, except these were tatty looking and dirty.

"It's creepy in here!" said Rachel, with a shudder, looking at a banner with a large gold cross with ragged edges stained dark red. "That looks like blood!" she said stepping back quickly.

"Yep, I reckon it probably is!" answered Gareth, inspecting it closely. "They all look as though they have been in a battle, or several by the look of them!"

Their footsteps echoed eerily as they made their way towards the altar. To the right of the platform was a wooden hatch door in the floor with a large metal ring. They stood around it and looked at each other.

"We can't!" said Rachel, reading their thoughts. "This is a church!"

"Well there's no-one here to see, and we can't find this tomb anywhere else," answered Gareth, his hand already closing on the ring.

It took Johnny's help to pull the hatch open, revealing a flight of stone steps leading into blackness. Johnny took a candle from the altar, lit it and held it over the steps and as they peered into the gloom they could see that there was a room below. The two boys started down the steps with Rachel following nervously.

The flickering candle gave them just enough light to look around and they saw that the room was almost bare, apart from a long stone carving on the floor in the middle. As they got closer they could see that it was a life-size stone knight lying on a stone platform. The knight was depicted in full battle dress with his arms folded across his chest. On closer inspection, it was obvious that the stone platform had been moved, as it sat crookedly, revealing a large space below it.

"Bingo!" said Gareth delightedly. "I think we've just found what we are looking for! This has got to be it!" He pushed at the stone carving to see if he could move it a bit more and see what was underneath. To his surprise it moved easily, sliding with a grating noise. Rachel stepped back again, shuddering as the boys held the candle over the side and peered into the tomb.

"There's some more steps!" said Gareth. "Right, all you need to do is go down them and leave the casket there, then we can close it up again, job done!"

"Me! I'm not going down there!" said Rachel, shivering at the thought.

"Well I would do it, but you're the one in charge of the casket!" Gareth answered. "Look there's only a few steps, just go down and put it somewhere."

"I'm not going down there! It's a grave! I don't care how many steps there are! I'm not going anywhere near them!" said Rachel, almost in tears.

"That will not be necessary," said a voice from behind them, making them jump out of their skins. They turned to see who had spoken, but there was no-one there. They looked at each other frightened, each of them wondering where the voice had come from.

"Listen, what's that noise?" said Johnny, as Rachel grabbed Gareth, terrified. The crypt began to fill with the distant sound of galloping horses, neighing, followed by terrible screams and shouts and the clashing steel of swords in combat.

For a moment it sounded as though they were back listening to the dreadful battle again, only from a distance as the noise was quite faint, and they clutched each other in fear. Suddenly the strange noises began to fade as a dark figure came towards them out of the shadows at the other end of the room. Rachel screamed as the figure drew nearer, still silhouetted by their candle light.

"Who are you?" asked Gareth trying to sound brave, although the wobble in his voice gave him away.

The light caught the figure, revealing a tall slim man with shoulder length wavy hair. He wore a long red tunic with a gold crest emblazoned on it, over chain mail leggings and sleeves. His face bore a kindly smile, and Rachel recognised him immediately.

"King Arthur," she breathed. A quick look at the expressions on her two companions faces told her that this time they could see him as well.

"I'm sorry sir, I didn't mean to … I mean I was only …" stammered a terrified Gareth, looking from Arthur to the sculpted effigy on his tomb, which he had just moved!

"You have no need to be frightened. I know why you are here," Arthur replied. "You are returning the Chalice."

"Yes sir," Gareth replied lamely.

"So let me look at you, the new Keepers of the Power and my distant relatives," Arthur said, inspecting them closely. "And you, young man, Johnny is it not?"

Johnny nodded, incapable of speech.

"You have served your friends well! You have shown great bravery, with no thought for yourself and I applaud you for that!"

Johnny nodded again, still speechless.

"Rachel. Always frightened by everything! Do not fear your heritage, it is a gift that you must learn to trust," he continued, his attention turning to her brother. "And Gareth, our newly elected knight, already showing the courage expected of you. There is much you can learn from those who are left, seize the opportunity and learn from them!"

"Yes sir," Gareth managed again, not quite knowing what else to say.

"You have all done well, and if you would like to give me the Chalice, I will return it to safety again before we part."

"Sir, Mordred has altered time, we have to ask the Chalice to put it right again," Rachel said, holding the casket out towards him.

"It shall be done, the Chalice knows that you have risked much to do this," he said, taking the casket from her and moving towards the steps of the tomb. Suddenly the ground started to shake, the walls appeared to vibrate and move and there was a rumbling noise that seemed to be all around them.

"What's happening?" asked Gareth, looking around worriedly.

"I hopes it's not thunder. I doesn't like the thunder, miss Rachel!" said Johnny clutching Rachel's arm. "I doesn't like it at all! I wants to go home!"

"Johnny, what's wrong with you, talk properly!" said Rachel, looking at him in concern. "What's the matter with you?"

"I is talking properly, miss Rachel, but I's frightened of the thunder!" he replied, looking around fearfully. "I want to go back to the farm! I don't like thunder, I never have!"

"He's going back to how he was before! That's exactly how he used to talk when we first met him!" said Gareth. "The Chalice must have corrected the time in Valonia!"

"No! Oh no! This isn't fair!" said Rachel. "Wait!" she shouted at Arthur, as he was disappearing down the steps. "Stop, I have a last request from the Chalice!"

Arthur stopped and turned back to them, his face solemn. "Think very carefully before you ask for anything else. You have heard of what can befall those who seek to gain from the Chalice," he said.

"Yes, I know and I don't care!" Rachel answered adamantly, holding out her hands for the Chalice. "I have to ask it for one last thing!"

"Very well," he answered, handing it back to her.

"Rachel, what are you doing? Have you gone mad?" shouted Gareth too late as she concentrated on the casket, her hands getting hotter and hotter until she thought she might drop it.

"I'm sorry but I have to ask you one last thing," she whispered to it. "Please don't let Johnny go back to how he was. Please let him stay the way he's been while he's been helping us. We wouldn't have been able to bring you back here without him, and if it hadn't been for Mordred trying to kill him in the first place, he wouldn't be like that anyway! Please make him better again." The casket appeared to cool again in her hands. "Thank you," she added, before handing it back to Arthur.

"That was a noble gesture, you are a very brave young lady," Arthur remarked, as he took it from her. "I hope the Chalice fulfils your request."

With that he turned away and retreated down the stone steps. There was a loud grating noise as the carved stone moved back on its own, and they were alone again in the vaulted stone room. The candle flickered as they all stared down at the stone effigy of the man they were talking to just a moment ago.

"Come on, let's get out of here before that candle burns out," said Gareth. "Come on Johnny, let's go," he said putting an arm round the tall boy's shoulder, leading him towards the steps. Johnny hadn't spoken since the rumbling noises that had frightened him so much, and appeared dazed, but he followed them back up the steps into the church, where Rachel helped Gareth lower the hatch again. Johnny followed them, stumbling back through the church and out into the brightness of daylight where Gareth and Rachel breathed a big sigh of relief. The main part of their mission was finally over.

They helped Johnny sit down against the church wall, concerned by his white face and dazed expression. He leant back and closed his eyes.

"I don't believe you sometimes," said Gareth to Rachel, as they leant against the wall outside. "You quiver and quake over the quicksand, but face to face with a very dead King Arthur, standing right next to his own tomb, and you're as cool as cucumber!"

"Don't forget that I've seen him several times before. I knew he wouldn't hurt us."

"I still can't believe that we've just been talking to him, right next to his grave!" said Gareth. "Anyway, do you think Johnny's all right?" he motioned towards their friend, who hadn't spoken since they had left the underground crypt.

"I don't know," she answered. "Johnny, are you okay? How do you feel?"

"I dunno, I feel a bit strange and I've got a banging headache, like you wouldn't believe!" he answered, quite comprehensively.

"He sounds all right, he's talking normally again," whispered Rachel.

"Yeah, but he doesn't look too good does he?" replied Gareth.

"Do you mind? I am here you know!" answered Johnny, indignantly, still holding his head.

"I'm sorry; we're just worried about you, that's all," said Rachel. "Do you think you'll be able to ride? We ought to try and get back as soon as we can."

"Yes, I'll manage," Johnny said, struggling to his feet. "I used to have a lot of really bad headaches like this after my accident, they go eventually. Catherine used to give me one of her remedies for them."

"If we can get you back to Merlin, he'll give you something for it, I'm sure," Rachel said, taking his arm as they walked back through the churchyard to the horses.

"Oh great!" Johnny replied, sarcastically. "I can't wait for that. I can still taste the last one he gave us!"

Gareth and Rachel laughed and mounted their horses, relieved that their friend seemed to be all right again. They all started back on their journey to the tunnels and Tyntagyle, hoping that they would find that they had been successful, and everything had returned to normal again.

Chapter Eighteen

Déjà- vu

The journey back up towards the pass was uneventful, even though the surroundings looked different by the beach, the pass was exactly the same, and the big rocks and stone cliffs were comfortingly familiar. Johnny managed the ride, even though his face was ashen. Although he didn't complain, they knew his headache was much worse than he was letting on.

"Do you think he'll be all right going through time in the tunnel?" whispered Gareth to his sister. "Merlin said it would be dangerous for him!"

"I know, and I do hope so! We couldn't have done any of that without him, he knew exactly where to ride on that quicksand," answered Rachel, looking at their friend with concern. "He's just risked so much to help us; it would be awful if something happened to him because of it!"

The entrance to the tunnel was open and the big stones were rolled back, much to their relief. They dismounted, intending to lead the horses through into the cavern but as they stepped inside, the figure of Mordred appeared in front of them, his white teeth gleaming in a sadistic smile. They turned quickly to retreat and found three of his men with swords drawn, blocking their way. Two more stepped out from behind the rocks either side and they were completely surrounded.

"So, I suppose that you have returned the Chalice and corrected time again. No doubt you think you have won and it's all over!" Mordred said, his voice containing a nasty edge.

"Yes we have, and you might as well just give up now, Mordred, there's no point in you continuing this. Let's just go our different ways," suggested Gareth, with only a small amount of satisfaction in his voice.

Mordred threw back his head and laughed. "No point in continuing? I have every reason to continue, I can still alter everything if I have a mind to," he said, bringing his face close to Gareth's. "Do you really think that you can take me on, with your sister and a farm boy? I think not. I can destroy all of you here. Three keepers in one go, all in the wrong time! I only ever wanted but two things, the Power and Tyntagyle. Destroying you here will give me one of them at least and once I have that, the Power will give me Tyntagyle! I admit that I was distracted by Morgause's greed. She wanted the Chalice, she wanted even more than I." He drew a long silver sword out of its scabbard. "No, I will be more than satisfied with your deaths!" he finished, as he pointed it towards them.

Mordred's men moved in closer behind them, and they glanced at each other in despair, realising that they had no defence against them. Johnny had an axe but it was attached to the saddle on his horse and out of reach, along with Gareth's sword on his horse. Neither of them had any weapon within reach.

"Now then, who shall be first?" said Mordred, running a finger down the blade of his sword, his evil smile widening. He peered first at Rachel then at Johnny, raising the tip of his sword at each one of them in turn, enjoying every moment of his power over them.

"Maybe the boy," he laughed manically, and one of his men grabbed Gareth, thrusting the boy towards him. Mordred carefully aimed his sword at Gareth's throat, sliding it carefully back and forth, not marking him. "Let his sister watch him die! Oh, and this will be such a pleasure!" he declared. "I once said I would slit your throat like that of a squealing pig and I meant it! And it will be so satisfying!"

Before Mordred could say or do any more, galloping horses were heard faintly all around them and Gareth and Rachel recognised the same sounds they had heard in the crypt. The smell and the sounds of battle were creeping eerily around the tunnel.

"What is that?" said Mordred, nervously. "Who is with you?"

The same cries and shouts as before became louder and Mordred clutched Gareth even more firmly. "Answer me boy!" he shouted, and his men looked around fearfully as the battle sounds appeared to be coming towards the tunnel entrance.

Mordred's men moved away from the tunnel entrance in fear, as the sight of a figure in red and gold came towards them. Behind him were ghostly grey horses with the figures of phantom knights, long since dead, seated on their backs. Their lances held drooping colourless flags and the unearthly, unseen battle could still be heard faintly around them. Gareth, Rachel and Johnny knew instantly it was Arthur.

"The same old Medraut: just the way you like it, an unfair fight!" said Arthur as he came into the tunnel. "Your speciality as I remember, women, children and unarmed boys, easy pickings!"

Arthur was silhouetted against the light, and Mordred squinted to see who he was.

"Who speaks?" asked Mordred angrily, letting go of Gareth, as his men fell back, quickly withdrawing their swords in awe of the approaching figure. "You?" shouted Mordred in shock, his dark face paling. "It cannot be!"

"Why, because I am dead, Medraut?" replied Arthur. "But of course you would know that, since it was at your hand that I fell, unarmed and wounded!"

Mordred's men stepped back even further, terrified by the figure they recognised as their late King and the ghostly figures that blocked the tunnel entrance.

"So you did kill Arthur!" said Gareth, turning to Mordred. "Merlin was right, it was you!"

"Oh yes, I killed him! The great pious Arthur, who could do no wrong. It was possibly the sweetest victory that I have ever had," sneered Mordred.

"Indeed, look on your master, the great Medraut," said Arthur to Mordred's men. "He is naught but a coward, a man who fought side by side with us and when the battle was won, he came to me, one hand on my shoulder in congratulation, the other holding the dagger that he plunged into my heart."

The men backed away in confusion and fear.

"So, what are your intentions, to come back from the dead and avenge your own death?" asked Mordred, as his men looked from one to another, quite terrified. "Surely not even the great, noble Arthur can do this?"

"No, as much as I would like to take vengeance against the man who murdered me. I cannot. I will not! I will not upset the balance of the future, for which you have no regard. No, I am dead, that has already passed, but I will not stand by and see your cowardice destroy others. No, I merely intend to even things up," Arthur continued firmly, withdrawing the long shining sword from his side.

At the sight of the famous Excalibur held by the dead King, any loyalty Mordred's men ever had quickly vanished, and they fled past him into the tunnel and disappeared.

"Well now, that seems to have evened things up considerably, wouldn't you say?" Arthur smiled, handing the great sword to Gareth.

"Me, but I can't …" stammered Gareth, taking the shining sword from him.

"Yes you can. I give this to you as a gift. It is yours; it is your heritage, as it was mine. It will serve you well, just make sure that you extend it the same courtesy and serve it as well as it will you!" Arthur said with a purposeful look.

"But I can't fight him … he's ... got years of experience with swords!" stuttered Gareth.

"Yes you can, you already have swordsmanship. Use it, and what you don't know, this sword will soon teach you," he said resolutely, and turned to Mordred, whose previous bravado seemed to have suddenly left him, along with the departure of his men. He could be seen quivering as Arthur's smile left him and he looked at Mordred coldly.

"You see Medraut I don't need revenge, because I know what is in store for you. You will meet your maker soon enough, and when you do, be very frightened, for what lies ahead for you will be your penance for every bad deed you have ever done!"

With that, Arthur turned and walked away, his spirit knights on horseback following him - taking with them the eerie battle sounds. They walked towards the rocks in the pass until they simply disappeared into the landscape of hills as though they were a part of them.

Gareth turned back to face Mordred who was recovering rapidly from the shock of seeing Arthur, with the reality dawning on him that even though his men had deserted him, he only had Gareth to face now.

"Let us past, Mordred," Gareth said, much more bravely than he felt.

"Stupid boy!" snarled Mordred angrily. "I have fought the best and won, seasoned swordsmen all of them. Do you think that I am threatened by a mere boy with a sword? A boy that knows not even how to use it!" He threw back his head and laughed again, followed by a swift unexpected lunge at Gareth with his sword. Gareth leapt back quickly out of reach, and Mordred swished his sword from side to side, still laughing.

"Well, boy, your dead master wants you to learn from the best and this is your chance! Learn quickly, boy, for this will be your only lesson!"

Gareth's fear was beginning to be replaced by a rising anger and he positioned himself into an 'on guard' fencing position that he had learnt from his lessons at home. If Mordred was going to challenge him to the death, then he was going to have a damn good go at defending himself, he decided resolutely! He hadn't previously been able to use the swords here, as they were so heavy and took two hands for him to swing. The sword Excalibur was much larger than the sword Mordred was holding, yet it felt strangely light, almost as light as the rapiers he was used to wielding so easily in his fencing classes. He felt quite comfortable with it, almost as though the sword was adapting itself to him so that he could use it, instilling in him a great rush of confidence.

"I'm asking you again, Mordred, let us past!" he said firmly.

The large, dark haired man laughed, and lunged again at Gareth, who this time was prepared for him and met his blade with a swish that clashed heavily with his sword. Before Mordred could recover, he stuck another blow on the broadside of his sword, dancing back nimbly out of reach, with his knees bent and his left arm out to balance him.

Surprised by this, and puzzled by Gareth's moves, which were strange to him, Mordred backed off for a moment. His smile was now replaced by a look of pure hatred as he wondered for a moment whether this boy was actually going to be an opponent.

The moment didn't last long and he ran at Gareth with a roar, sweeping his sword with two hands, intent on bringing it down on his head. Gareth ducked back and blocked him again, meeting the blow so squarely that it threw Mordred off balance for an instant. Gareth immediately took advantage of this and delivered another thrust that slashed Mordred's shoulder and the big man staggered back.

Mordred clutched his shoulder, shocked that the inexperienced Gareth had managed to inflict a wound. He looked at his hand and saw that it was covered in blood and for a second seemed quite stunned. Gareth jumped back again out of reach, knowing that Mordred would come back heavily this time.

He was right; the sight of blood on his arm drove Mordred into an absolute fury. He roared again and came forward, swiping his blade to and fro at Gareth's head. Gareth nimbly ducked and moved, and ducked and moved again. He danced sideways with Mordred still making wild thrashing movements with his sword, forcing him back, again and again as he vented his anger. The heavy sword hacked left and right, but he still couldn't manage to strike him, as Gareth's well-practised fencing movements kept him out of reach. Each time he missed he grew more and more angry, the sweat was forming on his brow, and his face turned from red to an angry purple.

"Come on then, Mordred, teach me!" taunted Gareth as he leapt up onto a rock. "Teach me how to fight, because I'm ready to learn!" He balanced easily with his left arm out to steady him and his right arm holding the great sword Excalibur outstretched, taunting him with a circular movement, angering his opponent even more.

"I can't watch this!" said Rachel turning away with her hands over her face.

"He's brilliant!" breathed Johnny, as Gareth leapt down with a heavy blow towards Mordred's chest. The big man met it and their swords clashed, a furious duel starting as they faced each other. They clashed and withdrew, and clashed again and again.

"Where did he learn to do all that fancy stuff?" asked Johnny. "I've never seen anything like it!"

"He's been fencing for a couple of years now," Rachel answered, not looking.

"Fencing, what's that?" Johnny asked as they moved back quickly out of the way behind the rocks as the sword fight drew nearer.

"It's the only swordsmanship you can learn where we come from, but it's completely different to the way they fight here."

"Well whatever it is, it's brilliant. Mordred can't get near him!" said Johnny in complete admiration. "All that dancing around Gareth's doing, it's brilliant!"

"He's won competitions, he's really good at fencing, but not with a sword that heavy! He can't keep it up for long, not using it like that!" she answered, her voice muffled by her hands still covering her face.

"Well, the weight doesn't seem to be bothering him at the moment," answered Johnny delightedly as Gareth's blade slashed at Mordred's chest. "Oh yes, he's just got him again!" The duel was now heading back into the tunnel entrance with Gareth forcing Mordred back this time, thrusting and withdrawing out of reach as Mordred swiped at the air. He lunged forward in a series of controlled moves, forcing the big man backwards again and again. Gareth was looking tireless, but the older man was finding it difficult to keep up the pace now as Gareth lunged again and again determinedly.

This was not what Mordred was used to. His way was to maim with one heavy blow, not to be met again and again, forced to reign blow after blow that were successfully evaded. Gareth's skilful fencing moves taunted Mordred and kept him out of reach of the experienced swordsman's heavy strikes. Blows that swiped into the air yet again as Gareth nimbly ducked away. These were not skills that Mordred had expected or was even used to. Gareth's age was on his side as well, as each heavy blow sapped the heavy man's energy.

The frustration of it all was making Mordred worse, as he swiped wildly over and over again, only to be forced back by another expertly timed lunge from Gareth. It was he who retreated back into the tunnel, where he finally turned and ran down the steps into the cavern with Gareth close behind him.

"Come on then, Mordred. What is it you want to teach me?" asked Gareth from the top of the steps, his anger rising. "Do you want to teach me how to use a sword, or do you want to teach me how to kill my friends? People who fight with me, like Johnny or Bran? Or maybe you want to teach me how to be eaten up with jealousy for people who have what I want, like Arthur?" he shouted, advancing down the steps towards him sword still outstretched. "Either way, you have nothing to teach me that I want to learn!"

Mordred backed off again, completely thrown by the unexpected ferocity that this young man was facing him with. Rachel and Johnny followed with the horses into the tunnel, and paused to watch from a safe distance.

"I can't believe this is Gareth," she said quietly, to Johnny. "Galahad or one of the other knights, yes, but not Gareth. I've never seen him like this!"

It certainly wasn't what Mordred had expected either, because as Gareth leapt down the last few steps in one easy move, never taking his eyes off his opponent's angry face, Mordred turned and ran, through the cavern and into the tunnel that lead towards Tyntagyle, with Gareth in hot pursuit.

"Come on!" shouted Johnny, taking his axe out of the strap on the saddle. "This is brilliant; we need to keep up with them!"

The tunnel was dark and they followed the noise of the footsteps in front of them, leading the horses. Although the torches had come on involuntarily as they passed, the darkness still remained in front of them, apart from a glow, well down in the tunnel where Mordred and Gareth had disappeared ahead of them. They heard Gareth shouting. "Come on then, Mordred, come out and face me, come out and teach me whatever it is that you think you can, you coward!" and they hastened their steps towards his voice.

"They've turned towards the beach, these caves lead down there, I can hear the sea," said Johnny.

"Is that where we were with Morgana?" questioned Rachel, hearing the waves echoing, amplified by the caves.

"No, we aren't as far along as that, this is much closer, it probably leads to the beach where we rode over the quicksand."

They left the horses and followed the noise of clashing swords, as Gareth had obviously caught up with Mordred again. They arrived at a much smaller cave and had to duck as they entered it, to see the silhouette of the sword fight against the daylight in the cave entrance.

Mordred was still swiping heavy blows at Gareth who was still proving to be a fierce opponent, and was still successfully evading each of his strikes. Instead the large, angry man found himself forced backwards again and again as he missed Gareth and was counteracted by a blow even heavier than his own. They came together at the mouth of the cave where their swords locked. With a fast upward swipe of his blade, Gareth pushed him away, quickly regaining his balance by resuming the stance he had been fighting in. Mordred staggered back and Gareth lunged forward again forcing him back onto the sand. Gareth stepped out to follow him, springing forward with his sword outstretched.

"Gareth, no stop!" shouted Johnny. "You'll be on the quicksand, don't go any further!"

Gareth stopped on the edge of the sand and watched as Mordred tried to leap forward at him, only to find that he couldn't move, the quicksand already up to his ankles. Mordred struggled and tried to pull out his foot, but as he did so he slipped in further. By the time Johnny and Rachel reached Gareth at the cave entrance, his actions were getting frantic and he was up to his thighs. His face was red and he swore at Gareth, his struggling actions making him slip further and further into the sand, until he was up to his waist.

"I can't watch this, I know he deserves it, but it's still awful!" said Rachel watching in horror as he slipped further down, with none of them lifting a finger to help him. When the sand reached his chest he started pleading, offering Gareth anything he wanted to help him.

"Sorry, Mordred, but you don't have anything I want, and you're getting exactly what you deserve! This is for killing Arthur, Geraint, Bran's father and his brother and all the other people who've died because of you! Before the sand swallows you up, just think of all the villagers you've treated badly, and left with no food while you dined at your castle like a King. Oh, and let's not forget Johnny, who you didn't actually manage to kill, but you rode off anyway leaving him badly injured. He has more courage than you could ever hope for! This is for all of the people whose lives you've ruined to get what you wanted, and I hope for all of them, that you rot in hell!" said Gareth without a shred of remorse in his voice. "Come on, leave him to it!" he said to the others, turning away abruptly as he left Mordred to his fate and walked back into the cave.

Johnny and Rachel looked at each other and back again at the quickly sinking Mordred who was still struggling and shouting obscenities at Gareth.

"Do you think we ought to help him?" she asked Johnny, feeling guilty that they were doing nothing.

"I think it is too late for that, he is in too deep, we'd never be able to pull him out now!" answered Johnny sombrely, as he watched the sand creep up towards Mordred's neck. "Come on, turn away, don't look," Johnny said, putting an arm round Rachel's shoulder, leading her back into the cave.

Realising they were leaving, Mordred cursed them again and then he saw a woman's figure heading across the sand to him.

"Help me! Help me," he shouted, as the small lady approached. In his panic, he didn't even wonder how she crossed the quicksand so easily, until she drew nearer and he realised it was the ghost of his dead sister, Celia.

"Help you? No!" she laughed. "I have come to say good-bye, for you and I will never meet in the next world! You will be going somewhere where I can't help you!"

"I'm sorry! I'm sorry, I shouldn't have k…" the sand rose up, and Mordred sank, it covered his head and he was finally swallowed up.

Celia's ghost tossed a small bouquet onto the sand where he had been, the same as he had done after her funeral, before laughing and calling her a stupid woman. For a moment she looked quite sad and shook her head slowly. "Who is stupid now, Medraut?" she said quietly, before turning away and disappearing.

Rachel looked back fearfully and saw Celia's actions, but before she could say anything, the figure had gone and she somehow guessed who she was. She looked at Johnny and it was obvious he hadn't seen her, as he said, "Mordred's dead, Rachel, come on, let's go back."

Gareth was already by the horses as they approached and they took the reins from him and led the horses back into the tunnel.

"You were fantastic! That was so amazing!" said Johnny, slapping him on the back.

"Thanks, but if I hadn't had Excalibur, I wouldn't have been able to do it," said Gareth modestly. "I just hope that I don't ever have to do anything like that again!"

As they continued on their way, the horses' hooves clopped noisily, echoing round the vaulted stone as they walked. Their mood was not of exaltation, but more of a quiet horror at the turn of events, none of them used to taking another's life to save their own.

Mordred's death still played on Rachel's mind. However bad he had been, she still felt awful that they had left him to die without doing anything to help him, but she knew in her heart that as long as he were alive they would never be safe from him, while they were the Keepers. The only consolation was that they were all safe, it was all over, and they would be able to go home.

The entrance was getting nearer and they could see daylight in front of them. They blinked as they stepped outside the tunnel into the sunlight, where they were suddenly roughly seized by several men, who dragged them out into the open, surrounding them with their weapons.

"Bring them over here, let's have a look at them!" came a growling voice.

"I don't believe this!" said Rachel, recognising the men as Galahad's, and supposedly their escorts back.

"I am getting a very bad feeling of déjà-vu here," said Gareth as he was pushed hard in the small of his back. "This is exactly what happened when we first arrived here, and these are the same men!"

"I know they are," she replied. "They're Galahad's men."

"Do you think they ride with Medraut?" asked one of the men.

"They do not look like his men, maybe they are from the village," said another, as they found themselves in the middle of them, pushed from one to another.

"Look, just take us to Galahad will you, he knows who we are," said Gareth.

"The boy gives orders!" said a large man, and they all laughed menacingly.

"Aye, and he has a fancy sword for a knave so young!" said another, taking Excalibur from Gareth's horse.

"Stop, make way!" came a familiar voice, and as the men fell back they knew they would see Galahad on his white horse approaching through the middle of them as he did when they first got there. The men's words were different but everything else was identical.

"What goes on here?" Galahad asked.

"We caught them by the cave sire; we do not know for sure whose side they are on, so we have held them anyway!"

"Galahad, thank goodness!" breathed Rachel.

"You know my name?" he questioned, bringing his horse up close, looking questioningly at her.

"Oh, Galahad, please don't say that you've forgotten everything!" Rachel blurted out, close to tears. This was what Merlin had warned them about.

"Sir, we have to get to Tyntagyle, we have to get to the castle and Merlin," tried Gareth, silencing his sister with a hand on her arm. "We're friends of his, and our mother Bronwyn is at the castle with him."

Galahad looked puzzled for a moment and looked hard at Rachel as though trying to remember something.

"I believe I do remember you, and I will escort you to the castle," he said finally, signalling for the men to leave, apart from two who quickly mounted to ride with them.

The small party started off in the familiar direction of the causeway.

"What's been happening here?" asked Gareth cautiously, sharing his sister's concern about what they may or may not remember of the battle and events surrounding it.

"You do not know?" he answered in surprise. "There was a problem at a village by Mordred's castle; a servant girl there said she had seen a vision of a girl by the stream. They branded her as a witch and were going to kill her. A boy from the village saved her, and Mordred torched their village in spite. They came to us for help and once we had heard their stories it would seem that Mordred had been treating them all very badly and we offered them the protection of the castle. Mordred was furious and made a rather futile attempt on Tyntagyle. Needless to say they were defeated, all the knights came with men and most were finished in a final battle outside the castle. The rest scattered and we have been rounding them up, that's why my men were so suspicious of you."

They all looked at each other, astounded by the way things had altered.

"You came through the tunnels; did you have any sight of Mordred?" Galahad asked, "My men still look for him."

"Mordred's dead!" said Gareth flatly.

"Dead?" said Galahad, in surprise, pulling up his horse to a halt. "How do you know this?"

"Because I fought him, and he stepped onto the quicksand outside a cave," replied Gareth. "When I left him the sand was up to his neck, so unless there was some sort of miracle, I'd say he died there."

"You fought him?" said Galahad incredulously, "with Arthur's sword?"

"Oh, you recognise it?" said Gareth surprised.

"Of course I recognise it; there are no other swords in the land that look like Excalibur. Some say that it was never made by mortals! How did you come by it?"

"It was given to me, to fight Mordred," answered Gareth, hoping that he wasn't going to ask for too much more information, since it would all sound rather unbelievable.

Galahad scrutinised him carefully and nodded slowly, asking no more questions.

They went into single file across the causeway, and Galahad turned his attention to Rachel, riding beside him.

"'Tis strange, it is a long time since your last visit here and yet I feel as though I know you quite well. I have the strangest feeling I have seen you both since then, but I do not remember where, or when," he said.

"No, Merlin said you wouldn't remember, nor anyone else here for that matter," she said sadly.

The horses stopped outside the castle, and they began to dismount. Galahad jumped down and reached up to help Rachel down, looking at her strangely.

"You are a seer, aren't you?" he asked.

"You've asked me that before, and yes I am," she said, wishing he remembered the events they had all shared together. He looked puzzled, and she walked towards the turret entrance. "Thank you for bringing us back," she said, turning towards him. He pulled his helmet off, and her eyes were drawn to the livid semi-circle scar on his neck. She was surprised that he still had it, since everything there had altered so much.

"Wait," he said as she entered the turret stairwell. "What is it that Merlin said I would not remember?" he asked.

"Nothing, I shouldn't have said anything," she answered awkwardly, looking at the floor.

"It is something to do with this, isn't it?" he asked, touching the scar on his neck.

She nodded, but didn't know how to reply.

"Do you know how I got this scar?" he asked.

"Yes, I do, but do you know how you got it?" she asked cautiously.

"No I do not, I have many scars and I know exactly where and how I got all of them, save two."

"The one on your neck and the other one on your arm," she replied. "Do they still hurt?"

"No they do not pain me, apart from the fact that I have no recollection of how I got them," he answered.

"I must go," she said, hovering on the bottom step. "Maybe you aren't meant to remember and maybe it's best if you don't!"

She left him staring after her, still touching the scar on his neck, with a puzzled expression on his face.

Chapter Nineteen

Memories and Promises

As Rachel joined the others, she was greeted by Bronwyn with tears and a large hug, as she expressed her relief at seeing them all back safely. Gareth and Johnny relived the events of the day excitedly to Merlin who nodded and beamed profusely as they recounted everything.

"Oh well done, well done all of you!" he exclaimed finally hugging each of them in turn again. "I am so proud of you all, and I am so pleased that you have not suffered, Johnny!"

"He's got a really bad headache, he's had it since Arthur's tomb, but he's not saying anything about it. Can you give him something for it, Merlin?" said Rachel.

"Of course, of course, why did you not tell me, dear boy? I will find you a potion straight away!" he said pulling out his keys and unlocking a cabinet full of strange shaped bottles.

"Thanks," Johnny whispered to Rachel. "Just remember that it's your fault if I turn into a frog or something worse after I've swallowed it!"

"Here you are, my boy, this will make you feel better," he said, handing Johnny a small green bottle before returning to his former exuberance on hearing their success. "Oh, this is such a night to remember, such a night to remember!" he said rapturously.

"What do they remember though, Merlin?" asked Rachel seriously, trying to ignore Johnny as he took a sniff at the bottle, pulled a face and replaced the stopper very quickly.

"Ah, well now, this is where time is such a wonderful thing. It has carried on creating things in their natural course, and it has adapted itself in the most wonderful way!"

"We gathered that, but what exactly do they remember, or know?" asked Rachel again.

"Well there has been a battle here against Mordred, and the villagers have come to the castle as before, but there was no sorcery, no Chalice and no intervention by us. No-one has any memory of this, and that is how it must remain. We must not speak of this to any of them," said Merlin seriously.

"You're saying we shouldn't tell them, then?" asked Rachel guiltily, remembering the conversation she had just had with Galahad.

"No, we have all experienced things that, without Mordred and Morgause's spells, would never have happened. It was their intervention in altering time that caused them. Now that time has been set back on the correct course they haven't happened at all, which is exactly as it should be!"

"Galahad said that Sarah was going to be killed as a witch because she saw a vision of a girl by the stream. I think that was me when I went there through the Orb, so why does she remember that?" asked Rachel

"Ah now, the Orb is an entirely different matter, because time has no bearing on it. It works on an entirely different entity. That is why she may remember seeing you, because you went to her through it, but she will not remember why, and she certainly wouldn't have any recollection of seeing Gareth, Bran or Bronwyn in the fortress, as that would be governed by something in time that shouldn't have happened."

"This is all very complicated," said Rachel, still slightly confused. "But what about Galahad's scars, the ones that he got from Morgana when she attacked him as a wolf? He's still got them, but he doesn't know how."

"Galahad bears the scars from a shape shifter, in animal form. Wounds that would have caused certain death were it not for the Chalice. These are scars that will never fade and will never go away, and you must not tell him how he got them!" insisted Merlin.

Rachel nodded uncomfortably, as she had already started Galahad wondering about his scar and he would be certain to question her again about it.

"But enough of this we have so much to celebrate!" said the old wizard excitedly. "You are all back here safe and sound. The Chalice is returned, Mordred is dead, Bronwyn has been rescued and Johnny is still himself! Such a wonderful conclusion: and tonight the whole castle will be celebrating their victory against Mordred. We shall join them and make our own secret toast, to setting the course of time right again!"

"Hang on a minute, is this the same feast we went to last night?" asked Rachel. "Weren't they celebrating their victory against Mordred then?"

"Ah, well, yes my dear they were, and in theory it is the same one," he answered, as though it were quite normal. "But you must understand that now time has been set on its natural course again, the feast that you went to last night hasn't happened yet. It's happening tonight!"

"I can live with two feasts!" said Gareth. "The first one was quite good as I remember!"

"Yeah, me too!" said Johnny, now recovered from the spectacularly disgusting potion that Merlin had given him, which had made him feel better, even if it had tasted foul.

"Well I can't!" said Rachel adamantly. "I can't go down there and pretend that none of this ever happened, and not say anything to anyone!"

"Oh come on, Rachel, you really can be a kill-joy sometimes," replied Gareth. "It's all over, what's your problem? Just go down and enjoy it!"

"I can't, and I'm not going to!" said Rachel resolutely. "I'm not going to relive last night in a different way. It's just too strange, it's not right, and suppose people ask questions, I wouldn't know what to say! No, I'm not going."

"Oh come on, Rach, it's our last night here," said Gareth, in an attempt to persuade her, but she was having none of it, and it was eventually decided that the boys would go with Merlin, and Bronwyn would stay with Rachel.

Gareth didn't even complain about having to change into his fancy clothes again, as he was eager to see Bran and Sarah and join in the fun. They left Rachel and Bronwyn, promising to bring them a tray of food, and went off with Merlin in his elaborate robes to join the feast below.

The same smells and sounds were already drifting up, exactly as they had the night before, and Bronwyn and Rachel settled back in the turret room on their own, ignoring the sounds of merriment from below. They passed the evening quietly, sitting on the settle chatting until Johnny brought them a large tray of food.

"How's it going?" asked Rachel, as Bronwyn thanked him for the food.

"It's really good," said Johnny. "Well, it's exactly the same as last night really, apart from the speeches and Galahad, he was acting really strangely. He stood up and made a toast to the men, and waffled on about the battle, and then he lost the plot completely. He stopped talking and just stood there staring, and then he walked out! Fortunately Bors stood up and took over, and they were soon banging their tankards on the tables again and shouting out 'Aye, aye.' You know, like they did last time!"

"What was wrong with Galahad then?" asked Rachel.

"Search me!" replied Johnny. "Anyway, I'll go back now, are you sure you don't want to come down? You're missing all the fun?"

"No, I'm quite happy here thanks," answered Rachel.

After he had gone they tucked in to the platter he had left, until they were quite full. Rachel said that she might go to bed, even though the noise still rising up would prevent anyone from sleeping, however determined they were. They were disturbed by a knock at the door and Bronwyn went to answer it. Rachel couldn't see who it was, but she heard Bronwyn having a short, whispered conversation with them, before shutting the door.

"There's someone who wants to see to you," she said.

"Who?" asked Rachel, surprised, since no-one had come in.

"Galahad," answered Bronwyn, noticing Rachel's immediate worried look.

"No, I don't want to talk to him!" she replied stubbornly.

"I think you ought to, he looked quite troubled," replied Bronwyn. "He asked if you would join him on the battlements, I think he wants to talk with you in private."

"Oh no, I can't ..." said Rachel. "You don't understand, on the way back from the tunnel I asked him if he remembered anything: he didn't, but he felt as though he knew us. He's got a memory loss the same as the others, except that he knows it! He wants to find out why, and worse than that, he's still got the scars from Morgana! He doesn't know how he got them, but he knows that I do!"

"Is this why you wouldn't go down to the feast?" asked Bronwyn gently.

"Partly, I can't face him asking questions, since Merlin has told us not to say anything."

"I think you ought to ignore Merlin's advice in this instance," said Bronwyn. "If Galahad is going to carry the scars from Morgana's attack for the rest of his life, he deserves to know how he got them. I think you should tell him, if he wants to know."

"Do you think so?" asked Rachel uncertainly.

"I most certainly do, you owe him that. He helped all of us, and from what I've heard, would have done even more if he could. You have to tell him!"

"But what will Merlin say when he finds out?"

"You can leave him to me, you've asked my advice and I've given it. The blame lies entirely with me!" answered Bronwyn firmly. "Go and see him, and if he asks any awkward questions, just tell him the truth!"

"All right I will, thanks, Bronwyn."

"Don't thank me, that's what mother's are for," reflected Bronwyn. "I just haven't done a great deal of it before, because I haven't been able to!"

"Well you're here now, and that's all that matters," said Rachel, taking the cloak that Bronwyn handed to her. "Thanks, mum!"

She didn't see the tears in Bronwyn's eyes as she made her way up the stone steps towards the battlements. She stepped out, pulling the heavy cloak around her as the sea breeze caught her. She walked across into the moonlight that illuminated the battlements and cast a shimmering silvery pattern across the sea. Galahad was leaning against the parapet looking out to sea and he turned as he heard her footsteps.

"I did not think that you would come," he said awkwardly. "You did not join us at the feast."

"No," she answered.

"You leave tomorrow?"

"Yes," she answered, shuffling from foot to foot and looking at the floor, feeling very uncomfortable.

"Thank you for coming," he said, as she looked up warily. "I had to tell you before you left that I have remembered!"

"You have? What have you remembered?" she asked cautiously.

"All of it!" he answered. "When I awoke this morning I recalled a strange dream. It felt real; it felt as though it had happened, but most of it, on waking, escaped me. Then I found scars on my neck, shoulder and arm, scars that I had never seen before and had no recollection of how I got them."

"I'm really sorry, I shouldn't have mentioned them," she answered.

"'Tis not your fault, I have remembered how I got them and I know that, were it not for you, I would have died from them!"

"What made you remember? I don't think you're supposed to, Merlin said that no-one would remember what happened."

"I have puzzled ever since I met you again this afternoon. I knew that I had seen you since your last visit, but I couldn't grasp the memory! It was at the feast, when I stood up to make the toasts and saw two empty places. It was then that I remembered Bronwyn and yourself seated next to me, while I talked about the sorcery that had saved the battle. But there was none, the battle we had fought was like any other, there was no sorcery. Another battle came flooding back and I could not speak, because for a moment, I could not tell which battle had happened and which one had not. I'm ashamed to say I left the feast without a word, because I had no idea what was fact and what I was imagining!"

"You didn't imagine anything, it all happened," said Rachel.

"But how? I have paced the battlements for an hour or more, and gradually it has all come back to me, but I do not understand how or why! This is why I sought you out because I knew that you would be the only one who would tell me!"

"I'm not supposed to tell anyone about it, but I'll tell you, since you've remembered anyway," she said. "When you left us we were returning the Chalice to Avalon."

"I remember that, you were frightened," he said, as the memory came back to him.

"Well terrified really!" she said, managing a laugh. "We returned the Chalice and it put time back to how it should have been, which means that everything we went through never happened. That's why you woke up thinking you'd had a dream and then went out to fight the battle that should have happened. Does that make sense?"

"It does, and I thank you for telling me."

"Galahad, you mustn't tell anyone else, I wasn't even supposed to tell you. I'm glad that I have though, and I'm glad that you've remembered, even if you weren't supposed to, because we all went through so much and you helped us do it!"

"None shall hear it from me," he replied.

"Thanks," she answered. "I'd better get back to Bronwyn now."

"As you wish, I will walk with you," he answered courteously. "There is something else I must tell you before you retire. Your brother came to me at the feast; he has asked if we will teach him our ways if he stays."

"What? He can't stay!"

"I had a feeling you might not know about this."

"He can't stay; Bronwyn will have a fit, not to mention my Dad: he'll have a heart attack!"

"This is for you to discuss with them. He also asked me if Bran and Sarah can stay on at the castle. I know now that this is something that I promised before, when we fought against Morgause, and I will honour this, even though the boy has no recollection of what happened."

"Oh, I'm really pleased for them, they deserve it, and I'm sure Bran will be the best knight you've ever taken on."

"I have no doubt of it, but I feel that this may be why your brother wants to stay, along with a promise he says he made to Arthur, to learn the sword."

"This is awful, he can't stay," she repeated.

"If he does, you know that I would look out for him as though he were my own brother," Galahad answered earnestly. "I would make sure that no harm came to him."

"I know you would," Rachel answered. "But it is much more complicated than that."

He nodded as though expecting her to continue.

"I'm glad you've remembered everything," she said, as they reached the doorway. "We've got a lot to thank you for!"

"Gratitude is not a necessity, when one fights alongside kindred spirits," answered Galahad sincerely.

"Well maybe it isn't, but thanks anyway!" she answered awkwardly.

"We will escort you back in the morning," he answered, "I bid you goodnight."

"Goodnight," she answered, rather formally, as she left him. Walking back down the steps to Merlin's room she was reflecting on the staid adult conversation she had just had, so far removed from any conversation she would ever have with anyone in Chesterton at her age. Would anyone there ever refer to her as a 'kindred spirit', or 'bid her goodnight'? No they wouldn't, she thought, and the whole absurdity of everything that they had done there, flashed through her mind.

The last thing Rachel wanted to go back to, in the peaceful sanctity of Merlin's room, was a full scale argument. She had hoped to talk to Bronwyn on their own about her conversation with Galahad, in their new found mother-daughter relationship, but this was not to be, as the argument was already in full swing.

"You can't stay here, this is ridiculous, and what on earth do you think your father will say?" she heard Bronwyn exclaim, realising instantly that Gareth had already dropped his bombshell.

"Look, Bronwyn, I made a promise that I intend to keep. I said I would learn the sword, I said I would learn to use Excalibur. I can hardly take it home and learn it use it there, because there's no-one that can teach me!"

"Gareth, this is taking everything too far, you're not meant to be here!" Bronwyn argued.

"I'm sorry, Bronwyn, but I've made up my mind, I'm staying!" Gareth declared resolutely.

"You're not!" Bronwyn replied equally firmly. "You'll do as I say!"

"It would not be a great travesty if the boy stayed," interrupted Merlin. "Don't forget that time moves very slowly while you are here. In your time, he would only be missing for a day at most!"

Bronwyn looked helplessly at Rachel, in the hope that she would back her up, only to be disappointed.

"To be honest, if Gareth's made a promise that he feels he has to keep, I think he should stay," said Rachel. "Galahad has said that he'll make sure he's all right."

"Please don't tell me that you want to stay as well?" asked Bronwyn, looking really worried.

"Me? No, absolutely not! But if Gareth really wants to, I think he should," Rachel answered, looking at her brother, remembering his fight with Mordred in the cave. She realised how much he had changed and grown up since they had been there. The experiences over the last few days had affected them all, in different ways. She knew that Gareth had been frustrated a lot of the time. He had been powerless to do anything, as he was unable to fight like the men here and she knew that he had found this difficult. Although they were both Keepers, he hadn't taken to using the magic that she adapted to quite quickly. She remembered Argante's words, in the cave on their last visit; saying that as Keepers, she was to provide the intuition and Gareth was to provide the strength. This strength was to be with the sword and she knew that Gareth felt a strong desire to learn this, in the only place that he could. He nodded appreciatively that she had backed him up, knowing she understood why.

"The only thing that would worry me is that Gareth and I are supposed to stay together here for safety and Gareth would be on his own. Would that matter Merlin?" asked Rachel.

"No, no, my dear," answered Merlin. "The main threat here for you both was Mordred, and since he is no longer with us, it is no longer important. There is no threat to Gareth from anyone here."

Eventually, after more persuasion from Merlin, Bronwyn finally gave in.

"I don't know how I am going to explain this to your father!" she said, as they were retiring for the night. "He's not going to be pleased at all, when he finds out that we've left Gareth here!"

"I'm sure he'll understand," said Rachel consolingly, only to receive a look from Bronwyn that indicated that they both knew full well he wouldn't understand at all!

In the morning they got ready to travel back and found Galahad and Owain waiting with their horses by the arched castle entrance. Merlin decided to accompany them, and the party mounted their horses, riding out sedately through the castle gate on to the causeway.

Rachel took a last look over her shoulder at the magnificent castle, sitting high up on the dark ragged cliffs, and felt almost sorry to leave. They dismounted at the tunnel to say their goodbyes.

"Thanks, sis!" said Gareth, giving her a short uncustomary hug.

"Just be careful!" she said, and he nodded in reply.

Bronwyn was about to deliver a lecture about his safety there and was stopped abruptly by Johnny suddenly announcing that he wanted to stay with him.

"Oh no, not another one!" she said in dismay. "Johnny, what am I going to tell your family if we go back without you?"

"You could tell them he's staying with me! After all it would be the truth! Anyway, they aren't likely to be cross if he's with Merlin!" answered Gareth. "That's if he can stay of course! Can he Merlin?"

Merlin looked thoughtful and tugged his beard. "This was once Johnny's heritage, one he never had a chance to even know. So I do think, Bronwyn, he deserves a place if that is what he wishes."

"I do, wish it, I mean!" said Johnny, with a pleading look at Bronwyn.

"Oh dear, this puts me in a very difficult position," answered Bronwyn, knowing she was beaten already.

Rachel smiled, knowing it wouldn't be long before they persuaded her to let him stay.

"And what about you, Rachel?" came Galahad's voice from behind her, taking her attention away from Bronwyn's dilemma. "Now that your friend and your brother are staying, will you be reconsidering?"

"No, I want to go home," she answered. "It's different for me."

He looked puzzled, and she felt for some unknown reason that she should offer an explanation.

"We come from somewhere very different and when I'm there, I lead a normal life. I'm not a seer or a sorceress and I don't have to do any magic. It's only when I come here, that all these things happen to me. I don't like it, I have no control over it and it frightens me!" she said, surprising herself with her frank admissions.

"I have seen how frightened you have been, and I can understand that you are not comfortable with sorcery," he answered.

"That's why I don't want to stay," she said.

"This is where I was so wrong when I compared you with the other sorceresses. They would go to the ends of the earth to increase their powers, but you, you shy away from it. You are nothing like them, and although I do not hold with sorcery, maybe you are the one sorceress who ought to develop her powers. For I know that you would use them only for good," he said sincerely, making her blush. "Will you ever return?" he asked.

She really wanted to say, 'No, I will never come back here!' but instead she found herself saying. "Yes, I'll be back one day, I don't know when, but I have a feeling I'll return!"

"Then I shall remember you, and you will be welcomed back by all of us on your return," Galahad answered. "Whenever that may be!"

Other titles from

The Chronicles of Valonia

The Jewels of Valonia

ISBN 978-0-9548518-7-3
March 2009

The Golden Casket and The Spectres of Light

ISBN 978-1-906873-11-0
October 2009

The Battle of The Underworld

ISBN 978-1-906873-24-0
Due 2010

The Quest for The Immortal Walker

ISBN 978-1-906873-25-7
Due 2011

Katie Paterson

Katie Paterson, of Scottish descent, has lived most of her life in the Midlands.

As a mother of two grown-up children herself, she has an ambition to help keep reading 'alive' for children, and was inspired to write 'The Chronicles of Valonia' by a lifelong fasination with the Arthurian period and legends.